I0689724

Rose's War

The Maui Trilogy, Volume 3

Jill Engledow

Published by Maui Island Press, 2024.

Maui Island Press

1200 Mira Mar Ave. No. 511

Medford, OR 97504

www.mauiislandpress.com[1]

Publisher's Note: This is a work of fiction. Names, characters, and incidents (except for those of historical record) are a product of the author's imagination. Locales and public names are sometimes used for atmospheric purposes. Any resemblance to actual people, living or dead, or to businesses, companies, or institutions is completely coincidental.

Cover Design by Cynthia Conrad

ISBN 979-8-9857063-2-1 (ebook)

ISBN 979-8-9857063-3-8 (paperback)

---

1. http://www.mauiislandpress.com

Chapter One

D*ecember 1941*
     After it was all over, and you'd run into someone you hadn't seen for a while, the first thing they'd ask was, "How was your war?"

Because we all had one. No one on Maui could escape the war, with barbed wire on the beaches and military camps in the field next door, soldiers eating cheeseburgers in tiny towns, everyone scrimping with food shortages and doing jobs they'd never expected to try.

Maui wasn't the same after the war. Because none of us were.

· · · ·

IT BEGAN FOR ME ON a Sunday morning when Aiko came racing down the driveway. Lately, she'd been going to services at the church across the road, as much to socialize as to worship, I thought. After all, she'd been raised Buddhist and still participated with her family in the traditions of that religion. But every week, she left early to meet with her church chums before Sunday school.

Her running steps halted at my back door, and I looked up from the novel open on the breakfast-nook table where I sat in my bathrobe, cup of tea in hand.

"Auntie Rose, turn on the radio!" Aiko yelled through the screen door. "The Japanese wen' bomb Pearl Harbor! I gotta go tell my folks."

She turned and ran as I reached across the table to switch on the radio. Chills ran through my body as I leaned closer to listen. I could hear some weapon firing behind the official voice rattling off the facts of disaster. "This is no maneuver!" the announcer barked. "This is the real McCoy!"

As he described dive bombers raining destruction on Pearl Harbor, I realized the ships under attack there were the ones I'd seen during a visit to Lahaina in the spring of 1940 when I was in town for a friend's wedding. The U.S. Pacific fleet was anchored there, ship after ship strung out in a long line across the channel between Maui and Lanai. They had been holding war maneuvers in the calm waters where, once upon a time, Hawaiians paddled canoes and whaling ships came for rest between forays into the North Pacific. The maneuvers were part of a general ramping up in preparation for war that seemed just on the horizon, as Japan prowled the East and Germany ravaged Europe. War was in the air, and we must make ready.

I had gazed at those ships from the second-floor balcony of the Pioneer Inn, where I was staying in a room overlooking the harbor. The fleet was an impressive and reassuring sight. Down below, white-clad sailors on shore leave strode toward the picturesque little town, their faces bright. Now those fresh-faced young men, not much older than my own students, were in a desperate fight for their lives and for our country. How many of them were already dead, and how many of those great ships were aflame, or even sunk to the ocean floor?

We had known we were at risk and had prepared, territory-wide, for months, with blackout practice, first-aid classes, and aluminum collection drives. Now, here it was, sounding far worse than we could have imagined. Suddenly a quiet Sunday morning was filled with terror. We were only a hundred miles from Honolulu, close enough that the island of Oahu was visible from some parts of Maui. People on Maui's northwestern shores probably could see the clouds of black smoke that must be rising from Pearl Harbor and the air bases where the Japanese were strafing our fleet of warplanes.

The radio announcer said we were to avoid hysteria and remain indoors, except for those who were part of the provisional police corps or one of the other volunteer units formed as we prepared to defend ourselves. Then he signed off, and the radio went quiet. There would be radio silence until the government issued further orders for us.

I changed from my nightclothes into a *muumuu* and walked down the hill to the Tanakas' house. I stopped for a moment at their front steps, looking out over the gently sloping green pastures of my little farm. The chaos of war seemed impossibly far away, and yet I knew it could come here so easily. Inside, I found Masako sitting at the kitchen table, stroking the silken fabric of a kimono. She looked up teary-eyed as I entered. "He's going to bury everything," she said, holding her kimono tighter as if to protect it from the grave. Beside her mother, Aiko slumped in her chair, white-faced. The family's two youngest children, Henry and Iris, stood close behind Masako.

"Bury what?" I asked. Just then Masako's husband, Isao, stepped in the back door, glanced at me, and said, "Rose," his face wearing an uncharacteristic frown. Without pausing, he set down an old orange crate and began packing it with the family's heirlooms. He was calm and careful with these precious pieces, but he moved quickly. Hiroki appeared at the back door, a gawky seventeen-year-old. He stood gravely watching his father dismantle the family shrine, the *butsudan,* a carefully crafted cabinet with filigree doors carved by Isao's father. I knew that *butsudan* was the most highly treasured thing in this house, a connection to the family's heritage and ancestors. The distress on each of the Tanakas' faces deepened as Isao removed the candlesticks and the little bowl that held incense, then gently closed the filigree doors and wrapped the *butsudan* in an old piece of canvas.

I'd never met Isao's parents, who had gazed from a photo atop the *butsudan* next to the wedding portrait of Masako's folks, Yuki and Taka-san. I knew her parents well, from our growing-up days on the Spencer Ranch. In the picture, Yuki wore the same kimono her daughter now held. It had been Masako's wedding gown as well.

"Hiroki, take down that *bukkyo*," Isao said. "Roll it up nicely, but quick." Hiroki and his mother exchanged a look, but he obeyed his father, packing the cloth printed with Buddha's sutras that hung beside the *butsudan*.

I didn't have to ask why Isao was about to destroy his family's tiny inheritance—a few photos, a string of glass prayer beads, wooden plaques with the family name engraved in *kanji*, the hand-carved *butsudan*. The Japanese had bombed Pearl Harbor, catapulting us into the war we'd feared. All the preparation of the past year had done little to cushion today's shock, but at least it had allowed time to figure out what to do when war came.

Obviously, Isao had been doing his own planning, for now he moved deliberately, removing all evidence of any perceived loyalty to Japan. It wouldn't matter to the military authorities taking over that Isao and Masako had been born and reared right here. They knew no other home. But their faces matched those of the foreign bastards who'd bombed our ships and planes, and who might be coming for us. These remnants of their heritage could only make matters worse.

Isao turned and stretched his hands toward Masako. Her tearful eyes met his. The next thing he packed away would be her wedding kimono.

"I'll take them," I said, the words coming out of my mouth as fast as I thought them. "We'll hide them in my house. No one will ever look there."

Masako took a deep breath, and Isao turned, his face relaxing.

"Where?" he asked.

• • • •

THE TANAKAS WERE LIKE family to me, filling in gaps that otherwise would have left me alone, a spinster whose own family consisted only of my sister, her husband, and their son. They lived in faraway California, and I hadn't seen them in years. We were Scottish, and the island social structure automatically gave Caucasians like me a high status. The Tanakas' ancestors were more recent immigrants who had arrived in the Islands in the late 1800s. Island Japanese were still viewed as newcomers and laborers, and in the conventional way of things, we would have kept our distance. But we were all a bit unconventional, and we got along fine.

Masako, Isao, and I grew up within miles of here, Masako and I next door to each other on Spencer Ranch. Isao and Masako had adored each other since high school. Orphaned, Isao had to leave school early to support himself. When the aunt who took him in died, he found work and a home at Spencer Ranch. After Masako graduated, they married and moved into one of the ranch's tiny cottages.

Masako was pregnant with Iris, their fourth child, when I hired Isao to help me build a stable, and we found we worked well together. Isao and I shared an invisible bond. We both were the beneficiaries of the love and support of Vaughn Spencer. To Isao, he gave a steady job and the opportunity to develop his skills. To me, he bequeathed this land and the memory of a love so strong I believed I would never need another.

I felt at home here from the beginning, living not far from the ranch where I had grown up. My farm was uphill from the little town of Makawao, in an area of ranches that ranged from small homesteads to outfits with hundreds of acres. It was only a ten-minute walk down to the town, where shops had hitching rails for customers' horses and boot scrapers outside their front doors. I was close enough to Maui High to make it possible for me to ride my horse to work until I could afford to buy a truck.

I did my best to make the little farm Vaughn left me productive. But I could only do so much, teaching full-time and tending my growing collection of farm animals. When Isao told me how unhappy he was working for Vaughn's son, Pono, who took over the ranch after Vaughn's death, I made a deal with him. Soon after Iris was born, the family left the ranch to move to a house on my farm, built by Isao with materials I supplied.

The deal we'd made back then still worked out handily for all of us. The Tanakas had a comfortable home, I had the help I needed to run my little farm, and we all had plenty to eat, a boon during the Great Depression that had plagued the Islands as well as the rest of the world. This farm could be a lifesaver as we moved into this new crisis. I thought of it as ours, even though I owned the place. Theoretically, I could give orders or even kick them out at any time. I had no intention of doing either. We were a team.

Despite having to leave school at sixteen, Isao was one of those people who never stopped learning, whether by reading or by doing. His fine carpentry skills had earned him a reputation among the Upcountry elite. He made a good living for his family while also maintaining and expanding our farming efforts. He was a handsome man with straight black eyebrows. The strong planes of his face were lit with bright eyes and a smile that carved deep dimples in his cheeks.

I often thought of Isao as the sparky sun that energized his family. Masako was its moon, with a round, pretty face and a serene, gentle personality. She'd been a straight-A student at Maui High School and still loved to talk story with me about the latest novels. Masako dressed as most Japanese women in the Islands did, in simple cotton kimonos or dresses, with her hair pulled back into a bun. But she seemed most comfortable in her gardening overalls.

Life on the ranch, with its mixture of ethnic groups, had integrated Isao and Masako into the wider Hawaii society more than if they had lived in one of the plantation villages segregated by race. Isao was a dab hand with the ukulele and hula, having spent many hours with his Hawaiian cowboy friends. Masako had learned American-style cooking from her mother, the Spencer family's cook.

Aiko, their eldest child, had her mother's wide face and pulled-back hair, with her father's dimples and outgoing personality. She worked at the pineapple cannery in Haiku. Hiroki took after his father in looks but had been an intense, serious fellow since childhood. He was a senior at Maui High, where I taught, and headed for the University of Hawaii next year. Henry, a freshman at thirteen, still had the soft face of childhood, with horn-rimmed glasses through which he examined the world with interest, always busy, always with a project. And Iris was the baby of the family at age ten, still walking down the hill each morning to Makawao Elementary School. She wore her hair in long braids and would likely grow up to resemble her wiry father, with those engaging dimples and brows like wings over dark eyes.

Now all our futures were uncertain as war descended. I knew that some in the community already harbored suspicion about the loyalty of Americans of Japanese ancestry, but I also knew there was no question that the Tanakas were patriotic Americans. I would do whatever I could to protect them from the consequences of that unfounded suspicion.

• • • •

WE SPENT AN HOUR WRAPPING the Tanaka family treasures in clean rags and stowing them in burlap bags. We tucked the bags into a cabinet in the tool room next to my kitchen, a dark and grubby little room that kept my washing machine, tools, and other odds and ends from the rainy Makawao weather. As a Caucasian, a schoolteacher, and a farmer, I was not likely to attract an official search. The treasures would be safe in my tool room for as long as they needed to be.

We kept the radios on in both houses the whole time we wrapped and carried things up the hill to my house. Occasionally the static erupted into words, urgent commands in a strained voice: Stay off the streets and off the phone, keep calm, but shoot to kill if you come across a parachuter in a blue uniform. The governor had proclaimed a state of emergency before noon, and later the military took over. We were under martial law.

We worked in an eerie fear that day, as we waited for the next word of death and destruction on Oahu and listened for the roar of foreign fighters over our heads. Obviously, the killers who had cast death and destruction over Oahu on a peaceful Sunday morning would stop at nothing, so we had to defend ourselves as best we could.

After a hurried lunch, Henry and Iris came up to help me hang my blackout drapes. I'd cut and sewn them from lengths of dark denim when we had a practice blackout earlier that year. The tall windows in my house, so lovely most of the time, now were a liability. If I wanted any lights on in the evening, these curtains had to work.

I handed the hammer to Henry and climbed down the ladder. I had thought ahead enough to make the curtains so long that I could nail them along the top of the window frame, where the holes would not show when, someday, I'd be able to remove these necessary evils. Already the room was dim, though the sun shone brightly outside. It would be utterly dark after sunset, and who knew when there might be a power cut. I'd better dig out my flashlight and make sure the kerosene lanterns were full.

"Auntie, what about upstairs?" Iris asked. My house was big, with three bedrooms upstairs in addition to mine on the ground floor.

"No need," I said. "I'll put towels along the bottom of the bedroom doors so no light can get out. I never go up there anyway." A thought occurred. "Unless they have to evacuate Downcountry, or they send evacuees from Oahu, and I need to put people in those bedrooms. Dagnabbit—I only bought enough denim for downstairs. I hope we can still buy some if it comes to that."

"You can put pineapple paper," Henry suggested. When we'd had a blackout practice last May, some people had covered their windows with the heavy black paper used to mulch pineapple fields.

"Yes, if I have to," I agreed. "But it's too hot—can't open the windows at all at night. At least with curtains, some air comes in around the edges. Well, maybe it won't be a problem. Maybe nobody will need to evacuate, and it won't matter if the upstairs windows aren't blacked out."

With the curtains in place and hungry for information, I decided to walk down to Makawao town to find out what was going on in the wider world. Henry and Iris came along, staying close to me in the chilly December air. All of us looked up frequently to scan the sky for planes. Iris clung to my hand, and Henry edged closer as we neared the town.

"Look, Auntie, guards!" he exclaimed as we neared the intersection that was the main crossroads at the center of Makawao. Sure enough, a couple of Filipino men stood at one corner, clutching bolo knives, the long blades normally used to cut cane. Their faces were tense, but they nodded and greeted us as we passed.

The town was busier than it would have been on a normal Sunday afternoon, with people clustered outside a shop that must have opened for emergency buyers. We said hello to a few neighbors holding full shopping bags and looking worried as they shared stories. Off to one side, a woman comforted another, who was crying. A third woman stood near them, concern on her face. I heard the crying woman tell her, "My son is stationed at Hickam" and I understood her tears.

I spotted a plantation supervisor who I knew had been active in home-defense preparations and stopped him as he hurried toward his truck, arms full of groceries.

"Brad, have you heard anything about a local attack?" I asked. "Are they coming ashore anywhere on Maui?"

Brad paused, shaking his head. "Not that I know of. I'm taking food to the provisional police headquarters. I talked to one of the fellows there before I left home, and he says so far, so good. We're scattering around the island to keep watch on all the beaches."

"Good luck," I said as he turned to leave. I wished we had a local radio station and didn't have to rely on the Oahu broadcasts. Their focus of course was on the disaster there, and the Oahu stations gave the outer islands short shrift in the best of times.

I heard the clip-clop of a horse's hooves and turned to see a neighboring rancher dismount and tie his horse to a hitching post across the street. Bill waved as he crossed.

"How are you holding up, Rose?" he said. "A bad day for Hawaii, eh?"

"It is indeed. We're managing," I said. "Came for supplies?"

"Need a few things for my saddle-bags. Some of us are going to ride up Kula and keep an eye on the coast."

"Oh, thank you for doing that. We're all so afraid of invasion. What will you do if you see them come ashore?"

"Send one fellow to the nearest house to find a phone and call it in. And the rest of us will have our rifles ready," he replied, his face grim.

"Let's pray you don't have to use them," I said, and he nodded.

We stepped into the store to find it buzzing with customers. I was glad I'd done my shopping the day before; there was no bread on the shelves, and other items seemed to be in short supply. On the aisle that held canned milk, two customers reached for the last two cans, then glared at each other, each apparently having hoped to grab both cans.

Copies of *The Maui News* lay on the counter, the front page emblazoned with giant black headlines: JAPAN PLANES ATTACK OAHU. PEARL HARBOR-HICKAM BOMBED, followed by advice from Col. Charles B. Lyman, commander of the Maui military district: "REMAIN CALM."

I bought a copy of this "First War Extra" and skimmed the front page. Henry and Iris stood close to peer at the paper's rather disorganized mix of news about the Oahu attack and Maui's response. Pages 2, 3, and 4 were almost empty, except for large block letters: KEEP COOL. NO HYSTERIA. BLACKOUT TONIGHT, ALL NIGHT.

As we stood reading, a truck pulled up, and a man jumped out of the passenger seat and grabbed a stack of newspapers from the truck bed.

"Second war extra," he said to us as he passed. He tossed the papers onto the counter, and I went to buy a copy, hoping for more news. I could already see that the headlines were different, and, as I had feared, one of them reported, "Hundreds Injured." Like the first war extra, the front page of this one was filled with a patchwork of information in different-sized type. Rather than try to decipher it all standing on the street, Henry, Iris, and I trudged past the guards on alert at the crossroads and up the hill to home.

We walked along the driveway, where the tethered goats grazed, past my house, and down to the Tanakas'. Masako and Isao were at their kitchen table drinking green tea and looking solemn. Their blackout curtains were hung, pulled back to let in air and light.

Hiroki and Aiko sat on *zabuton* cushions next to the wall where the *butsudan* had stood. Masako got up to pour me a cup, and I sat in an empty chair at the round wooden kitchen table Isao had made for his family. I spread the newspapers on the table, the two older siblings left their cushions to join us, and we all pored over the papers.

Obviously printed in haste, the first war edition still had the date of yesterday's regular edition—December 6—and typos scattered through the stories. Usually, those errors would have sent the English teacher in me searching for a red pencil. Today I was just grateful for the information.

We'd known since early that morning that our lives were going to change a lot, but the newspapers gave us details. Mr. Wentworth had been appointed coordinator of civilian defense and now was "virtually dictator of all civilian activities and property." We were to avoid assembly in groups, take cover in the event of an air raid, and refrain from hoarding food.

"Hey, they wen' cancel the Punahou game," Henry said, pointing to a box at the top of the page. The Oahu football team had been scheduled to play Maui's Baldwin High School in Wailuku that afternoon, but now the much-anticipated game was off. Interisland sailings and airplane flights had been canceled. The Punahou team was stranded, probably going to camp on Maui family couches for the foreseeable future.

The two front pages were jammed with reports of mayhem on Oahu, attacks on the Philippines and Guam, the British declaring war on Japan, and President Roosevelt's preparations to speak before our own Congress tomorrow. The paper also said, in tiny print at the bottom of the page, that schools would open as usual on Monday unless we heard otherwise from our principal.

"I need to go call Mr. Crowder," I said, pushing my chair back. "I've been gone, and he might have tried to call. Things are still so uncertain. I can't believe we're expected to go to school tomorrow, but I'd better find out."

"Yeah, what if planes come and bomb us at school?" Henry said, pushing his glasses up on his nose.

"That probably won't happen," I reassured him, as everyone looked up from their reading, alarmed. "I'll let you know what Mr. Crowder says."

The principal's phone was busy, so I hung up and sat considering the possibility of an invasion. How many American soldiers could fit into an airplane, and how fast could they travel from the mainland to defend us? It took days to get here on a ship, and the Japanese had shot up so many planes and killed so many men on Oahu that maybe there wouldn't be anyone to take care of us on Maui.

How could this have happened to our little Islands? Most of the world had never heard of Hawaii, never mind Maui. We were the remotest place on earth, farther from anywhere than anywhere. Visitors were so rare that the newspaper reported their arrival. I supposed that great harbor full of ships must've attracted Japan's attention. And maybe there had been spies, somewhere, sometime. But surely not here. We were the back of beyond, barely on the map, tiny, isolated, rural. And undefended.

I dialed again, and this time Mike Crowder answered. He had spent the last hour contacting teachers and students, he told me.

"We're staying out until Wednesday, as long as things remain calm," he said. "We'll need a faculty meeting Tuesday, to get us ready to deal with the situation. Can you spread the word?" He gave me a few numbers to call, families who could share the news around their own neighborhoods. After I made the calls, I went back to the Tanakas' and sent Hiroki and Henry out to let students know in the few houses near us.

"Be home before sunset," Isao warned as the boys took off. "We have curfew now."

"If the schools are closed, I don't know if I should go work at the cannery," Aiko said as they left.

"Stay home until you hear something. Maybe call first thing in the morning," her father advised. He stood up. "And we gotta go do chores."

"I'll help you," I said. Normally the boys would have done some of the work, but I had preempted them.

"Milking time," Masako said, pulling clean buckets from a cupboard.

I brought in the goats, and Iris fed the chickens and checked for eggs, while Masako milked and Isao did the heavier work. I stopped to pat my old mare, Penny, who nuzzled me as I stroked her neck. I no longer rode Penny, and she spent most of her time grazing in the pasture with the milk cow, Lani, and her calf. Penny had been replaced in her old age by a Ford truck. It kept me a lot drier than I had been when I had ridden Penny to school on rainy days but was not as much fun. Not to mention that horses ran on pasture grass and oats, not gasoline. That would have been helpful in our current situation.

That reminded me.

"Isao, do we have black paint for the headlights?" I asked as he filled the water trough that supplied the larger animals.

"Sure," he said. "I'll paint them first thing tomorrow."

"I hate to think of driving with only a little slit for light," I said, then shrugged. "But with the curfew, I guess we won't be going anywhere at night anyway." I peered into the barrel where we kept oats. It was half empty. "How about feed? Are we short of anything? Who knows when we'll get more, and the pastures won't be enough with this drought."

"We're okay for a month or so," he replied. "More bags in the storeroom. But we better get together tomorrow and go over our planting plans, for the animals and for us too. Gotta speed 'em up."

And so ended our first day of war as the boys came running down the driveway, Isao latched the stable door, and I headed up to my place to settle in for a long, dark night, broken by dreams of fire and smoke and shattering glass.

Chapter Two

"We gotta make the garden bigger and plant some sorghum for the animals," Isao said when we sat down to plan the next morning. "Maybe we could start on that today, while the boys are here to help me clear out some pasture. I'm going to get Watanabe's tractor later, open up that field above your house." He glanced at Hiroki. "No roll your eyes, boy. You gonna be happy we did that if the Japs cut off our food supplies."

We were silent for a moment; I was surprised to hear Isao use that word, but I guessed we were in a different world now. I changed the subject. "What about water?"

Makawao was rain country, but we were in a drought, and every rancher I knew was moving cattle and worrying about feed shortages. Buying feed from the mainland was expensive and might be impossible now that war had begun, but growing feed crops without water was hard.

Isao frowned. "Gotta build more tanks or get empty drums. Probably a bomb shelter, too. You boys gonna be doing a lot of digging."

"I'll lend you my gloves," I said, patting Hiroki's hand. "We have plenty of seeds?" I asked.

"Plenty pigeon pea seeds," Isao said. "I've been saving them, and I've got about a hundred sprouting already, so we can plant them all over the place, yeah? Rows wherever we can, and chop branches for the animals."

"I have a bunch of seedlings ready to go into the ground," Masako said. "And I've been saving vegetable seeds. Plenty tomatoes, green beans, peppers, cabbage. Corn for when the days get longer."

"What should we do about the new house?" I asked. We were in the material-stockpiling stage of building a third structure between my house and theirs. My plan was to rent it to teachers, perhaps

16

colleagues who wanted to move out of the small on-campus cottages the schools provided. "We have almost enough materials, right? Might be hard to get more with the war on."

"Most of it, but better to hold off, not start until we see how things go." Isao looked up, suddenly alert, and I heard footsteps on the porch. Through the screened top half of the door, I saw Sergeant Kalama, our neighborhood cop, and two tall *haole* men in suits.

Isao rose slowly and went to the door. The rest of us froze, our eyes on that screen.

"Eh, Tanaka," the sergeant said, and backed away, allowing the *haole* men to move forward.

"Isao Tanaka?" one asked.

"Yes."

"Could you come out, please." His tone of voice said this was not a request, but an order.

The man opened the door and Isao walked onto the front porch.

"We are taking you into custody on suspicion that you are a danger to the security of the United States," the man said.

Isao glanced at us as they put handcuffs on him, his face tense with fear. We were all standing now, crowding the door. Beside me, Masako was breathing fast and clutching my hand.

"Wait, what are you doing?" I demanded. "This man is my farm manager. He was born here and is a good American. You can't just take him like this. What is he charged with? Where are you taking him?" I put on my best schoolteacher voice. "Stop this right now and explain yourselves."

Kalama, whose daughter Mildred was one of my students, dropped his head and took another step back. But the taller of the two *haole* men simply paused, his hand gripping Isao's arm, and said, "Ma'am, it's martial law now, and we're doing what we have to do to protect the country."

"Can I put my shoes on?" Isao asked. It was the first time he'd spoken since acknowledging his name.

"Bring them," the taller man told Kalama. "He can put them on later."

Abashed, Kalama waited for Aiko to get her father's shoes and socks. Masako, tears on her cheeks, grabbed Isao's jacket from its hook by the door and handed it and his old fedora to Kalama.

"Sorry, eh, Missus" he whispered as he accepted them. "Get martial law now, cannot help."

"Where are they taking him, Sergeant Kalama?" I whispered back. He glanced at the men escorting Isao down the steps, muttered, "Haiku," and turned quickly to leave. Stunned, we all stood on the porch, watching them go. Isao's shoulders slumped, something I'd never seen.

Around me, the kids started to sniffle at the sight of their father being marched barefoot to the jeep parked up the drive. Iris started forward as if to follow him. "Wait, where are you taking my daddy?" she cried, and Aiko grabbed her sister's shoulder and pulled her back.

"Hush, baby, you like they take you too?" Aiko said, wrapping her arms around Iris, who began to sob.

The men settled Isao in the back seat and handcuffed him to one of the struts supporting the jeep's roof, then came back to the house. Kalama stood by the jeep with Isao's belongings still in his hands, looking off into the distance.

But the two *haole* men were not finished. "We have to do a search now," the taller one said. "Please step back inside and take a seat."

In shock, we all did as told. For the next ten minutes, we watched through the open bedroom doors as the men turned out dresser drawers, lifted mattresses off their frames, rifled through closets, and generally made a mess of Masako's tidy home. They randomly pulled dishes and pots out of the kitchen cabinets, took one last look around, and left. I was so glad Isao had had the foresight to clear out all the Japanese memorabilia yesterday. But they still had taken the most important part of this household, Isao Tanaka, and we had no idea why, or what would happen to him.

When they had left the house, we all rushed to the porch to watch the jeep drive away, with the two *haole* men in front and Kalama in the back next to Isao. The jeep accelerated up the driveway and over the hill. "Haiku?" Hiroki said. "What's in Haiku? It's only one small little town, not too far. Maybe we can go get him."

"Let's all sit a minute and think," I said, putting my arm around Iris's shoulders. She was trembling. Masako, who had said nothing since Kalama banged on the door, plopped into her chair, face set and pale. The whole family looked terrible, with yesterday's shocks now compounded by the sudden loss of Isao, our bedrock. If I was terrified, I thought, how must poor Masako feel? And the kids—their faces broke my heart. They were trying so hard to maintain the composure they knew their dad would expect, but their glittering eyes and wet cheeks gave them away. Hiroki stood rigid, gripping the back of the chair.

"Mom," he said, his voice choked with anger. "I gotta go get him. They cannot do that, take him away. Let me use the truck. I'll go find him."

"No." At last, Masako spoke, turning to her son. "No, you cannot go. What if they take you too?"

"Wait, Hiroki, let me try to find out what's going on," I said. "Tomorrow morning, I have to go to a teachers' meeting, and I'm sure I'll be able to find out where they took him, and what we can do about it, whom to talk to. We can figure this out, so please wait. Your mother is right. We don't want to lose you too."

"You're the man of the house now, until your father gets home," Masako said in a soft voice. "Please stay and help me take care, son. No make trouble. Stay home."

Hiroki's shoulders dropped, anger softening into despair. He pulled out the chair at last and sat with us as we each grappled silently with this new reality.

• • • •

THE NEXT MORNING, WE were all out at dawn, taking on chores Isao usually did. On any morning, we all had our jobs, but today we were missing our strongest worker. My mind jittered over Isao's fate—where the hell in Haiku was he? I tried to picture the rural acres and small commercial areas around the Haiku pineapple canneries, a few miles down the road from us, and I couldn't imagine where the authorities might be holding prisoners. As I worked, I cast frequent glances at the sky and stopped to listen for the faraway roar of planes. I didn't know much about our military situation, but I knew we didn't have enough soldiers and guns on Maui to stave off a Japanese invasion. And Oahu was busy taking care of the mess there. What if the attackers came here next? Were we going to be bombed too?

Still, the animals had to be fed and milked and managed. Aiko helped Masako milk the cow and two goats, and the boys filled food and water troughs, then led cow and calf to pasture, as Isao would have done. They checked on the steers, making sure the cattle had water and that the fence wire was tight in the big pasture that stretched back on the *mauka* side of my land, ten acres I had leased a few years ago.

Meanwhile, I slopped the pigs that lived in the pen we'd put at the *makai* corner, far from our homes and noses. I filled their water trough and headed back up to clean and refill the chickens' water cans. Iris gathered the eggs and tossed grain and the kitchen scraps from our two kitchens to the chickens, her usual job. Then the two of us took on another Isao chore: leading the goats out of the stable and tying them on the lines along both sides of the driveway.

Isao and I had laid concrete on the driveway between the house
and the road a few years ago, and he had edged the concrete with
cypress trees. Alongside were strips of land where we tied goats, each
goat attached to the long line with a shorter tether that allowed her
to graze along the strip. Set out of their reach on one side was a big
vegetable garden, and on the other side a field also used for grazing.
Isao had a system and lines of different lengths set at different places
to which the goats' short tethers could be attached. He rotated the
grazing sites so that the goats kept the driveway and field trimmed
and the lush grass around our two houses short and neat.

At least the soil in the grazing field would be well fertilized, I
thought, as I hooked a tether to the line that stretched between two
pegs at opposite ends of the driveway. The goats left their droppings
all along the line as they cropped the grass in the field. Unfortunately,
that also meant the grass would be thick and hard to break up, and I
had no skill with a tractor. Nor, for that matter, a tractor. Isao usually
rented one from his buddy, Mr. Watanabe. In fact, Isao had planned
yesterday to pick it up, before those men took him away. Would Mr.
Watanabe let me or Hiroki use it? And was he even home, or had he
been arrested too?

I stood up and watched Luna stretch her neck to nibble the lush
grass at the end of her tether. Isao probably would've moved the pegs
today so that Luna and her sister, Lily, could graze another strip of
lawn in some other area. But I didn't have the time, or the heart, to
move the line today.

I shook my head. Tractors, goat-grazing lines—never mind
trying to figure out how to get by without Isao, I told myself. Go find
out how to get him back.

"Anything else, Auntie?" Iris had gotten Lily on her line and
walked over to stand with me. I put my arm around her shoulders,
and she leaned in. Iris was my favorite. I loved all the Tanaka
children, but Iris had lived down the hill from me since she was a

baby. I had started raising goats because her tender tummy needed their milk. When she was just learning to crawl, I'd been her willing babysitter, held and comforted her, and cuddled her in my lap to read a picture book.

Iris had done a lot to stave off my yearning for a child in those years when, by rights, I should have been settled with a husband and children of my own. But things had not worked out that way for me, and I was grateful for my *hanai* family. For much of my life, I had depended on families that were not biological but tied with love and friendship. Because of them, I had been able to make a good life for myself, even if it was as a spinster schoolteacher in a rural community far from the big outside world. Now we seemed to be disturbingly close to that outside world.

"Auntie, what do we do now?" Iris asked, gazing up at me, and I knew she wasn't talking about morning chores.

"We're going to carry on, take care of each other, and figure out how to get your dad home. In fact, I need to go get ready for my meeting. And I'm sure I'll learn more while I'm there. When I come home, we'll plan our next move. Can you be strong and patient, help your mom and me keep things going while we work on it?"

"Uh-huh," she replied, nodding. She didn't sound very enthusiastic.

I got myself cleaned up, put on a dress, and tied my hair back. I didn't bother with more than a glance at the mirror. It didn't really matter how I fixed my hair today; there were more important matters at hand. And anyway, I knew how I looked, with gray hairs now among the dark waves and fine lines on my sun-browned face. I'd been a pretty girl, and I thought I still looked good, with dark lashes and brows setting off my hazel eyes. I'd stayed fit and slim, doing farm work all these years, but I'd be forty-two soon, no longer a girl. What mattered now, though, was that I was strong enough to do what had to be done. I straightened my back, pulled on a sweater, climbed into my pickup, and headed to school.

Chapter Three

Maui High was my alma mater and my second home, the place where I'd spent years teaching kids to love literature, or at least to write a complete sentence.

I parked in front of the school and climbed the steps quickly. This building with its wide, welcoming flight of stairs up to vine-covered arches was nothing like the simple two-story wood-frame building of my school days. But the view was the same. I stopped to look back, down the mountain's flanks to the flatlands of bright green cane and the little towns that edged the shores. No sign of military action, so all was well, at least for the moment. That beloved view was as green and blue and peaceful as ever. I turned back to the school and went straight to the teachers' lounge.

"Mike, I'm so glad you're here," I said, closing the door behind me. Our principal, Mike Crowder, looked up from a pile of paperwork. We had taught in adjoining classrooms for years, until he chose to climb the administrative ladder.

"Oh hi, Rose. You're early. How are you holding up?"

"As well as can be expected. You folks?"

"Scared and angry, but determined to do everything we can," he replied.

I pulled out a chair at the table where we teachers held meetings, sipped coffee, graded homework, and gossiped. "Actually," I said, "I came early because I need some help."

Mike raised one eyebrow.

"My farm manager, Isao Tanaka, was hauled off by someone yesterday—someone official. I don't know who they were, but they were with Herman Kalama. We heard they were taking him someplace in Haiku. Do you know where that would be? And what they might be doing to Isao?" A wave of anxiety washed over me when I thought about the possibilities.

Mike clasped his hands and stared thoughtfully at them, then flicked a glance at me.

"Rose, I'm not sure you should get involved here. We're at war, you know, and there's a lot of suspicion about our Japanese neighbors."

I shook my head angrily. "I'm sure Isao had nothing to do with spying or whatever those people think he might be doing. I've known him since high school, and he and Masako have lived on my land for almost ten years. You know their sons—Hiroki and Henry. They're a great family, and in no way do they support this terrible attack."

Mike nodded. "I know them. Good kids. But isn't Isao pretty wrapped up in the Japanese school?"

Of course he was, I thought, with his children attending all these years after regular school, as did most of the island's Japanese kids.

"Yes, but so what? Mostly he does their repairs, *manuahi*, for free, to support the school. What's wrong with that?" I asked, indignant.

Mike shrugged. "Maybe nothing. Just being a good parent. But I do know they're picking up Japanese school teachers, as well as doctors, priests, newspaper editors—leaders, in other words. Would you consider Isao a leader in the local Japanese community?"

"Well, he's certainly respected and well-known. Isao is such a friendly guy. He is involved in community events, and he helps a lot of people, so I guess you could consider him a leader, but I don't see why that's such a bad thing."

"That's who they're gathering up," Mike said.

"For what? For how long? And where are they?" I demanded.

Crowder sighed and leaned back.

"I hear they took them to the jail in Wailuku, but they're building a prison camp on the playing field *makai* of the cannery in Haiku. I drove by there yesterday. There are men putting up a fence, and a bunch of National Guard fellows with rifles standing around."

Mike must have read my mind because now he leaned forward and said, "Rose, you mustn't go nosing around there. This is serious business. No telling what the military will do if you start kicking up a fuss."

I folded my arms, fuming and fearful at the same time. "But he's my farm manager! We've built that place up together, and we had plans to increase production just for this time when we might have to get along without help from the outside. How am I supposed to do that without him? Not to mention, how is his family supposed to manage? Masako has three kids still in school and no income except for Aiko's cannery wages if Isao isn't there."

Mike rubbed his chin, looking thoughtful. "You might have an argument with the farm manager thing. I doubt they'll give a damn about the family. More than a thousand of our families lost someone in the attack yesterday, I hear. What about them? But maybe you can get someone in authority to do something based on the farm-manager argument." He stopped, frowning. "If, that is, you're sure Isao had nothing to do with this, nothing to do with helping Japan."

"I'm sure as the day is long," I said, and right then the door opened, and two teachers came in. These early birds lived in the teachers' cottages next to the school. They were both looking pale, hair tucked up into turban-style headscarves. I could see I wasn't the only one not interested in fixing my hair that morning.

"Mike, what's going on? Do we really start classes tomorrow?" Adele Mounts asked as she pulled out a chair. She was our registrar and taught home economics as well.

"Depends on whether we get through today without another attack," Crowder said, straightening his papers and sitting back in his chair. "Let's wait a few minutes and see who else shows up, and then we'll discuss it. How are you getting on, Lettie?" he asked Mrs. Hadlow (French and Latin). "And you, Adele?"

Ten minutes later, a few more teachers had straggled in, and everyone seemed to be talking at once: how they'd heard about the attack, stories about Oahu's damage, and rumors.

"They think a submarine is cruising Paia Bay," one said.

"I hear there are signal lights blinking over in Pauwela," said another. "Maybe it's the local Japanese sending signals!"

"I heard they're going to fill up that camp in Haiku with suspects," said the first. "I bet they've been sending information to Japan for years!"

"And they've been our neighbors for years, so why would you think that?" I countered, my voice tight with tension. The others turned to stare at me, and Mike cleared his throat.

"All right, let's get started." He glanced around the room. "Usually, we fill every chair in here," he said, "but either people are at their emergency stations or just scared to leave home."

"My husband is out patrolling the shoreline," Adele said.

"And mine had to report to the hospital yesterday and still isn't home," said Elsie Butler, whose husband was a doctor. She dabbed her eyes and looked down at her lap.

"Well, we'll all have to buck up and do our bit and hope for the best," Mike said. "Here at Maui High, that means protecting our students and ourselves while cramming as much knowledge as possible into their heads and doing all we can as a school for the war effort." Several teachers nodded.

"First priority is safety, of course, so we'll rely on the military and the government to tell us if we should start. So far, they say it's okay to get back to class, but if that changes before tomorrow morning, you'll receive a call. And we need to follow the plans we've made, keep up our safety drills. At this point, for the students' sake we should get back to class as soon as we can. We'll need all the teaching time we can get, because we'll be doing a lot of nonacademic things as well. It will be better for the students' morale, not to mention our own, to be doing something constructive rather than cowering at home.

"Now, we've all feared this was coming," he continued, "and we have our plans to deal with it. I see Mr. Stevens is absent. I guess he's out with the provisional police. But I assume he'll show up tomorrow to get the boys to digging trenches for air-raid shelters. You'll need to excuse them from your classes until we can get that done. And we'll be holding drills, probably every day for a while. March the kids out under the big trees—the same class locations we use for fire drills. Soon, I hope, we'll have the trenches to hide in."

"Filthy, especially when it rains," Adele Mounts muttered.

Mike shrugged. "I'm sure they will be. Better than the alternative, however. Now—Mrs. Mounts, what's the plan for home economics? You're in touch with the Red Cross about what they'll need, I presume?"

So the meeting settled into some sort of normalcy, each teacher reviewing plans to keep the school going on a wartime basis. I'd taken on the girls' service club that year, and we were already selling war stamps, while the boys' club sold bonds. We'd been doing well with sales; now, we must do better.

Mike outlined plans for return—first-aid classes, military drills for the boys. None of it too surprising; we had been preparing for war for months. But now war was a jolting reality, and fear shadowed every minute.

The meeting ended, and the others left in twos and threes, their worried voices echoing in the empty hallway. I busied myself with examining the contents of my inbox until everyone was gone except Mike, standing now as he reached for his jacket. I picked up my purse and stood facing him.

"Mike, what do you think I should do about Isao? Do you know anyone in the military? Or is that even whom I should talk to? Who's in charge of this?"

Mike put his jacket on slowly, frowning. He shook his head. "I don't know, Rose, but you could start with Wentworth, the head of the disaster council." He looked at me. "I still am not encouraging you, understand? And if you do try, I suggest you get a man to go with you, back you up." He plopped his hat on his head and opened the door, bowing me out. Reluctantly, I walked ahead and waved goodbye as Mike's Buick pulled away.

Get a man, huh? I noticed he hadn't volunteered. I sat for a moment, my engine idling, as I thought about whether to go look for this place where they might be holding my friend. I glanced at the gas gauge. Fortunately, I'd gassed up while running Saturday morning errands. No doubt gasoline would soon be in short supply, so I'd better be frugal. But Isao was worth using a little gas. I'd go look.

Instead of turning around to go back up to Makawao, I headed the truck down the long tree-tunneled road to the ocean. Just past the school, a couple of grubby barefoot boys in ragged pants waved as I passed the road to Hamakuapoko, the plantation village that was across the gulch behind the school. Yes, I thought, Mike's right. We might as well get these kids back to school.

Ahead, I saw a glimmer of blue sea. Haiku was only a few miles away on the road that ran along the shoreline. I took a right and pulled off the road, though there were no other drivers in sight. I scanned the shoreline for as far as I could see, stared out at the ocean, and up at the sky. Nothing untoward. I pulled back onto the road and drove with the ocean at my left, fields of sugarcane on my right, and the flanks of Haleakala rising above them.

Get a man. Hmmm. That might be good advice. But who should it be? Pono Spencer? No, he still held a grudge from years ago, when I had offered Isao a chance to work part-time for me and develop his own business as well. Isao had been the favored jack-of-all-trades at Spencer Ranch, and Pono had been angry when he left.

I could go straight to the top and ask Harry Baldwin. He owned the sugar plantation where Isao's father had been the mechanic who took care of Mr. Baldwin's cars. The plantation, and Harry Baldwin in particular, had a habit of continuing benevolence toward employees and their families and survivors. Surely Mr. Baldwin would know Isao's name from his well-respected carpentry work for many in the Baldwins' social circle, if nothing else. But he was a big man, running companies that were the main industry of this rural island out here in the Pacific. A very big fish in this tiny community, and probably busier than ever as war descended upon us.

I'd have to think about Mr. Baldwin. I'd met him socially, of course, and knew Mrs. Baldwin from her community work. But how far could I presume on this acquaintance?

I glanced over at Maliko Gulch as the road began its curve to the bottom of the green valley. No sign of smoke or alien landing gear on the beach, but no reassuring presence of U.S. khaki and guns either, to guard this little bay.

Another right, and I was climbing the hill to Haiku, where the big pineapple-packing company canned the local crop for export and Aiko toiled at trimming pineapple. A few buildings lined the road—a store, the bank, factory-worker dormitories. And back behind one of the dormitories, the shocking sight Mike Crowder had described, men putting up a fence and setting up tents in a field, and armed men standing guard at its perimeter. I pulled up in front of the store across the road and climbed out, trying not to look too nosy as I glanced over toward the camp.

It was just after noon, and the store had reopened after the mandatory closure that began yesterday, when storekeepers had been required to do an inventory. Inside, several women clustered around the counter. They were all Japanese, as was the clerk. All of them looked scared as hell, and I couldn't blame them. When they saw me, the shoppers scattered to browse the shelves, heads down.

"You need help, Missus?" the clerk asked. "We only supposed to sell food to regular customers."

I was there for information, not groceries. I had no intention of hoarding food. But I saw the store had copies of two new war extras, so I bought those. Then I decided to be forthright, though she might be too afraid to tell me anything.

"I'm trying to find my friend, Isao Tanaka," I said in a low voice. "Have you seen him over across the street?" I noticed one of the shoppers glance my way, and the clerk looked surprised. She probably wasn't expecting such a question from a strange *haole* woman.

"No, I don't know him. I don't know anything about that place," the clerk replied, and suddenly she was very busy with her dust-rag, turning to clean the radios and lamps on a shelf behind the counter. I looked around and saw that the shoppers were also busy, absorbed in examining the cans lining the shelves. No one looked at me. I left.

Outside, I couldn't simply drive away. I had to get closer. I headed down the road a bit until the dormitory would block my view of the soldiers around the camp (and their view of me) as I crossed the road, walked along the front and finally turned the corner to observe more closely.

Now the figures I'd seen from across the road were clear. I could see faces. Was that Dr. Doi? Another man looked familiar—the principal from the Japanese language school the Tanaka kids attended? It sure looked like him. Maybe I could get close enough to call to him and ask about Isao. I took a step forward and almost ran into a Guardsman with a rifle over one shoulder. He was a local boy who didn't look much older than Hiroki.

"Where you going, ma'am? You can't be here. You'll have to leave."

"I'm looking for my farm manager," I said. "I can't run my farm without him. Isao Tanaka? Do you know if he's here?"

"I don't know ma'am. Now, please leave."

"Okay, I'm going. But do you know how I can find out? Whom can I talk to? Who's in charge?"

He shrugged, looking worried. "I don't know. Just leave, will you? I don't want to have to arrest a lady."

I turned and walked away. But as I reached the front of the dormitory, I looked toward the fence builders again, and then I saw him. The face was hidden, but those were the khaki trousers and denim shirt Isao had been wearing, and I'd know that straight back anywhere, even from a distance greater than this.

Elated, I headed back to my truck, turned the key, and took one last look at the camp. I had to talk to Masako. We needed to figure out the next step. But at least I knew for sure where we could find Isao.

Chapter Four

"**I** saw him," I said as I let myself in the Tanakas' front door, setting off a chorus of questions.

"Where was he?"

"Is he okay?"

"How did he look?"

"Did you talk to him?"

Iris said nothing but burst into tears and ran to clutch her mother, who turned to me, her own eyes brimming, holding the mayonnaise-coated spoon with which she had been mixing canned tuna for sandwiches. Standing next to her at the kitchen counter, Aiko stopped chopping celery and stared at me. Hiroki jumped to his feet from his seat at the table. Henry's chubby cheeks quivered with the effort not to cry.

Quickly, I filled them in on the little that I knew. "I'm not sure they are actually staying at that camp," I said. "It looked as if they might be setting up tents and so forth."

"Mrs. Yoshioka said Mr. Yoshioka and some other men are in the jail down Wailuku. Maybe he's there," Hiroki said. He had gone over to his Japanese teacher's house to check on the teacher and to find out what was happening to others in the community. No one wanted to talk about this shameful situation, but everyone was so hungry for information that, at least for now, the teacher's wife was willing to share that, like Isao, her husband had been arrested.

Masako had abandoned her tuna mixing to sit at the table with Iris huddled, sniffling, on her lap. "Mrs. Kealoha came to pick up goat milk for her baby," she said, "and she told me they're doing the same thing to other Japanese men, taking them away, with nothing, only what they have on." She stroked Iris's shoulder. "Thank goodness Isao asked for his shoes, or he'd be barefoot."

"What will they do with the people they arrest?" I asked.

Masako's eyes filled with tears again. "No one knows."

"If Dad is right there, by the cannery, maybe I can see him when I go work tomorrow," Aiko said. Like everything else, the cannery had stayed shut today.

"Don't get too close, Aiko," I said. "We don't want you arrested too. One of the guards threatened me today. Who knows what they might do to a young Japanese girl?"

"Please, Aiko, listen to Auntie Rose," Masako said. "Don't do anything to call attention to yourself. I don't want to lose you too. And I need you here in case they come and get me."

We all sat silent, frowning. Surely that wouldn't happen. Or would it? No one could say. Only a few days ago we'd never have expected Isao to be arrested.

I turned to Masako. "Mr. Crowder says I need to have a man to back me up, once we figure out who is in charge. We need to find an advocate, some high muckamuck *haole* man, to speak up for Isao. Would any of Isao's customers do it?"

She thought for a moment. "How about Mr. Breeze? He's a manager at the sugar plantation. Isao has done a lot of work for him."

I drove down the hill that afternoon to one of the managers' houses on the road to Paia and knocked on Mr. Breeze's door. He didn't invite me in, just opened the door enough to give me a puzzled look, so I stood on his porch and explained the situation.

"How do I know he's not one of them, sending messages home to the emperor?" he responded, scowling.

"Isao would never do that," I replied. "He's a U.S. citizen by birth, and he's lived here all his life. Maui is his home, not Japan."

Breeze snorted. "For God's sake, Miss McKenzie, don't try to get him out. We could be looking at an invasion here, and we need fellows like him safely locked away. I bet his parents registered him with the Japanese government, so he's probably a dual citizen."

I was getting nowhere with Mr. Breeze, so I thanked him for his time, trying to ignore the frown on his face, and took my leave.

When I got home and asked Masako, she confirmed that they were both dual citizens. Their parents had registered them at birth, as most *issei* parents did in those days. That complicated things. Breeze's suspicion was discouraging. I feared others would have the same response; maybe I needed to go it alone, without seeking a man to help me. I still didn't know who had the authority to free the men in the camps. Tomorrow, after school, I would go in search of Mr. Wentworth, head of the Maui Major Disaster Council.

It was close to sunset now, and we needed to start early on the evening chores. Masako invited me to come for dinner afterward, but I decided to settle into my blacked-out home, eat whatever came to hand, and try to prepare myself for tomorrow's classroom full of frightened teenagers.

• • • •

WE STOOD THE NEXT MORNING, hands over our hearts and eyes on the flag rising up the pole as the buglers played "To the Colors." There were fewer students than usual standing at attention between the wide entry steps and the school's vine-covered walls. And the ones who were here were absolutely still, with no side glances or stifled giggles. War had intruded on their childhood. Some of them, I supposed, would be swept up in that war just as they began their adult lives. I closed my eyes as the last notes faded and prayed that this would be over soon. Then I turned around and went to greet my homeroom class.

They all looked a little peaked, tight-jawed and wide-eyed. The few empty seats all belonged to students of Japanese ancestry. But most of the Japanese kids were here. If they'd all stayed home, we'd have half-empty buildings.

We pledged allegiance and listened to Mr. Crowder on the PA system. He repeated the plans for trench digging and first-aid classes, said the older boys would be forming a fire brigade, and ended with a little pep talk.

"It's up to us to carry on and do our bit," he said. "This is the time to dedicate yourself to being a good American, to speak English, and help your families to do the same. Whatever race you are, remember that we're all in this together. We'll all work together to win the war. And we'll do it while maintaining our aloha and the Maui High Saber spirit. Let's make this a time we're proud to remember and show the world that the students of Maui are good Americans and patriotic citizens."

The students seemed somewhat buoyed by Mr. Crowder's speech. It always helps to have a mission in a crisis. They set off for their first-period classes, but one student lingered. Lillian Tanimoto was a quiet girl, more reticent than ever in the past year.

"How are you doing, Lillian?" I asked.

"Soldiers came to our house, Miss," she said, her voice almost a whisper. "They were looking for my dad."

Impulsively, I put my arm around Lillian's thin shoulders, now slumped in despair, and she leaned against me a bit. Her father had died last year. "I'm so sorry that happened to you," I said. "It must make you and your mom extra sad."

"Thank you, Miss," Lillian replied, then plodded off to her class. I watched her go, making a mental note to stop by the Tanimotos' with some eggs and vegetables the first time I had a chance. The little family must be struggling with only Mrs. Tanimoto's salary from the plantation store. And now these suspicious authorities had added insult to injury with their intrusive visit.

My first-period students trickled in and settled at their desks, the now-familiar worried looks on their faces. I'd been planning to continue a lesson from last week when we had been preparing for an oratory contest. But I had decided to go off schedule, at least for today. We were all in shock still, trying to understand what had happened to us and our country, and my Core classes, a combination of English and social studies, were the perfect place to discuss the situation.

"Congress formally declared war yesterday," I began. "We'll all need to work hard to make sure we win the war. Let's make a list of things we can do." I turned to the board and picked up a piece of chalk. "Anyone have ideas?"

"Look out for invaders on the beach," said a boy who lived near the shoreline in Paia.

"Grow plenny food," said a girl from Kula, where the soil was dark and rich.

"Plenty of food, Charlotte," I reminded. "Because remember—we all need to speak good English, not pidgin." That got a few giggles, aimed at the chagrined Charlotte.

"Buy war stamps and bonds," said Nalani, a high achiever when it came to the stamps the girls' club was selling. She smiled and waved a handful of stamps. "I can sell you some after class." The giggles turned to laughs.

Finally, I gave them an assignment, to write a page about what they personally would do to help win the war, and told them to turn in a final, error-free draft the next day.

As the first-period class filed out, once again, a single student lingered. It was Mildred Kalama, whose father had been the policeman accompanying the men who took Isao.

"How are you doing, Mildred?" I asked, the standard question that started so many conversations in those trying days.

"I so shame, Miss," she replied, ducking her head in the same gesture her father had made on Isao's front porch two days ago.

"You're ashamed?" I replied, emphasizing the non-pidgin usage.

"Because of my father," Mildred said. "Because he helped them do arrests. My friends are mad at me."

"I'm sorry to hear that, Mildred. I guess they'll cool off after a while. It's not your fault he had to do his job."

"Yes, Miss." Mildred stared at her feet. "Do you think we have spies here, Miss?"

"I don't know, Mildred. I certainly hope not. But it's war, and the enemy sneaked up on us at Pearl Harbor, so we have to be careful." I patted her shoulder. "You keep being a good student and a good citizen, and we'll all work together to win the war." Despairing, I watched her trudge down the hall. I had to keep my Good Teacher face on, even for the daughter of the policeman who'd helped arrest my friend. But I was having a hard time dealing with the loss of Isao, whom I could guarantee was no spy. How I could prove it, I had no idea, but I knew I had to, and I planned to start that afternoon as soon as school was over.

I still had classes to teach, so I put Isao out of my mind and went about my day. At lunchtime, I walked outside to find Tom Stevens and his gang of seniors digging air-raid trenches. Tom and his wife, Harriet, were prospective tenants for my new rental cottage if we ever got it built. Perhaps he would know something as an officer with the provisional police that had been set up in the months before the war to supplement the regular police force.

The ditch diggers were halfway down the gulch that separated the campus from Hamakuapoko Village. Tom was swinging a pickax, breaking up the ground so the boys could follow along behind with shovels. They all took my arrival as an opportunity to rest for a moment.

"Look, Miss McKenzie, blisters!" said one of the boys.

"Me too!" Others chimed in, showing me their hands.

"Maybe tomorrow you can all come with gloves," I suggested.

"Keep digging, boys," Stevens ordered, but he rested his pick on the ground for a moment and turned to me.

"Never thought digging trenches would be part of my job," he said. He wiped sweat from his forehead, leaving a muddy streak.

"We live in an unusual time," I replied, then lowered my voice. "Tom, can I talk to you privately for a moment?"

Stevens glanced back at the boys, once again busily flinging dirt into piles alongside the trench. "Okay," he said, moving a few steps away.

"I'm trying to find out whom to approach about getting my farm manager released. I saw him working in that camp over in Haiku. Any suggestions?"

Stevens frowned, leaning on his pick. "I'm not sure. But you could start with the police in Wailuku. They're holding men at the jail, you know."

I nodded, thanked him, and headed back inside. I'd get through the afternoon's classes, drive to Wailuku, and try to see Mr. Wentworth and the police. At least I had two leads now.

• • • •

AT THE BANK IN WAILUKU where Wentworth was manager, I approached a woman sitting at a desk near the loan department. "I'm sorry, Mr. Wentworth is in a meeting and cannot be disturbed," she said. "As you can imagine, he is very busy. Would you like to leave a message?"

I wasn't sure how much good that would do, but I gave her my telephone number and left. Outside the bank, I hesitated. I'd save gas if I walked the few blocks up to the police station. The town was quiet, though most of the stores were open. I noticed that some Japanese-owned stores now had American flags hanging prominently near their entrances. I stepped into one to find there were two newspapers bearing today's date, a fifth war extra and the regular Wednesday "home edition." I bought both. The salesclerk (clad in a dress rather than a kimono, I noticed) bowed as I handed her my coins, then seemed to catch herself and stood straight, trying to smile.

I paused on the sidewalk, skimming through the news crammed onto every page. Terrible battles were happening across the Pacific. Locally, the Red Cross sought volunteers to sew, knit, fold bandages, or lend sewing machines. First-aid stations had been set up in various places. All firearms and ammunition must be turned in—but stores were allowed to sell limited amounts of liquor again, which I knew would make some people happy. Sighing, I tucked the newspapers under my arm and headed up Main Street.

At the police station, I went to the front desk and made my usual speech. "Can you help me? I'm trying to find out where my farm manager is—he got arrested the other day for no reason—he's done nothing wrong. His name is Isao Tanaka. Do you know where he is?"

"Sorry, ma'am, can't help you," the bored-looking police officer behind the desk said, pausing briefly as he flipped through papers in a file folder. He barely made eye contact with me. "We aren't giving out any information on the situation."

"Well, who can help me?" I asked, trying not to sound impatient.

He shrugged. "Can't say. Sorry." He turned, opened a file cabinet, and deposited the file. I was dismissed. Now what? I hated to go home with nothing, but I had no idea where to turn next. It was getting late, and I had homework to grade and chores to do before dark. I took a deep breath and headed back to my truck.

• • • •

HALF AN HOUR LATER, I pulled up at my backdoor, and Iris walked out, looking like she was in a hurry. When she saw me, she stopped in her tracks, a startled look on her face. Like all the Tanakas, Iris had the run of the place and could come into my house any time; the door was never locked. Sometimes I'd open the fridge to find that Masako or Aiko had been there to bottle and store milk. But in general, the family came in only when I was there.

"What's up, Iris?" I asked as I walked around the truck to pull the pile of books and homework papers from the passenger seat. She hesitated, hands behind her back, eyes on the ground, and dragged the toe of her shoe through the dirt.

"Oh, nothing," she said.

"How come you were in the house? Did you need something?"

"Um, I was looking to see how much vegetable scraps you had for the chickens tonight."

"Oh. Not a lot, huh? I'll have more after I make dinner."

"Okay." She said, still not looking at me. "I'll come back later. Bye!"

And she was gone, off down the hill to home. I watched her go, puzzled. Inside, I glanced around. Everything looked normal. No telling what was going through Iris's little mind; she usually picked up chicken scraps at chore time, which was an hour or so away. I shrugged and dumped my books on the table, put the kettle on, and turned my thoughts back to the conundrum of how to free Isao.

Chapter Five

Hiroki was going to be "Sam" from now on, he informed us as Masako and I sat drinking tea after chores that evening.

"I gotta show I'm American," he said. "And anyway, it's my name. We just never use it."

Isao and Masako had given all their kids both English and Japanese names, and the two youngest, Henry and Iris, had always been called by their English names. It was a sign of the gradual transition from a purely Japanese culture into which Isao and Masako's immigrant parents had been born to the increasingly American one in which these children were growing up.

Aiko, however, was having none of it. "I'm Aiko, that's who I am," she said, dumping chopped tofu into the pan where she was frying vegetables.

"Yeah, but you don't go school with a bunch of *haole* teachers anymore," Sam said, frowning. "You're *pau* with that, working with other local girls at the cannery, and they know how to say your name. Every year, I get a new teacher who takes a month to learn how to say 'Hiroki.' Anyway, get one war now. Gotta show our patriotism."

Stubborn, Aiko shook her head and kept on cooking. Masako bit her lip and looked at me with sad eyes.

We were all disappointed and discouraged. I wasn't sure where to turn next. I'd try again with Wentworth, of course, and keep asking around, but this whole thing was so unexpected. Why on earth would they have grabbed Isao, a carpenter and farmer thoroughly integrated into life in this American territory?

Sure, the Tanakas cherished the mementos of their family's past and tried to keep their culture and language alive, but so did everyone in Hawaii, and we blended those traditions, overlapping customs to make our own kind of culture. Those shared traditions gave flavor and color to our tiny community. We did small-town things, grew our food, and knew each other from childhood days. But when we gathered for a party, our little community showed its international roots, from all the cultures that made up our island population.

I remembered Frances De Silva's wedding, a few months ago. Late in the evening, after the ceremony and the food, folks had pulled out their instruments to *kanikapila*, playing and singing in the old Hawaiian style. Voices blended over strings in a language and rhythm that belonged to this place, and one by one, the dancers joined in.

Isao was a favorite, with his agile, sometimes naughty hula, a smile always on his face. And, when he wasn't dancing, he was playing ukulele, his fingers rapid on the strings, his eyes bright, singing songs learned from the Hawaiian cowboys he'd worked with from the time he was sixteen.

One of those cowboys was our host that night, our neighbor Frank De Silva, father of the bride. He bent to give greeting kisses to me and Masako as he worked his way through the crowd after overseeing the big grills where he and a line of cowboys had cooked steaks while their wives and daughters served a cornucopia of food from a half-dozen cultures. On long tables decorated with ferns and hibiscus stood bowls of *poi,* rolls of sushi, and great glass dishes full of English trifle.

The diners sat scattered across the lanai and the broad lawn, with stars twinkling in the dark sky above. Frances and her new husband held hands amid a circle of young friends under a giant poinciana tree. The musicians were taking a break, some tuning their instruments, some wandering off for a drink or a smoke.

Frances looks lovely, Frank," I said. "And she and Robert seem very happy."

"Yeah, he's a good kid. He get a good county job too, water department. Cannot go wrong with that. Job for life. Only thing, they going live down Wailuku. Only me and Momi up here now." He laughed. "Too bad. I could use some help, and I was hoping for a cowboy son-in-law, but Frances had her own ideas."

Isao appeared, having taken a bow as his dance ended and the musicians declared a break. He clapped Frank's shoulder. "No worry, Braddah, you call us if you need help. I bring my boys. We take care."

Frank smiled, but I knew he was wishing he had boys of his own, if not a daughter who had fallen in love with a cowboy rather than an accountant. But he and Momi had produced only one child. It wasn't going to get any easier, as time went on, for Frank to run his place by himself.

I'd be in even worse shape than that, all alone, if Frank hadn't shown up at my place one day years ago with two bleating goats slung over his saddle, their feet tied, and recommended that I hire Isao to build a shelter for them. From that job, our partnership had grown.

In those days, Isao still worked for Pono Spencer on the ranch where Frank, Masako, and I had grown up, the children of ranch workers. Our childhood gang ranged from the ranch owner's children to Masako, daughter of the cook and the stable man; me, daughter of the foreman; and Frank, whose father kept the gardens. Uncle Joaquin De Silva was Portuguese, and his wife, Auntie Napua, was full-blooded Hawaiian. As in many island families, their cultures had blended. Joaquin grew taro and pounded it into *poi* for the whole ranch family. And his Hawaiian wife baked sweet bread in a dome-shaped brick Portuguese oven. In the afternoons, famished from play, we would run to Auntie Napua to beg for bread.

Now, the ranch kids were all grown up, still friends and neighbors, still sharing the dishes and dances of our various homelands, on these green mountain slopes above a quiet town. I loved my place in this community and the roots that fed me from many cultures. Gatherings like the De Silvas' celebration filled me with joy and contentment. I was home.

My mind snapped back to the present as Iris set the table with bowls and chopsticks, and Aiko brought the rice and stir-fry to the table. Masako filled our bowls, and we ate, hungry after a long day that began and ended with farm chores we were not used to doing. No one said much. We were tired as well as hungry, carrying a heavy load not only of physical labor but of fear and uncertainty about what lay ahead, our ears always tuned to hear foreign planes in the sky.

Then there was grief for Isao. What was happening to him? What was he eating tonight? Would he sleep in a tent in the damp December chill of Haiku? No one spoke of it, but I knew we all wondered and worried.

Dinner finished, I said good night and headed home. I'd wrapped a piece of blue cellophane around my flashlight to dim its beam, and once at the house, I looked back to be sure no light showed around the edges of the Tanakas' windows.

I still had homework to grade, the Friday assignments most of the kids had remembered to bring when they returned to school this morning. But it took me a while to get in the mood. My heart hurt, imagining Masako facing the giant hole Isao's arrest had left in her life. Thank God she and the kids were safe here, with food from the farm and a roof over their heads, unlike other families who I knew would be thrown into poverty as well as despair by the loss of their breadwinner.

• • • •

OF ALL THE LATEST WARTIME restrictions, the one that bothered me the most was the rationing of gasoline. No more than three gallons were allowed, and only for a vehicle that held less than half a tank. My tank was still at three-quarters full, but I knew that wouldn't last long if I kept going all the way to Wailuku in my campaign to free Isao. And three gallons was nothing, barely enough to keep me driving back and forth to school every day. I'd have to switch tactics and use the phone to find out who to talk to and what to do for Isao.

So after school each day that week, I sat with the phone book, trying to reach someone with authority. I focused on Wentworth, since he was head of the disaster council, but he was never available and never returned my calls. I'd keep trying, badgering him until he found time to talk to me, I thought as I dialed his number on Friday afternoon. Wentworth's secretary was beginning to sound a bit miffed with me as she explained that, no, Mr. Wentworth was still unavailable, but I cared only to the extent that I wanted her to keep taking my messages and passing them along. Maybe I should drop off a dozen eggs for each of them next time I had enough reasons to expend the gas for a trip to Wailuku, I thought as I hung up.

Now what? I still had no idea who was in charge of these arrests and the camps where the men were held. Maybe it was the military. I looked through the phone book, hoping to find a number for the camp in Paukukalo where the National Guard had been on active duty for the past few months. There was no listing. Then I remembered that my hairdresser had a son in that unit. She might know how to reach them.

"Oh yeah, I get one number," Gladys said. "Try wait, I go look." A moment later she was back with a number for the Guard and a suggestion. "Try call the airbase at Puunene too. Maybe they might know something."

"Do you know their number?"

"Ah, no, sorry. But maybe National Guard folks can tell you."

"Sorry, ma'am I cannot help you," said the Guardsman who answered the phone. "I don't know who is in charge of that. And I cannot tell you the air station number. They not taking calls from civilians."

I hung up and sat drumming my fingers on the tabletop. This was so frustrating.

Then the phone rang. It was Wentworth. I sat up straighter as relief surged through me.

"Miss McKenzie, I'm sorry it has taken me so long to answer you. As you know, there's a war on, and we're quite busy. I understand you want information about your farm manager."

"Yes, Isao Tanaka. I have no idea why he was arrested, and I need him here to help me run my farm. He's a loyal native-born American, and we were making plans for increasing our food production when they took him away. How can I get him released?"

"I'm afraid you can't, Miss McKenzie," Wentworth replied, his voice cold and impatient. "Tanaka is on the list the FBI compiled of potential saboteurs, and he'll be held by the military for the foreseeable future."

"Isao is not a saboteur," I said, trying to keep my own voice calm. "He's lived here all his life, works hard for his family and the community, and is a patriotic American."

"Well, be that as it may, as I understand it, Tanaka was on the planning committee the last few times *Shintoku Maru* visited, which makes him suspect. I'm afraid you're going to have to manage without him, Miss McKenzie. And now I must get back to work. Good afternoon." Wentworth hung up before I could respond.

I sat staring at the phone. An answer at last. Isao had been active with the local hospitality committee when the Japanese naval training ship *Shintoku Maru* made its annual visits to the island in the years before things became so tense between Japan and the United States.

I stood up and headed straight to give Masako the news.

When I told her what Wentworth had said, Masako dropped her dish towel and sank into a chair, burying her face in her hands. Aiko stepped closer to put a hand on Masako's shoulder, and Iris looked from her mother to me, distressed.

"But, Auntie, that was just for fun," Sam said, a disbelieving frown on his face.

"Yeah, fun to visit the ship, and we got to help make one *luau* that night," Henry said, looking confused.

"And all the handsome sailors ..." Aiko's voice trailed off. "Now they shooting at us."

Masako looked up, her face pale.

"Rose, this makes me think. Remember how we brought some sailors back here for tea a couple of years ago? And then took them on an Upcountry tour?"

"Oh my God, of course," I said. Chills ran down my back as the possibilities dawned on me. "And now those sailors know exactly how to get here, and that we have gardens and livestock. Not good."

Masako nodded. "Plus, we drove them up to Kula, where you can see the whole central valley and the beaches on both sides. Great landing spots. One sailor even took photos." She covered her face again. "Oh, what have we done?"

"But you didn't mean to do anything bad. You were just being hospitable, and we had no idea Japan would attack us. Not a good reason to throw Isao in prison," I insisted, then paused. "I guess the U.S. government might look at it differently, though."

"I guess they do," Masako said, shaking her head sadly.

Sam spoke up, his face grim. "We need to be ready to defend ourselves if they invade. They could come straight up here looking for food. Maybe we should all keep a pickax or something by our beds every night."

"I need to make sure the locks on my doors actually work," I said. "I've never used them, but they might help slow down anyone trying to come in." I shivered at the thought of enemy marauders invading my house and finding me there alone. "You folks don't even have locks, right?"

"I can make a bar across the door," Sam said. "At least if they have to break a window to get in, it will wake us up and we have time to get ready."

Iris's eyes widened, and Henry gulped as we all exchanged fearful glances.

Masako cleared her throat and dabbed her eyes. "And Mr. Wentworth wouldn't say how we can get him out? Or when we can see him?"

I shook my head. "No, he said we can't get Isao released. And he hung up before I could ask about visiting."

We sat glumly for a while, as dark clouds covered the sunset. The room was gloomy; the air, December chill. The walls seemed empty, with the blank spots left where Isao had removed the family's heirlooms to hide away in my tool room.

"We'll keep trying," I said. "I'll do everything I can, Masako. You know that. At least we know where he is, and eventually, we'll find out what's going on. But it doesn't look like it's going to be quick or easy. I think we have to get on with our work, help win this damn war, and keep advocating for Isao any way we can."

"You right, Auntie," said Sam. "The more patriotic we are, the better for Pop." He tapped one foot impatiently. "I only wish I could sign up for the Army. That would show them."

"No, no, Hiroki," Masako said, clutching his arm.

"Sam, Mom. It's Sam."

"Hah!" Aiko said. "They throw your father behind barbed wire, and you want to go fight for them?"

"Fight for us, Aiko, not them!" Sam said angrily, standing from his seat at the table to face his sister.

"They not going let you get your hands on a gun," Aiko responded, clenching her fists. "They think we're traitors, no matter what we do. You're wrong, Sam! Don't even try to sign up!"

"You folks calm down," Masako said, reaching to grasp her children's hands. "Sit, both of you. We can't let this mess make us fight each other."

Scowling, Sam plopped back onto his chair, while Aiko angrily yanked out one next to her mother and sat with arms folded, legs crossed, and lips pressed tightly together.

"It's a mistake that they took Pop, a misunderstanding," Sam said in a calmer voice. "Sooner or later, they're going to realize that and let him out. But we gotta help by being as American as we can."

"I thought we already were," Henry said. "How can we be more American? We already know, no more *Shintoku Maru,* no more Japanese school, no more nothing Japanese." He frowned. "We hid the Boys Day carp flags and the Girls Day dolls at Auntie's house. And I guess no more bon dance this summer. What else we gotta do?"

"Like I said, keep on with your life and help win the war," I replied. "Go to school, study hard, make good grades. Just what your parents always tell you, *ganbatte*—do your best. I'm sure things will come up that we'll all be asked to do, and we'll do them, whatever it takes."

"You folks already help with the garden and the animals," Masako said. "If we can feed ourselves, and maybe have food to share or trade or even sell, we'll be doing our bit." She paused, and her shoulders slumped as if they strained to hold a sudden burden. "Auntie is right. I need you folks to do your best. Your father made all the important decisions and did the hardest work, but now we have to do things for ourselves." After a moment, Masako turned to look out the window. "And right now, we're almost out of daylight. Let's go get the animals in." We all stood and set off to do the evening chores.

· · · ·

THE MAUI NEWS, which once had featured stories of tea parties, sports, and the Board of Supervisors, now provided one shocking headline after another, astounding news of the world aflame and our island chain's efforts to cope. On Saturday, I walked to the store to see if the paper had published a "war extra" that day.

They had, and the news was awful, as usual. "GUAM TAKEN!" filled the top of page 1, another blow to the hope that we might win this damn thing anytime soon. Japanese airplanes were pounding the Philippines and leapfrogging across the Pacific, taking island after island. Could we be next? Would they try again, and maybe invade this time? In Honolulu, civilians were being evacuated from coastal areas, and the U.S. West Coast was strengthening its defenses in fear of attack as well. With so much uncertainty, we needed to be as self-sufficient as possible.

The next morning, Masako and I sat and made a long list, trying to prioritize and parcel out the jobs that lay before us. We'd already discussed what to plant, but Masako had a few more suggestions: peanuts, sweet potatoes, more papaya trees. We were in for a lot of work, but there was no way around it. We had to be ready to survive on what we could grow.

"I guess we have to be realistic," Masako said after a while. "Isao might be gone a long time." Her voice broke. "I don't know how to live without him."

"No wonder. You've been together since you were sixteen," I said. "You've been a couple for most of your lives, longer than anyone else I know."

"Now I have to run the house and keep the family going." She looked at me, her face distressed. "How am I going to do that, Rose? I can hardly move right now, never mind taking Isao's place. I barely slept last night."

I leaned across the table to place my hand on her arm. "You're strong, Masako. Maybe we can figure out how to get him free. Meanwhile, you tell me how I can help, and I'll do my best."

She nodded, sniffing. "I know. I appreciate your help, especially with people like Mr. Wentworth. He probably wouldn't even answer if I called. But I have to figure out how to be the head of the family. Hiroki is so strong-willed and so angry! They all need their father, and I can't be him.

"And there are practical things, like money," she said. "I'll keep up my end of the farm work, but I gotta have cash too. I don't want to spend all our savings to survive. I'm going to have to go to work, somehow, doing something."

"Maybe you can find something part-time."

Masako nodded. "Something in the neighborhood, so I don't have to use the truck and spend money for gas," she said. "Maybe something in Makawao town, at one of the stores."

"We'll have to keep our eyes open for possibilities," I replied. "Meanwhile, why don't we go take a look at the garden?"

Outside, Masako and I surveyed the area where we grew vegetables now, on the *mauka* side of the driveway. Before they arrested Isao, we'd talked about expanding the garden closer to the driveway. On the other side of the driveway and the cypresses that lined it was the grazing field that also could be planted.

"We're definitely going to need Mr. Watanabe's tractor," I said. "All that thick grass—too hard to dig up. I know Isao taught Sam how to drive it, so maybe we should go ask if we can rent it."

We took off in my truck to the Watanabes' place, up the road a few miles. A fine mist began to wet the windshield as we climbed the mountain.

Mr. Watanabe was working on his pickup truck in a cluttered open shed near the house. Dressed in greasy overalls and holding a wrench, he looked up as we pulled into the driveway but did not come to greet us.

"Why don't you stay here and let me ask him. He knows me," Masako said, and got out of the truck. She walked quickly in the mist to the shelter of the shed. Mr. Watanabe didn't smile as Masako approached, and his face didn't change as she spoke. The truck's windows were up, so I couldn't hear his reply, but it was short. Masako immediately turned and headed back to the truck, her head down.

"Let's go," she said as she climbed up onto the seat.

"What happened?"

"He said no."

"What? Why?"

"Please, let's just go," she said, her voice thick.

"Maybe he'll listen to me," I said as I opened the door and stepped out. Mr. Watanabe glanced up as I strode toward him, then looked at his car engine and avoided my gaze as I came closer.

"Mr. Watanabe, could you please let us rent your tractor? I am willing to pay, of course, and you know that Isao has trained Hiroki to use it. We only need it for one day, and we'll bring it back."

Watanabe glowered as he looked up at me, wrench still clutched in grubby oil-stained hands.

"I no like get in trouble with the FBI," he said. "They might be watching, you know. Bumbye they come take me away too." He shook his head and bent over his car engine again. "I busy now, cannot talk."

Amazed not only that Isao's friend could refuse his wife's request for help but that he would turn down even my request, I walked slowly back to the car. Fear permeated our lives now. Local Japanese afraid of being arrested. The rest of the community afraid of some secret saboteur hidden in plain sight. All of us afraid that the enemy would return.

Masako stared straight ahead as I backed out of the driveway and headed home. Both of us were silent.

At home, I met her in front of the truck, where she stood in the mist that had followed us down the hill. "Masako, what did he say to you?"

"He said, 'I no like end up in one jail because I wen' help you folks,'" Masako replied, her eyes downcast. She blinked and pressed her lips together. "I guess he thinks this sabotage nonsense is contagious." She lifted her eyes to mine, then looked away again. "I'm sorry, Rose, I hope we don't contaminate you too."

Impulsively, I threw my arms around her, and for a moment Masako rested her head on my shoulder, but we were neither of us the hugging type, and we quickly stepped back, a bit embarrassed. I grabbed her hand, though. This was way too painful for my old friend to let her stand alone.

"You are not contagious, or for that matter, in any way to blame for this mess," I said. "Someone else will lend us a tractor, I just need to think of whom to ask." It had never occurred to me that a local Japanese American would turn on his neighbor. I hoped Watanabe wouldn't try to get Masako and the rest of the family into trouble with the authorities.

"You know," I continued, "it's probably best if you folks keep your heads down for the time being. Let me deal with the outside world until things settle a bit. And meanwhile, as I told the kids, we'll just carry on. That's all we can do."

Chapter Six

It took only one phone call. Our neighbor Frank De Silva said he'd be happy to bring his tractor over and help us that afternoon. Tall, silver-haired, and reassuring, he showed up not long after lunch. Masako and I watched as he turned up the long strip of grass between the existing garden and the driveway and the patch on the other side, both well-fertilized from goats grazing there over the years. I tried to pay Frank, but all he would accept was the box Masako had put together—some vegetables, a pineapple Aiko had brought home, a loaf of yeast bread Masako had baked, and a chunk of butter wrapped in waxed paper.

"Ho, Masako, thank you," he said. "Bread as good as my mother used to make!"

We all smiled, remembering Auntie Napua and the golden loaves we'd enjoyed as children.

"Maybe not that good," Masako demurred. "Frank, thank you so much for helping us."

"Yes, thank you, Frank, we so appreciate it," I said.

"No worry," he replied as he mounted his tractor for the short ride up the road to his own homestead. "I help you out anytime you need. You folks take care—Isao is one good guy. They gonna turn him loose soon, and we gonna win this damn war."

Both of us were teary-eyed as we watched Frank drive away. But there was no time to waste, and we both knew we'd feel better if we were busy. Masako went to call the kids, and soon we were all raking and hoeing to get out the roots and bits of grass, preparing the soil for new crops.

By Sunday afternoon, we'd managed to cultivate the new section of the original garden and haul up wheelbarrows full of compost from the pile where Isao and the boys tossed manure and straw when they cleaned the stables. When I left for school Monday morning,

Masako was already out with a hoe, carving furrows in the soft soil. And by the time I came home, pigeon pea seedlings marched in a tidy row along the edge of the garden. In a few months' time, they would grow into deep-green bushes as tall as me.

I was pulling my blackout curtains closed that evening when I heard faint booms in the distance. I froze, fear flooding my body, trying to determine the direction of the sounds. Quickly, I turned on the radio's police band. Kahului was being shelled. I rushed outside and up the driveway toward Kahului, hoping to get a better sense of what was happening. Masako and the kids were not far behind me.

Masako pulled Iris and Henry close, and we stood listening, but the booms had stopped.

"Is that it?" I asked. "Or are they coming back again?"

"I don't know," Masako said, wide-eyed. "What if this is the beginning of the invasion?"

We stood huddled together, straining our ears to hear any unusual sound, from explosions like those of a moment ago to an airplane overhead. There was nothing. Just the usual flutter of leaves in the night breeze.

"I don't want to be home alone," I said, shivering in the cool December air.

"Yeah, safety in numbers," Masako said, tightening her hold on Iris and Henry. "Do you want to come to our place, sleep on a futon?"

"Or you could come to my place. We could bring mattresses from upstairs, put the kids on the couches, and you folks could have the whole living room."

"I think we should do that," Sam said. "Your house has a darker roof, and all the big trees around kind of camouflage it. Our house is more out in the open, easier to see."

"Fine with me," I said. "Plus I have real locks on the doors, for what it's worth." I shivered again. "And don't forget to bring your weapons."

"I have an old hoe, Auntie," Iris said. "I practiced hitting the compost heap with it, and I'm pretty good."

"Atta girl," I said. Iris could make me smile even in the worst of times. "You'll be a brave woman warrior if we ever need it." I patted her shoulder. "But let's hope we don't. Still, I would feel so much better if we were all together, at least overnight."

While the Tanakas went to change into their night clothes and gather their makeshift weapons, I filled pots and buckets with water in case Japanese shells reached as far as our little farm. Those few gallons might have been useless, but I needed to do something. Inside, I turned the door keys back and forth in their locks to make sure they would work. Sam and Henry dragged the two big mattresses from the upstairs bedrooms, and Masako and I distributed blankets and pillows. I made cocoa, and we pulled out a deck of cards and a Monopoly game so we'd have something to do until bedtime besides worry.

Once we went to bed, I tossed and turned, ears tuned to hear sounds from the sky. But there were no more explosions, and eventually, I fell asleep. The morning light woke us, and the Tanaka family went home, leaving the mattresses in place. They would stay over at least one more night, just in case.

That day, most of my students were back in their seats, some still downcast, others gung-ho, aiming their youthful energy to win the war. All of us kept glancing out the classroom windows toward the sea below and the sky above, waiting for the worst. The students buzzed with details of the attack.

"We saw flashes from my house," said one Kahului student. "It was one submarine, firing at us from way out at sea."

"My dad and I climbed up on the roof," said a boy from Puunene, several miles from the harbor. "Plenty loud bangs and fire out on the ocean."

"Even us," said a farmer's daughter from Kula. "We could see it from outside in the backyard. Ho, da scary, but!"

Mr. Crowder reassured us in his morning address. "Very little damage was done," he said. "Only a hit to the Maui Pine smokestack and roof. No homes were hit, but a few chickens got their feathers blown off."

That brought uneasy laughs from my homeroom class, but they were somber as they packed up their books and headed off to first period. Everyone was jittery all day, and rumors flew.

Later that morning, the PA system sputtered to life, and we all looked up from our lesson. It was Mr. Crowder.

"Students and teachers, we have been instructed by the military governor that there will be no school, effective tomorrow morning, until further notice," the principal announced in a solemn voice. "When you leave today, be sure to take all your belongings with you. We don't know when we'll be back in class. Meanwhile, keep your chins up, help any way you can in the war effort, and keep an eye on *The Maui News* for notification of our return. All school activities are canceled, of course, and it's likely we won't be back until after Christmas, so I'll sign off by wishing you a Merry Christmas and a Happy New Year, and I hope you and your family stay safe until we meet again."

Shoulders relaxed and expressions eased around the room. At least we wouldn't be sitting ducks, here in this big building in the middle of the cane fields.

When the final bell rang that afternoon, I locked my classroom and headed to the teachers' lounge for a meeting Mr. Crowder had called.

"I hope you realize that we're on our own here on Maui," the principal warned as we clustered around the big table in the middle of the room, all of us tense. "There are only a couple of hundred National Guardsmen on duty at Paukukalo, plus however many men building the airport at Puunene. I doubt they have much in the way of arms or ammunition to defend us if we're invaded, so think defensively. Get your place in order, plant a garden, set up a first-aid kit and a system for fire control." Teachers exchanged anxious glances as we gathered our belongings, and conversations were muted and sober. Ten days into the war, and we were still treading water in a sea of uncertainty.

• • • •

THE NEXT MORNING, AFTER Aiko left for the cannery, Masako and I, plus the three school-age kids, got to work. We still needed to break up the soil in the field behind my house, so the boys and I worked on that while Masako and Iris planted vegetables in the garden expansion.

It was a little overcast on this December day, and the air was cool and crisp, scented with upturned soil and eucalyptus, good working weather. I breathed deeply; as bad as things were, the beauty of my home lifted my heart.

Sam, Henry, and I swung picks and hacked at clumps of soil with hoes, then raked to create a fine layer of soil suitable for seeds. By noon, we were ready to sprinkle tiny sorghum seeds in the furrows. They would grow into plants whose parts were all edible for our livestock, from the foliage the goats and cattle would gobble to clumps of grain for the chickens.

I had just scattered my first handful of grain when we heard the airplane. Everyone stopped working and looked up at the sky, then rushed to the cypress trees along the driveway. We squeezed between their branches, hoping to be invisible. Airplanes rarely flew over this part of the island, so this sudden appearance was terrifying.

"Auntie, is it Japanese?" Iris asked, whispering through the branches as if the pilots might hear her from high in the sky.

"No, I see a star on the wings, not a rising sun," Sam said as the plane passed directly overhead. "I don't know what they're doing way up here, but it's one of ours."

Relieved, we headed back to plant the sorghum field. Explosions in the nighttime and airplanes in the afternoon. It was nerve-racking.

Once the seeds were scattered, we stopped for lunch and a rest, then went back to the field. Sam and Henry loaded the wheelbarrow with bagasse, the fiber left after the juice was extracted from sugarcane. Sam pushed the wheelbarrow up to the sorghum field, and we scattered handfuls of bagasse over the seeds we'd just planted. I was hoping that cover would deter birds from digging them up. We needed this crop, and I wasn't sure when we would be able to get more seeds.

"That was a lot of work. I'm not used to it these days," I said as I collapsed onto a porch chair that afternoon, cup of tea in hand.

"You'll sleep well tonight," Masako said, and sipped the cup I'd just handed her.

"I hope so." Automatically, I glanced at the sky and cocked an ear to listen for planes. I saw nothing out there but clouds and heard only the voices of the kids sprawled on the lawn below my front porch. "I'm finding it hard to sleep these days, what with submarines shelling the harbor."

"Me too," Masako said. "That and worrying about Isao and wondering how he is."

"Has Aiko been able to see anything from the cannery? Or heard any rumors about what's going on over there?"

Masako shook her head. "No. She sees the barbed wire and says there are guard towers at the corners and armed guards, but it's far enough from the cannery that she can't see who's inside. I keep warning her not to get too close." Her face clouded over. "I just wish they'd let me take him some clean clothes. I know he's going crazy, wearing the same clothes all this time."

Isao was as meticulous about cleanliness and his clothing as he was about his work. Every afternoon, he fired up the *furo* he'd built behind their house and got in for a long soak in steaming hot water. "It keeps my body moving," he always said. "Steams out the wrinkles." I was pretty sure he wasn't getting baths in that makeshift prison. I clenched my jaw, frustrated. We knew where Isao was, just down the hill, so close. And yet we were unable to do anything to help him.

· · · ·

A COUPLE OF DAYS LATER, I glanced up from chopping vegetables to see Frank De Silva's red truck pull up. I stepped out the back door, always happy to see his kind face and glad of an excuse to be outside as the late-afternoon glow turned the landscape golden.

"Rose, you heard about the pasture order?" he asked, climbing out of the truck.

"No, what's that?"

"The military government says we gotta block off our pastures—put one old car or one tree—so Japanese planes cannot land."

"Oh dear, how am I going to do that?" I said. "How would I get a tree into the middle of a pasture?"

"I was wondering if I can borrow Isao's boys, and with my tractor fix my pastures and yours, same time," Frank said. "Pull some trees down, spread 'em out."

"That would be swell, Frank," I said, relieved. "Thank you for thinking of me. Though, actually, I suspect my pastures won't need much, since they either have fences crossing them or are on a steep slope. Why don't we walk over to look and, on the way, stop at the Tanakas' to draft the boys."

Sam and Henry were playing what looked like a not-very-interesting card game, but they perked up when I stuck my head in the door and told them I needed them to help Uncle Frank with some defense work. We followed the fence line to get a good look at my pasture. The grass was a brilliant green against the sky turning orange with sunset. The cattle wandered closer, hoping for a handout.

"I think you're right, Rose," Frank said, stroking his mustache as he looked at the steep slope to the gulch. "Only that one place over there."

"Could you pull out a small eucalyptus with your tractor?" Vaughn had planted the row of eucalyptus at the pasture's edge years ago.

"Easy," Frank said, nodding. He turned to the boys. "Harder at my place. More trees, maybe need some sawing to get big branches off to spread across," he warned.

"We can do it," Sam said, standing straight and looking serious. "Yeah, we can," Henry chimed in.

The next day, I handed the boys a bag of sandwiches to share with Frank as they set off to walk up the road, and in the afternoon, Frank drove his tractor over to pull a few small eucalyptus trees across our pasture. Enemy planes would be hard put to land in our neighborhood now.

Frank's tractor would be no help in digging an air-raid shelter, and I knew no one who owned a backhoe. So the boys set to work with shovels. They followed a diagram the newspaper had printed showing a trench six feet deep and two feet wide, with a slope on one end for entry and exit. Masako and I embellished the trench with short walls of old lumber, reinforced on the outside with the excavated dirt. We shaped the sloping entryway into steps with a shovel and hoe and topped the shelter with corrugated iron and dirt. "I'm going to plant sweet potatoes on top," Masako said as we contemplated our new shelter.

"Good idea," I said, and chuckled. "Camouflage and food, all in one place, greens at least. Probably not deep enough for the potatoes."

"And I have another idea, Rose," Masako said, turning toward me with her hands on her hips. "I'm going to take a couple of quarts of milk and some butter over to Frank and Momi tomorrow, to say thanks for his help, and I would like to take some milk to Mrs. Harada. You know her husband got arrested too, and she has those three little kids."

"Of course," I said. "And whatever else you think she might need that we have."

Masako nodded gravely. "We're so lucky. Even with Isao gone, we have more than enough to share with families who need help."

Those women, struggling in these terrible times to raise children without their men, haunted my thoughts as I lay down to sleep that night. A gift of food could mean so much to them, as it had to me when I was a young teacher starting out and Vaughn came to visit, bringing me baskets of eggs and vegetables and banana bread made by Masako's mother, Yuki. Those visits and those gifts had sparked our romance.

It had been a most unlikely courtship.

I grew up on Vaughn's ranch, calling him "Uncle." Only after he was widowed, and I returned from four years of schooling and teaching in California, did our feelings for each other develop into a love affair. The twenty-plus years of difference in our ages didn't matter to us. We were engaged, though informally. We knew the little world where we lived would be scandalized, and so we waited, talking about how we would tell his children, how society would react, but mostly spending our limited time together simply enjoying being in love.

Then I realized I was pregnant. Before Vaughn could tell his children that we would marry, he was fatally injured in a fall from his horse. In the stunned aftermath of his passing, his daughter revealed that he had, with his last breath, left me this little farm, with five acres and a four-bedroom house. Heartbroken, pregnant, and alone, I went to California, hoping to return years later with a plausible explanation for the child I had borne.

But then I lost the baby in a bloody and painful miscarriage. The doctor told me I'd never carry a child to term.

Eventually, I returned to Maui and the farm. I would be eternally grateful for the security Vaughn's bequest had given me. But much as I loved my life here, I would have traded it in an instant for more time with Vaughn. I knew what it was to live without the man you loved, and now Masako did too. We'd share all we could of our farm's bounty with those women deprived of their men in a time of peril.

Chapter Seven

Two weeks after Isao's arrest, Masako finally got word that she could drop off clean clothes for her husband. She bustled about choosing what to take, almost as excited by this opportunity to care for her husband as she would have been to see him. I drove her down to Haiku and walked with her to the porch of one of the old pineapple workers' dormitories, the one farthest from the barbed wire fence where Isao was imprisoned. We stopped to gaze over at that compound, hoping to glimpse Isao, but we could see no one except the guards on the towers. We climbed the steps to the dormitory porch, where more guards were collecting packages from families for their men. Masako handed over her neatly wrapped stack of clean clothes, Isao's favorite shirts, a warm sweater, khaki pants, socks, pajamas, and underwear. One of the guards ripped open the package for inspection. Masako flinched at the sight.

"I hope everything in that package gets to my husband," she said to the soldier who was recording the deliveries, a pudgy fellow in an Army uniform.

"As long as there's no contraband, it will," he replied in a bored voice. He kept his eyes on the page where he was busily recording the contents of the package as the other man spread them on the table.

"When will I be able to visit him?" Masako asked, her voice anxious.

"Can't tell you, ma'am. You'll be notified."

"It's been so long," I said. "I hope it's soon."

He looked up at me, frowning. "What's your interest here, ma'am?"

"He's my farm manager, and we need him to expand our food production to help the war effort," I replied. The "farm manager" argument seemed to be the only leverage we had.

"Sorry, ma'am, can't help you. It's up to the brass. We're just doing our job."

We watched in dismay as the guard stuffed Isao's clean and pressed shirts and pants into the tattered package. Reluctantly, trying again to catch a glimpse of Isao as we passed the barbed wire fence, we trudged back to my Ford. Masako's shoulders drooped as we headed up the road home, and I had no words to comfort her.

• • • •

IN THE GRIM ATMOSPHERE of those first few weeks of the war, none of us was in a holiday mood. But a few days before Christmas, my friend Jeanette called. "Darling, will you come over Christmas Eve for drinks and a meal with a few friends? We were going to skip the festivities but decided to go ahead with just the nearest and dearest. After all, why should those damn Japs steal all our fun? We'll start early, so everyone can be home before the blackout."

So early Christmas Eve afternoon, looking forward to a bit of normality, I fixed my hair for the first time in days, taming my waves with fancy barrettes. I put on red lipstick and a moss-green party frock that complemented my eyes and headed to the Thorntons' place.

Jeanette and her husband, Jim, lived in one of the plantation managers' homes down the hill from Makawao, a lovely house with wide windows that looked over a manicured garden and the long green slopes to central Maui. Jim worked for the sugar plantation, an Oahu boy from an old island family who'd met Jeanette when she was a teacher at Maui High. Jeanette had rented a room from me when she first arrived on Maui, and we'd become best friends. I was the maid of honor at her wedding and godmother to her twin daughters. Jeanette was the only person on Maui who knew the whole story of my love affair with Vaughn, my dreadful miscarriage, and the doctor's warning that I should never become pregnant again.

Jeanette was famous for her parties, and I was a regular guest. Today's gathering was relatively subdued, with only a couple of cars parked on the lawn. I did my usual scan of the sky and chose to park my Ford under the shelter of a poinciana tree just in case Japanese bombers flew overhead while I was inside.

Jeanette greeted me at the door. She looked lovely, as always, with her honey-blond hair in waves to her shoulders, and a full-skirted red dress whose tight bodice showed off her tiny waist. She reached to give me a hug, pulling me close, then leaned back, still holding my shoulders. "How are you doing, darling? It's so dreadful, isn't it? We hear terrible stories about what's happening on Oahu, and it's all so frightening."

I nodded. "Yes. I doubt I would be celebrating Christmas at all if you hadn't called."

"Well, as you can see, I did put up some greenery, and of course we have our tree, but this will be our only social gathering until who knows when."

I could smell the scent of a pine tree, harvested from one of the plantation's mountain properties. It stood in a corner, tinsel-clad, and greenery framed the doorways. Outside the windows, poinsettias bloomed, and inside Jeanette had placed lush red, gold, and green arrangements of anthuriums, ginger, and palm leaves.

I handed Jeanette a plate full of cookies and cinnamon rolls I'd baked that morning, and she handed it to the maid, who I noticed was in a crisp white uniform instead of her usual kimono. "Merry Christmas, Shizue," I said. Shizue smiled and bowed her head, then took my offering to the kitchen.

"Darling, come, have a drink. Thank God Jim had a few bottles stashed away. Who knows when we'll get enough for another party." Jeanette linked arms with me and led me to the table where her yard man, all cleaned up and dressed in a white shirt with a red bow tie, was acting as bartender.

"How are you, Alfredo?" I said as he handed me my usual gin and tonic. "*Mele Kalikimaka.*"

"Doing our best to win the war, Miss," he replied, looking serious. "And *Mele Kalikimaka* to you too."

Jeanette turned at the ring of the doorbell, releasing my arm. "Sorry, darling I've got to answer the door," she said, and she was off in a whirl of skirts and a whiff of perfume. I turned to survey the room. The crowd was sparse. Jim's cousin, who worked with him at the plantation, stood near the front window, deep in discussion with the old man who lived next door. Frowning, they looked out the window, searching the sky, as we all did so often lately. Their wives sat in easy chairs across the room next to Jeanette's daughter, Carolyn. Jim's mother, Mrs. Thornton, sat on the couch across from them. The women all wore serious expressions. This was not the usual festive atmosphere of Jeanette's holiday parties.

Carolyn, seeing me look her way, gave me a wave; she and her twin sister, Madelyn, would graduate next year. They were smart girls who'd skipped a grade in elementary school and were some of the best students in my literature classes. Until December 7, their future had been predictable. After high school, they had planned to go off to a private girls college on the mainland. From there, most girls of their social set would come home to the matrimonial track that likely would lead to marriage with rising young stars of the plantation world. But with the war on, such certainty seemed gone.

Jim appeared with several dusty bottles of wine and handed them to Alfredo, who pulled out a cloth and began cleaning them.

"Red wine, roast beef for dinner," Jim said, bending from his six-foot-three height to give me a kiss on the cheek. "Ought to have had them open breathing earlier, but I suppose we'll be here drinking up the hard stuff a while longer." He turned to greet the guest who had just arrived, an old Punahou schoolmate who lived up the road.

Across the room stood a table filled with *pupus*—hors d'oeuvres— olives, stuffed celery, and crackers topped with seasoned cream cheese or deviled ham, all arranged artistically amid ferns and halved pineapples filled with little pineapple cubes wrapped in bacon. If it was going to be a while until dinner, I needed something in my stomach to soak up the gin, so I filled a little plate and sat beside Mrs. Thornton. She was wearing her favorite dressy black silk, with a lace collar to match her pure white hair, piled high in a pompadour.

"Oh, my dear, did you hear about the freighter that was torpedoed?" she said, turning to me. "I was sitting with Mittee on her porch in Spreckelsville when the lifeboat came ashore, and the sailors stumbled onto the beach."

"My goodness, you were there when the lifeboat landed?" I said, leaning closer. "I read about it in the paper. How amazing that you were right there."

"We could barely believe our eyes, as these filthy men came ashore right in front of Mittee's house, all skinny and exhausted," Mrs. Thornton said. "Some collapsed as soon as they reached the sand, so Mittee called her servants, and we all helped them get up onto the grass and into the shade. They were dreadfully sunburned, poor things. Of course, we gave them water, and the cook went to work making coffee and sandwiches while the poor fellows waited for the ambulance to come."

"They must've been starved, after ten days at sea with only the little bit of food they managed to grab before the freighter sank," I said, imagining the scrawny survivors sprawled across Mittee's lawn. "How many of them were there?"

"Thirty of them made it ashore in that tiny lifeboat," Mrs. Thornton replied. "Four were lost, and the survivors were in terrible shape. Once they got them to the hospital, the doctor told the nurses to give them all a shot of whiskey, tuck them up with warm blankets, and let them sleep. When they woke, the hospital staff fed them whatever they wanted." Mrs. Thornton shook her head. "What a time we're having. I never thought I'd live to see another war, and this one in our backyard."

I nodded, sobered by the thought of more people suffering from an attack by a nation whose young sailors had been on my own property, so friendly and interested in our farm, only a couple of years ago.

Suddenly, Mrs. Thornton's face brightened. "Oh, look, it's little Teddy, up from his nap."

I smiled, always happy to see Teddy. He was what plantation folks called a ratoon crop baby—named for the second crop of sugarcane or pineapple that sprang up after a harvest. Teddy had been a surprise, born when his older sisters were already in high school. Now the baby clung to Madelyn, one of those sisters. She came toward us, and I stretched out my arms. Madelyn set the baby on my lap, and I pulled him in close while Mrs. Thornton smiled indulgently and reached to tickle his bare feet.

"I've done my duty," Madelyn said, giving a mock salute. "Now I'm off to eat *pupus* and talk story. How are you, Auntie Rose, I mean Miss McKenzie? And *Mele Kalikimaka*!"

I smiled. "I'm Auntie Rose when I'm here, but remember to stick with Miss McKenzie when we're at school," I said. "*Mele Kalikimaka* to you too!"

Madelyn smiled and headed for the hors d'oeuvres, and Mrs. Thornton and I turned our attention to young Teddy, blond and plump and rosy-cheeked. He still looked a bit sleepy, and somewhat puzzled about all the strange people in his living room. I knew I would have to let Mrs. Thornton hold her grandson, but I relished this moment of feeling that soft, dense weight, that silky skin.

Such a gift, a child, and one I never would receive. I brushed those thoughts aside and focused on the child in front of me, happy to have even the temporary gift of his company on Christmas Eve.

Chapter Eight

January 1942

J   We all expected New Year's Eve to be a subdued affair, since we were confined to home after sunset with blackout curtains tightly drawn. But the Japanese Air Force decided to surprise us with a little show.

That afternoon, I had dragged the garden hose to top up the various buckets and bins I'd placed around the edges of the house. How strange to be preparing for something as preposterous as a bomb falling on my house. The authorities had tried to reassure us, saying that only military installations and public buildings were likely to be bombed in the event of another attack; civilian residents needed to beware only of machine guns. That was frightening enough. But no matter what the authorities said, it was even worse to imagine planes overhead, dropping bombs, and there was no guarantee the enemy would not do that.

And then, in the wee hours, I heard a familiar sound: dim booms far away, like that first shelling that had struck the cannery in Kahului.

I tensed and pulled my covers close, huddled alone in the home that always had seemed so secure, straining my ears to hear more sounds of attack. We were not safe, not by a long shot. I would keep my buckets full.

Word spread quickly that the booms had indeed been shells shot from a Japanese submarine. *The Maui News* had stopped publishing its war extras and gone back to its regular, twice-weekly schedule, so I had to wait until Saturday to find out what the paper might say about the attack. I stood outside the store, scanning the pages.

A couple of neighbors on their way up the street stopped to peer over my shoulder. "Anything on the shelling?" one asked.

"Not a darn thing," I said. "Lots about the rest of the world, and more orders of what we can do and not do, but nothing on that shelling."

The neighbor snorted. "Everyone on this side of the island must have heard it. I don't know what they're trying to hide. Do they think the Japs subscribe to *The Maui News*? Damn censors."

"It only takes one saboteur to give them all they need," her friend said. She turned away, then looked back to give me a contemptuous glance. "It could be anyone, even someone we think we know well." The first neighbor shrugged apologetically, then followed her friend, leaving me with my heart pounding and my jaws clenched.

• • • •

BY THE TIME SCHOOL reopened on January 12, we had planted every available inch with something edible. Masako always kept the little greenhouse tables filled with seedlings of all sorts. Many were now in the garden, in corners, and along fences, anywhere we could find that was out of reach of our menagerie's sharp teeth. If victory gardening could win the war, or at least feed us, we were off to a good start.

Water was our limiting factor, though we had tanks collecting rain from every roof. We'd be hard put to produce grain crops if the drought continued, and we might find ourselves slaughtering more stock than usual to limit the amount of grain we needed. On my last shopping trip, there had been no chicken scratch at all, and we could not let our hens hatch new chicks that would require even more feed.

"Make sure you get all the eggs, Iris," Masako said as we did chores one morning. "We don't want any hens going broody." She turned to me as I stood stretching my back after a particularly challenging bout with the goats when I'd dragged them to the place where I wanted them to graze, rather than the flower beds they found more interesting. "What about some chicken katsu this weekend, Rose?" she asked.

"Sounds good," I replied, rubbing a sore shoulder and wishing we had Isao here to manage the livestock. At least I wouldn't have to slaughter the chicken for Sunday lunch. Isao had made sure both boys were adept at that unpleasant job.

• • • •

I CAME HOME ONE DAY to find Masako aglow. She appeared on their front porch waving as I pulled into the driveway, then hurried up to meet me.

"We can go see Isao!" she said. "Visitor passes came in the mail today. We go Sunday afternoon."

"Thank God," I said. "The whole family gets to go?"

"Yes, they sent passes for all of us, and you should be getting one in the mail too, as his employer."

"I'm so happy for you! And so glad I can go too! What can we take? Clean clothes? Food?"

"Clothes, I'm sure, but I have to find out about food." She clasped her hands, eyes shining. "Oh, it will be good to see him. I'm so relieved."

So was I. It was as if a door had opened the tiniest bit, and a sliver of light peeped through. The next day that light seemed still to be shining, showing the way to the next step.

"I might have some news for you," Tom Stevens told me in a low voice as we crouched in an air-raid trench for one of the school's regular drills. The plantation had come by with big equipment while we were out and had enlarged and completed the "scare holes" Tom and his boys had labored to dig in the first days of the war.

I peered over the edge of our trench to see whether everyone was out of the building and safely tucked into the earth. A couple of classes were still hustling across the lawn to find their shelters, so we would be here for a few minutes. I relaxed and looked back at Tom. "What's the news?"

"There might be a way to get Tanaka out of the calaboose."

I swiveled quickly on the muddy ground, turning to face Tom. "What? That's big news! How? What is it?"

"There's going to be a hearing process. I don't know much about it, but there might be a possibility of release if Isao can prove he's a loyal citizen."

"Finally, some hope! Thank you," I said, beaming, then thought about the reality of proving such a thing. "Although it does sound challenging. But certainly worth looking into, Tom, thank you. Do you know how to start the process? Who would I talk to?"

The all-clear signal sounded, and we stood and began climbing up the sloping entrance wall. The students' murmur of conversation grew louder as they left the shade of the poinciana tree that camouflaged our shelter.

"Sorry, I don't know the details," Tom said, looking apologetic as he stood to one side so his class could line up behind him. "I'll let you know when I find out." With a wave, he was gone, and I turned to do a quick once-over of the line behind me before leading my students back to class. It was all I could do not to run to my truck and rush home to tell Masako.

• • • •

SUNDAY AFTERNOON, WE all piled into my truck and headed for Haiku. I was getting good at strategically going into neutral on hills to save gas, and much of the road to Haiku was a long, satisfying glide. I arrived at the camp buoyed by the excitement of getting to see Isao. My first close look at the place popped that bubble.

It was stark. Barbed wire stretched tight between fenceposts, just as we fenced the cattle in our pastures. But here there were two parallel fences surrounding the camp, with a few open feet between them. The fences were perhaps ten feet tall. At the top, Y-shaped braces bent inward, so that even if someone managed to climb the strands they'd run into a ceiling of barbed wire. The strands were far enough apart to reach through, but they would shred a human body trying to squeeze between them.

Armed guards were in lookout towers at the corners of the fence, with one of the pineapple workers' dorms at the end of the compound and assorted tents scattered around. A few men sat on benches under the tents, wistfully watching us and a couple of other families who had arrived to visit.

We could see Isao inside the fence, grinning as he waved at us. We returned the grins and the waves, and Henry and Iris hurried forward. Armed guards stopped us before we reached the fence. We handed over our food baskets and a bag of fresh vegetables for one of them to search, while Isao stood watching. Finally, the guards waved us on, and we spread blankets on the soft grass outside the fence and set down our baskets of food. A guard opened a gate in the inner fence, and Isao came through it and settled to face us in the narrow space between the rows of barbed wire. I hoped my face did not show my shock at how thin he was, and how gray the stubble of his unshaven beard. I manifested a smile and moved back so Isao's family could get closer to him. The two younger children began to chatter, crowding close to the fence and reaching to touch their father, while Sam stood back, gazing at Isao, his hands in his pockets and his shoulders slumped, and Aiko dabbed at her eyes.

Isao turned first to Masako, and his grin faded to a gentle smile as their eyes met. They joined hands through the fence, bowing slightly, and sat simply looking at each other for a moment. Next, Isao turned to each of the children, his smile widening, holding each one's hand in both of his. Then he reached to shake hands with me. I had busied myself with putting some of the food we'd brought onto plates, and now I handed one through the fence to Isao, who immediately downed half of a rice ball.

"It's so good to see you all," he said when he'd finished that first bite, his gaze traveling from one beaming face to another.

"Dad, what's been happening? How is it here? Were you here all along?" Sam asked.

Isao shook his head. "No, they took us to the Wailuku jail at first." His face was serious, his eyes unfocused, as if he stared at a place we could not see. "When the jeep pulled up there, I thought I was going to be executed, or at least in a jail cell for a long time. Next day, they brought us to put up the fence and tents here and moved us into the old dorm. At least it's not too uncomfortable, and we can come outside, even if get barbed wire around." Frowning, he glanced around the area, a flat, mowed sports field in a green rural neighborhood. Then he forced a smile. "Thank you for the clean clothes, Masako, and for this good food. Getting pretty tired of canned stuff, nothing fresh. And not enough rice!"

That got a chuckle out of the kids.

"Did you know there might be hearings, maybe a chance for parole?" I asked.

"I heard rumors. We had one hearing when they picked us up, but I think the next one might be more fair, not so rush-rush. I was hoping you folks would know more."

I shook my head. "I've been asking around, but no one can tell me anything, except for Tom Stevens. At least he's one person who's willing to help."

"And we learned they picked you up because you helped with *Shintoku Maru* visits," Masako said.

Isao sighed. "Yeah, we kind of figured that out. Some other guys in here helped too." He took a bite of chicken katsu and chewed for a moment. "It's tough, not knowing what's going on. They don't tell us much. And they've been sending people to Oahu from here. It doesn't sound good."

Masako gasped. "Oh no! Are they sending everyone? Will they send you?"

Isao shrugged. "Who knows?" He leaned closer and lowered his voice. "I'm trying to get assigned some carpentry work. I've been doing little odds and ends, as much as I can without tools, to show I can do things with my hands. Maybe if I can do some jobs around here, they'll let me stay longer." He tilted his head toward the workers' dorm down the road from the fence that enclosed the camp and the dorm where the prisoners stayed.

"That building is where the soldiers sleep, and they need someone who can fix it up. That's me. Most of the guys here are more academic types—teachers, priests, like that. I'm the only one with carpentry experience. So, worth a try."

"Good idea," I said. "And I hear you can have witnesses at the hearing, so think about who we should ask. I'll be there, of course. Write as soon as you come up with ideas of people to approach, so I can get to work on my end."

"Okay, that sounds like a good strategy. We just gotta wait. *Shikata ga nai*—cannot be helped." Isao briskly changed the subject and turned to the kids. "Tell me some news from home. Henry and Iris, you folks doing good in school? Helping your mom around the house? Helping take care of all the animals?"

That set off another round of chatter, as Henry reported on his science experiment and Iris on the maps she was drawing for geography class. Isao nodded and smiled, his eyes moving from one child to the other, occasionally glancing up at the older children and Masako. It was as if he was soaking up the sight of them all, storing the memories of this moment to savor later. I stayed back, moved by this reunion of a family that never before had been apart. Masako sat simply staring at her husband, the food on her plate untouched. Like her husband, she was thinner than I'd ever seen her.

After the kids had all had a chance to talk, Isao turned to me. "Now, maybe we should go over some business. You folks managed to get the planting done? How is everything? Any problems?"

Isao listened intently to our descriptions of our planting and concerns about water and feed, nodding occasionally.

"Sounds like you folks have done a good job on the planting," he said at last. "But I think you're going to have to send two steers to slaughter this year, instead of our usual one. And sell the calf so you can use all Lani's milk. I hear butter's hard to get."

"What about the piglets?" Masako asked. "All seven made it, so we're having trouble coming up with enough garbage and scraps to feed them all, plus we can't spare much grain."

"Keep one, sell the others, get the sow bred again. You still have some bacon left from the last one we slaughtered, yeah? So let the one you keep get to about two hundred pounds, then send 'em to the slaughterhouse." He smiled. "That way, you folks don't have to haul so much heavy feed every day."

"Or smell the stink!" I said, and we all chuckled.

One of the guards approached. "Time's up, you folks," he said.

Isao's face fell, and I sighed. The time had gone so quickly.

I passed the paper bag of vegetables and a plate of leftovers through the fence, gave Isao my hand again and told Masako and the kids I'd see them at the truck. I gathered up the empty food baskets and left them to have a final hand clasp or even, if Isao was feeling brave, a careful quick kiss between the strands of barbed wire.

I glanced back to see the kids trailing behind me, and sure enough, Isao and Masako were just drawing back, each smiling, and the guard was carefully gazing in the other direction. It looked like a post-kiss situation to me.

• • • •

"ROSE! WAIT UP!"

I turned around to see Tom getting out of his car, parked next to my truck in the teachers' parking area. He slammed the door and strode up the steps to me.

"I found out a little more about this hearing thing," he said as we turned toward the school. "They can ask to be paroled, but it might take a while to schedule the hearing for that. Apparently, they're overwhelmed with cases."

"For heaven's sake, how many cases do they have?" I asked, stopping to stare as Tom pulled open the door.

"A lot. Maybe dozens here on Maui. So maybe hundreds territory-wide. And they have the hearing in Wailuku, but the final decision gets made higher up, on Oahu."

"But he might get released, right? Can I be a witness at the hearing? Or can others?"

Tom shook his head. "Don't know. But I'll let you know when I find out more. Sorry." He gave me a sympathetic grimace, then was off to his classroom.

It was a lovely morning, with a clear blue sky and no wind, birds twittering in the monkeypod tree outside my classroom. I raised the windows to let in fresh air and began my morning routine, thinking about this parole hearing. I didn't even know who to ask for further details. For all the news in the paper, I had yet to see anything about who controlled the fate of the Japanese-American men like Isao who had been hauled away from their homes. Or, for that matter, much at all regarding the men who were in this situation. It was as if the incarceration of our neighbors was not news. And *haole* or Japanese, in official channels or neighborhood chats, no one wanted to talk about it.

· · · ·

I WAS WALKING ALONG one of the back halls after lunch that afternoon when I heard angry voices. I quickened my steps, heading in the direction of what I knew had to be a fight.

Around the corner, youngsters clustered, some shouting to urge on the combatants, others standing back as if afraid of being swept up in a riot. I pushed my way through the tight-packed crowd around the fight and saw with shock that one of the fighters was Henry.

"Stop this right now!" I shouted, reaching for the shoulder of the fighter closest to me, a tall *haole* boy. Henry's glasses had slid down his nose and were in danger of falling off his face. Still, he swung at his tall blond opponent, undeterred. As I grabbed the shirt collar of the blond boy, Sam appeared behind Henry and grabbed his brother, wrapping his arms around Henry's chest. He dragged Henry backward, shouting, "Stop that, you stupid idiot! You like get expelled?"

The kids in the crowd had begun to back off at my arrival, and I got a good grip on the *haole* boy's shoulder. He turned as if to attack me, but stopped himself when he saw who I was. The boy was Johnny Breeze, the son of the plantation man who had refused to help me when Isao was first arrested. His mouth twisted with contempt as he looked back at Henry and called, "Serves you right, Jap. Your father's where he belongs, and you should be there too!"

"Stop that immediately," I said, tightening my grip on his shoulder. "Henry, to the office, now. You too, Breeze. March." And I gave him a push in the direction of Mr. Crowder's office. Around us students edged away, disappearing down the hall at the sound of the word "office."

Several other teachers had appeared by this time, their presence and stern faces reinforcing my order. Both boys headed for the office, still giving each other angry looks. Sam followed close behind his little brother. He'd have made a better match for the Breeze boy than Henry, and by the look on his face, it wouldn't take much to start another fight. I was relieved when we reached the front office. The clerk looked up in alarm at the sight of the two boys, their hair disheveled. Henry's shirt was torn, and a drop of blood smeared Breeze's upper lip. At least Henry had landed one good punch.

"All right, boys, what's going on?" Mr. Crowder demanded when I ushered the two into his office. Sam sat steaming on a chair outside, forbidden to enter the inner sanctum with his brother.

"He said my dad was a spy!" Henry said. "And he called me a dirty Jap!"

Breeze inspected his fingernails, affecting nonchalance. "Well, where there's smoke, there's fire," he said smugly. "Once a Jap, always a Jap."

"We'll have no more of that," Mr. Crowder said, frowning. "We're all good Americans here. And I won't have Maui High students insulting others because of their race. Do I make myself clear, Breeze?"

Breeze shrugged and looked away. "Yes, sir."

"I'm serious, Breeze. We have a war to win, and I don't want you or anyone else trying to bring it here. It's not a war with our neighbors, it's a war with another nation that attacked ours. Understand?"

"Then why is old man Tanaka in jail?" Breeze asked defiantly.

"That's something for the Army to answer, and no business of yours. You're here to learn and to be a good citizen, and you'd best spend your time and energy trying to get your grades up, not picking fights.

"The same goes for you, Tanaka," he said turning to Henry. "Next time somebody says something like that, you put your hands in your pockets and come straight to the office to report it. I'll deal with the troublemaker. Your father would not want you fighting and getting suspended."

He stood looking from one boy to the other. "However, that's exactly what is going to happen today. You're suspended for the rest of the day. You will spend the afternoon at home, writing a two-page essay on the subject, 'Why violence has no place at Maui High School.' Report to the office first thing tomorrow morning to hand it in."

He opened the door to the outer office where Sam still sat glowering. "Mrs. May, please call both these boys' parents and ask to have them picked up as soon as possible." He looked at Sam. "You can go back to class, Sam. We'll look after your brother until your mother gets here."

Reluctantly, Sam left, and I followed close behind. Mr. Crowder had directed the two combatants to chairs on opposite ends of the front office and left his door open so he could keep an eye on them. I'd done my job as a teacher and authority figure; I'd broken up the fight. As much as I knew that fights, for whatever reason, were bad, I couldn't help feeling a tiny bit of satisfaction. Little Henry had shown his spunk and defended his father, and a bully had been denied his triumph. It seemed only fair.

Henry's mother, of course, had to show the same stern disapproval I had of her son's behavior. But her eyes twinkled when I saw her at milking time. "Who would have thought our Henry would turn out to be a fighter?" she said. "I'm sure Isao will scold him too. But I think he'll be secretly proud that Henry stood up for his dad." The twinkle dimmed, and Masako looked away. "It's just so sad that he has to," she said as she clamped Lani into her stanchion and got on with the task at hand.

Chapter Nine

February 1942

Masako and I sat fidgeting, dressed in our best, in a row of chairs off to one side of the little table where we figured Isao would sit. We chose those seats so we could see his face, and he could look over to see us. It had been a full ten weeks from the time of his arrest to his hearing. Isao had given Masako a list of possible character witnesses. Of course Masako would be there, and I would, so we had two of four allowed witness slots to fill.

The first two people we approached had agreed to speak for Isao. One was Dr. Hamilton, a longtime Upcountry doctor who had been the Tanaka family physician for years and was also an occasional carpentry client. The second was Tom Stevens. Both *haole*, of course, to impress the high-and-mighty men who would decide Isao's fate.

Masako and I had arrived early to be sure we were there in plenty of time. The hearing would take place in the courthouse, not in an actual courtroom but in a large meeting room furnished with one long table facing the smaller one. Tom came in after we'd been sitting there for a while and took the seat next to me. Dr. Hamilton arrived and greeted us, then sat next to Tom. Soon a clerk bustled in and arranged piles of paper in front of the four chairs that edged the larger table. A door to one side opened, and Isao came through, with two armed guards behind him. He was wearing the clean suit Masako had taken him, though it hung loosely on his thin frame. His whiskers had grown enough to be called a beard, and his hair was neatly combed. He bowed slightly in our direction, gave us a smile, and sat at his table.

Another door opened, and four men filed in, three civilians and one in Army uniform. I knew who all the civilians were—pillars of Maui society. I had met one of them socially some time ago, but these were Wailuku fellows, all engaged in the business and social life of Maui's capital, while my life was Upcountry. I'd never seen the soldier before. His first act was to pull a revolver from his holster and lay it on the table in front of him. Isao sat up straight and scooted back in his chair, and Masako and I instinctively did the same. What on earth? Did he expect Isao to make a break for it? Attack the hearing board?

One of the civilians tapped the tabletop with a gavel, called the hearing to order, and introduced the hearing board. He identified himself as Vernon McArthur, board president (and, I knew, an attorney who was active in all sorts of community groups). The other civilians were Ezra Jones, head of the local electric company; and Bill Harrison, a sugar mill manager who'd been a guest at a couple of parties I'd attended. The military man, Capt. Alex Adams, would record the hearing on a yellow pad. I was glad his attention was there instead of on that gun.

McArthur, a portly fellow with a bald head, looked at Isao with an expression of distaste on his face, then peered through wire-rimmed glasses to read from a file. "Case number 76 involves an internee named Isao Tanaka who lives a half-mile above Makawao town, where he works as a farmer and carpenter. Tanaka, what do you have to say for yourself?"

Isao started, as if he had not been expecting to speak so soon in the hearing. But he squared his shoulders and took a sheet of paper from his jacket pocket.

"I am born and raised here on Maui," Isao read in a voice so quiet that McArthur interrupted him. "Speak up, Tanaka. We can barely hear you!"

Isao cleared his throat and repeated himself in a louder voice. "I am married, with four children, and my wife and I are both native-born citizens of the United States and loyal to this country. I have never been disloyal and never would be. I pay my taxes, and I am active in all kinds of community projects. I help organize the county fair agricultural display and do volunteer work for my children's schools. I was on the planning committee for the visits with the Japanese navy ship, but those visits were innocent entertainment for us and for the sailors and nothing to do with the war. I don't want my family to become a burden on the community. I want to go home to grow food for my family and neighbors and to help however I can in the war effort."

Isao stopped speaking and bowed his head. Mr. McArthur frowned and said, "You may be seated." He aimed the frown at Dr. Hamilton. "Doctor, I understand you're here as a witness for the internee. Go ahead, please."

"I have been the Tanaka family's physician since their oldest child was a toddler, about twenty years," Dr. Hamilton said in his deep, gentle voice. "I know Isao Tanaka to be a kind and responsible father and husband, reliable in paying his bills, and well liked in the community. He has done carpentry work for me in the past, and I've been pleased with his work habits and his skills."

McArthur interrupted the doctor.

"What about his loyalty?" he said. "Have you ever heard him talk about going back to Japan, or express an opinion on Japan's behavior in China?"

"No, can't say that we've ever talked about politics or world affairs, and I can't imagine Mr. Tanaka going back to Japan," Dr. Hamilton said, sounding irritated. "He's as much a Maui man as you or I."

McArthur pulled his double chin into his collar and scowled. Maybe he disliked his citizenship status being compared to Isao's. I didn't like it either; after ten minutes in the room with McArthur, I much preferred having Isao as a neighbor.

"Very well," McArthur said, his tone icy. "You may go back to your patients, Dr. Hamilton." The doctor patted Masako's shoulder as he left and nodded gravely in response to Isao's smile.

"And you would be Mr. Stevens?" McArthur cocked his head at Tom, who stood. "Go ahead," he said, then looked off into the distance as if whatever Tom had to say would be of no interest to him.

"I know Mr. Tanaka from his participation in school activities as a parent," Tom began. He looked as if he was trying to keep a pleasant tone in the face of McArthur's disdainful attitude. "He's had three kids attend Maui High, and he's always willing to help. He and Mrs. Tanaka have brought drinks and snacks for our football team. And when the agriculture department needed stones for a foundation we were building, he and his two boys pitched in to haul several loads in their truck." Tom paused, turning his hat in his hands. "That's just a couple of specifics, but I know I can always call on Isao and he'll help me, whether it's for football or ag or whatever his kids get involved with." He sat, still nervously turning his hat.

"And is that it? I keep hearing what a great parent he is, but does that prove he's a patriot and not a spy?" McArthur demanded, waving his hand dismissively.

"I don't have any doubt that Isao Tanaka is a loyal citizen of Maui, the Territory of Hawaii, and the United States of America," Tom said tersely.

McArthur turned to me. "I believe you have something to say, Miss McKenzie?"

I stood, smoothing my skirt, summoning the strength for my speech. This had to count.

"I've known Isao Tanaka since we were freshmen at Maui High. I got to know him better when he moved to Spencer Ranch, where I lived, after his parents died. I know that the ranch owner, Vaughn Spencer, thought a lot of him, and Isao lived up to that. He married my childhood friend Masako." I glanced at Masako, who was gazing at me, her hands tightly clenched in her lap. "And they have lived on my land for nearly ten years, as neighbors, tenants, and employees. So you see, I know Isao Tanaka pretty well by now," I said with as much conviction as I could muster. "I can tell you he is no spy, no traitor, nothing but a loyal citizen of the United States.

"In addition, I petition you to release Isao Tanaka because his work is essential to my farm. We've been building up our capacity in the last couple of years for a time such as this. But without my farm manager, I will be unable to produce all the food necessary to help feed ourselves and our neighbors."

I tried to think of what else I could say to persuade these men of the government's error. It was plain to me, and I hoped it would be to them. I sat, and Isao turned to give me a warm smile.

"And I assume the wife would side with her husband, so we won't ask her to testify," McArthur said. Masako looked at me, startled, then stood and said, "But I want to speak." McArthur stared at her, his face sour. "All right, go ahead," he said grudgingly, and proceeded to page through the papers in front of him.

"My husband is a loyal American, native-born, and the U.S. government has no right to arrest him without cause," Masako began. All the men on the committee looked up, and the Army officer stopped his notetaking, leaning forward as if he wondered whether he had heard correctly.

"The law in the United States requires that there be evidence of a crime before someone can be charged and held, and my husband cannot be charged because there is no evidence, since he has committed no crime," Masako continued. Isao had turned to look over his shoulder at his wife, an expression of dismay on his face. Masako ignored Isao's expression and the frowns on the faces of the men behind the table and plowed ahead. "Therefore, since there is no evidence of a crime, my husband should be released immediately."

McArthur banged his gavel.

"I believe you are referring to the writ of *habeas corpus*, Mrs. Tanaka, which is suspended under martial law, so your point is moot. Please take your seat so we can proceed. This committee is too busy to waste time listening to amateur lawyers."

Masako sat. Isao gave her a sad smile and turned to face the front, and Masako looked at me again, her face stricken.

Then the grilling started. The members of the hearing board took turns questioning Isao. McArthur began.

"Who would you like to see win the war, the Japanese or the United States?"

"The United States, of course," Isao replied, his voice strong.

"You are a citizen of Japan, are you not? Yes, I know you were born here, but you are also a Japanese citizen." Isao nodded. "Why did you never take steps to expatriate yourself?"

"All the parents registered their babies with Japan, back when I was born. It's complicated to expatriate, lots of paperwork, takes a long time. It never seemed that important. I never thought about it much."

McArthur snorted. "Not that important, eh, to be a complete U.S. citizen?" He shook his head, ruffled papers in his file, and nodded to Jones.

"You do know, do you not, Tanaka, that as a Japanese citizen, it was your country that sent diplomats to Washington to lie," Jones said, glaring at Isao. "How do you feel about what Mr. Nomura and Mr. Kurusu were doing in D.C. while your government was launching a terrible attack against the United States?"

"I am very angry Japan attacked the U.S., and I'm very angry they deceived our country pretending they want peace when they're sending planes to bomb. But that is not my government," Isao said emphatically. "I am a loyal U.S. citizen by birth, and I don't like what Japan did."

"Then why play host to *Shintoku Maru?*" Jones demanded.

Masako looked at her hands, still clenched in her lap. This was it, the single thing that apparently had put Isao on whatever list some government men had been building of whom to arrest when war began.

Isao's voice was quieter. "Now I wish I never had. I didn't know what was coming. It was a community event that many people enjoyed. I thought I was being a good citizen by helping with the luau, making people happy. And visiting the ship was something fun for my kids to do, climb around on the ship, and they could practice their Japanese."

Jones pounced on this with a new line of questioning.

"Why do you people insist on sending your children to Japanese school to learn Japanese, if you're such staunch Americans? Aren't the teachers telling them to be loyal to the emperor?"

"No, no," Isao said, then hesitated. "No, *sir*. The teachers tell them to be American, to be obedient, to work hard, and show respect. They pledge allegiance to the United States flag. And why I want them to learn Japanese ... well, it's just tradition. To speak with the old people, or to remember our ancestors, they need to speak Japanese."

Harrison took over the questioning.

"Tanaka, you can do a lot of good for yourself if you share with us the names of anyone you know who favors Japan. Any neighbors who would be happy to see the Japs win?"

"No, I don't know anyone," Isao said, shaking his head, his voice tense.

"Think hard. It's a small community, and you know everyone around here, don't you?" Harrison insisted, leaning forward to frown at Isao. "Things could go easier on you if you help us out, you know."

But Isao was steadfast. "I don't know anyone who is disloyal. Everyone wants the U.S. to win and the war to be over fast."

"What about the men on the *Shintoku Maru* committee? How many of them are loyal to the emperor?"

"They are all loyal to America," Isao insisted. "The committee wanted to entertain Maui people, not support Japan."

The men on the committee exchanged glances, faces grim.

"All right, we've heard enough," McArthur said. "Guards, please escort Tanaka from the room. And the witnesses will leave while we deliberate."

The soldiers took Isao out the door where he'd entered, one soldier holding each arm. Isao strained his neck to look over his shoulder at Masako as he left.

Outside the hearing room, Tom shook our hands. "I wish I could stay, but I have to pick up Harriet for her doctor's appointment," he said. "Masako, I'll be thinking of you folks and wishing you luck. Rose, please call me later to let me know what happened." He looked down, then back up with an apologetic expression.

"You know," he said hesitantly. "I remember telling you, Rose, that the final decision gets made on Oahu. But recently I heard that the Oahu board almost always follows the recommendation of the local board." He looked down again. "So, whatever they decide today—that's probably it."

I gulped. So final. Masako was breathing quickly, looking from Tom to me and back. I closed my eyes for a moment, then said, "Thanks for letting us know, Tom. Better to be prepared."

After he left, Masako turned to me, her knuckles white as she clasped her hands. "Rose, did I make it worse, saying what I did? They all seemed so angry that I would imply they weren't following the law."

"I doubt anything any of us said made a difference to them," I said. "We just have to hope their sense of fairness and justice guides their decision."

For what seemed like a long time, Masako and I paced the hallway outside the hearing room. When the clerk finally opened the door to let us in, Isao stood at his little table, the guards on either side of him. Isao half-turned to lock gazes with Masako as we entered the room, facing forward only when McArthur called the hearing to order and began to read the board's decision.

"We find the internee to be a subject of Japan who owes allegiance to that country and whose activities have been pro-Japanese," he intoned, "though not necessarily anti-American."

That last phrase sounded hopeful: Not necessarily anti-American. But McArthur's next sentence shattered that hope.

"The board determines, therefore, that Isao Tanaka will be interned for the duration of the war."

McArthur hit the gavel again, and the soldiers seized Isao's arms and marched him toward the exit door. His face was shocked and pale, and Masako groaned as she dropped into her chair and covered her face with both hands. Across the board table, the men all kept their eyes busy collecting their papers, checking their watches, preparing to hear another man's story and ruin another man's life, all part of a day's work. The clerk stood politely by the door waiting for us to leave. I took Masako's elbow and guided her out, down the stairs, and into the truck for the long drive home. She sobbed for most of the way, stopping only to curse the hearing board in words I rarely heard her use. "Damn them," she said. "How dare they do this to an American citizen! What the hell is happening to this country?" She sobbed again, tears streaming down her face as she stared out the window in despair.

· · · ·

AT HOME, I STEERED Masako to the kitchen table, put the kettle on, and took a pile of clean handkerchiefs from a drawer. In all the years I'd known her, the only time I'd ever seen Masako cry like this was when a horse stepped on her toes back when we were kids. Now, between bouts of tears, Masako was angry. "What about what that general said when he took over before Christmas? That they were going to do things the American way? That the men they arrested wouldn't be treated as prisoners of war?" She pulled a clean handkerchief off the pile and blew her nose. "They're locking him up without a trial, without evidence—nothing! Whatever happened to innocent until proven guilty? The general said nobody needed to worry if they weren't doing anything subversive. Well, Isao wasn't! This is not the American way."

"It's this damn martial law that gives them that power," I said as I filled Masako's cup with hot tea. I was angry too, about Isao, about the way our home had turned into a military dictatorship, about the enemy who had locked us in this prison. "I can't believe this can happen here either, but we've never had an attack or been in such danger. That's making the men in power clamp down. They're clamping down on the wrong people, though."

Masako wiped her cheeks, nodding. "I understand the why," she said. "But I hate the how. And of course, the who."

"I know. They have your sweetheart," I said, reaching to pat her shoulder. Her beloved, locked up for who knew how long.

The two of us sat, sipping tea, waiting for the kids to come home and learn the fate of their father.

"Why? Why would they do that to our Pop?" Henry asked, his eyes filling with tears, and I patted his shoulder, shaking my head, for I had no answer that would satisfy him.

"Yeah, why?" Iris said fiercely. "It's not fair! Daddy didn't do anything wrong." She slumped in her chair and began to chew on a cuticle, a new habit she'd acquired in the past month or so.

Sam bit his lower lip, stood looking at the floor for a moment, stomped out and strode off into the pasture, whacking fence posts with a stick, burning off his anger with action.

Aiko sank into a chair, blotting her eyes on her sleeve, and said, "Damn *haole* dictators—sorry, Auntie Rose, not you. It's those guys who rule Hawaii and think they're the boss." She patted her mother's hand. "I'm so tired of it. This war just made it worse."

Chapter Ten

Now we settled into the hard business of living without Isao. Masako stopped crying, at least in front of me, but I could tell she pined for him. She drifted through the day, doing her own chores as well as a share of those Isao had left behind, all of it without a smile.

The internees were allowed to write a couple of letters a week, and those helped Masako keep going between visiting days. Isao's next letter cheered her up. A few days after the hearing, she came over after I came home from school.

"Here, Rose, read this," she said, handing me the single sheet covered with Isao's tidy handwriting.

The officers are impressed with my carpentry, and they are paying me ten cents an hour to fix up the building outside the fence they use for offices and sleeping. Our dorm also needs work, so maybe I can fix that building when I'm pau with this one. We sleep two men to a room. The rooms are small, just big enough for the pineapple workers who were at the cannery all day. Now that we are here, we mostly stay outside under the big tents in the daytime if it's not too wet and windy. Nighttime, some of the smart guys entertain us with stories. Some people are writing poems, but you know me. More better I build something!

I chuckled. Isao was indeed a man of action more than words, though ten cents an hour was a ridiculously low wage. I decided he must be putting on his most cheerful face in this letter, probably to protect his family's feelings. "Sounds like he's making the best of it," I said, handing the letter back to Masako.

"I hope he doesn't work too fast, so they keep him," Masako said, trying to smile. "My friend told me some more men were sent to that awful camp in Honolulu." She squeezed her eyes shut, just for a moment. "I hope they don't send Isao over there."

But for now, he seemed to be safely occupied in Haiku, in green and peaceful surroundings. The guards were from other parts of Hawaii; the small group of internees were acquaintances, interesting, educated people; and they all seemed to be doing as well as could be expected inside a barbed wire fence.

But they wouldn't let him come home. The best we could hope for was that Isao stayed within easy visiting distance.

• • • •

MEANWHILE, THERE WAS a war on, and we were all doing as much as we could to win it. We were busy, those early days back to school. We had barely had time to adjust to wartime teaching and learning in the few days between Pearl Harbor's bombing and our abrupt dismissal after the submarine shelled Kahului.

This week, we were working on essays, and the subjects were all war oriented.

"Wilma, your turn to read," I said as we combined lessons in writing and public speaking one day. Looking shy, Wilma came to the front of the class and ducked her head to read from her essay. From the list of subjects I offered them, she had chosen The American Way.

"I live in a democracy, with the responsibility to live up to and preserve the precious heritage of that democratic principle," she read. "Though I come of alien parentage, I am a citizen. Yet I uphold the ideals of my family. The difference between the teachings of my parents and the American way of life may conflict, but I adjust myself to these conditions. I try to make my home a democratic institution, just as my nation is."

"Good job, Wilma," I said. "You may be seated." I looked around the room, where many students were fidgeting and avoiding eye contact. They didn't care much for reading their first drafts aloud in class.

Next up was Tad, short for Tadashi, a peppy fellow who was a member of the student council. He had chosen Defending Our School as his topic.

"We defend our school in many ways," he read. "All the boys got blisters digging trenches." He glanced up, smiling. "We were happy when some pretty home-ec girls came to bring us cookies and juice." That got a few giggles from the class. "The boys in the student fire department wear old steel helmets when they practice firefighting, but sometimes we wonder how much fire they can put out with a few buckets of sand and water." More giggles. "In PE classes, we learn first aid and do military drills, and the girls practice home nursing. The farmers in our agriculture classes plant more land for victory gardens, and we all buy war stamps and bonds." His face sobered. "And some of our friends in the senior class left without graduating to sign up for nursing classes or to go fight the enemy. They are brave, and we hope they come home soon." Tad took his seat, and students throughout the classroom traded glances.

"Like my Johnny," one girl whispered.

I cleared my throat and called on the next student. Better to keep moving. We all had work to do, no matter how we hurt.

• • • •

EVERYONE HAD A JOB, even society ladies, in this new world. Anyone who didn't know how to pitch in went to the Labor Department downtown, which promised to find them something to do.

"You know, it's like we're living in a dictatorship," my friend Jeanette said when I saw her in Makawao town one day. We met as I was leaving the grocery store and she was arriving, with her sleeping baby on one shoulder. "All these rules we have to follow. And have you seen what they did to the golf course and the polo field, for heaven's sake? Concrete posts every which way, so the Japs can't use them as landing strips." She shifted her baby to her hip. "I should calm down. I'm waking Teddy." The baby looked up, sleepy-eyed, and Jeanette went on in a lower voice. "I know those things are necessary. I'm as afraid as anyone, and we must protect ourselves. But this martial law!"

She shook her head, face grim, but she wasn't finished.

"You know Fred Walls, Velma's husband. They stopped him for driving a few miles over the speed limit the other day and dragged him in front of a military court, proclaimed him guilty, and sentenced him to give a blood donation! It was that or fifteen days in jail, so of course he donated blood. Have you ever heard of such a thing?"

"A blood donation as punishment—that sounds barbaric!" I said, aghast.

"And it was like a court-martial," Jeanette continued, "run by armed soldiers, not even a judge or a jury, no lawyer, five-minute trial, *pau*! I thought this was supposed to be America. It's like we're all in jail! We didn't start this damn war. Why are we being punished?"

She leaned closer, lowering her voice. "Jim's brother works for the governor's office in Honolulu, you know, and he said on December 8, the military moved into Iolani Palace, took over offices, and simply shut down the government. Our governor had no choice but to let it happen. And now the military government is in control of everything. The civilian governor is powerless." She grimaced, exasperated. "How can this happen in a territory of the United States?"

"I had no idea it was so bad," I said, feeling helpless in the face of such injustice. "Fred's trial sounds like the supposed trial they held for Isao. Not what we're used to at all. You should have heard Masako—actually, you sound like she did after they sentenced him, raging about the lack of due process."

"I don't blame her. How is she doing, anyway? And how's Isao?"

"He's making the best of it. Masako and the kids can visit him now. He's working on the old pineapple-cannery dorms—for ten cents an hour."

Jeanette rolled her eyes. "Ten cents an hour for a carpenter with skills like his. Field laborers make four times that picking pineapples." She frowned. "Listen, is Masako all right for money? Would she like to work? I'd pay her more than ten cents an hour, that's for damn sure."

"She might. You'd have to ask her. I know she's been looking, hasn't had any luck with the stores here in town. She says some people would hire her to help with their gardens, but she already has enough of that to do around our place, and she's hoping to find something different. What would you want her to do?"

"Take care of this one." She bent to rub her nose on the baby's head, threw her own head back and laughed, and the baby laughed in return, a game between them, I supposed. The familiar wave of longing washed over me.

"May I hold him?" I stretched out my arms. "Teddy, may Auntie Rose have a cuddle?" The baby considered me for a moment, then leaned from his mother's arms to mine.

"Maybe I should hire you as a babysitter," Jeanette said.

"I would love it," I replied, breathing in that sweet baby scent. "But I already have a job. Why do you need a babysitter?"

"Because I want to go to work at the Civilian Defense Office, or roll bandages, or do anything I can to get this damn war over. We've suspended meetings of the women's club, you know. And everyone is supposed to find some defense work to do. I'm raring to go, except for this one."

I looked at Teddy, who was contemplating the beads of my necklace. Jeanette reached over to stroke his blond curls, then stopped and cocked her head.

"You know, I'm not the only Upcountry gal who would love to go downtown and work but who has a baby or toddler. What if a few of us got together and paid Masako a decent wage to watch the kids?"

I looked up from little Teddy and shrugged. "She might enjoy that. Why don't you stop by and ask her? She's usually home."

A little while later, as I was getting ready to start dinner, I saw Jeanette's car drive past my house on the way to Masako's. It left a few minutes later, and Masako appeared at my door, looking excited. "I'm going to work for Jeanette and her friends, taking care of babies a few days a week," she said. "I'm so glad you ran into her today! Perfect timing!"

Within a week, Jeanette managed to line up two friends with small children who would chip in to pay Masako and to give a raise to Jeanette's maid, Shizue, to fix snacks for the toddlers and generally be a backup for Masako. Jeanette contributed the use of her large sunroom, where strategic furniture rearrangement created a play space, and a wide *punee* provided a place for naps.

"We talked the supervisor into letting us work the same days, three six-hour shifts a week," Jeanette told me when she dropped in after bringing Masako home the first day. "It's not a big job, just sewing for the Red Cross, and of course it's volunteer, but at least we're doing our bit to get this thing over with," she said, smiling proudly.

"How is it going?" I asked Masako when I stopped at Jeanette's after school a few days later. I had volunteered to pick her up whenever my schedule permitted, since it was on my way and would conserve everyone's gas ration. I was looking forward to spending some time with the small fry in the half-hour or so until their mothers arrived from Wailuku. Now I stood and watched as two of the little ones toddled around their improvised play space, while Teddy napped on the *punee*.

Masako laughed. "I forgot how tiring it is to keep up with toddlers. But they're so sweet, you know, and I miss being around babies. Plus, Shizue and I are happy to spend some time together." Her smile faded. "And it takes my mind off Isao." I patted her shoulder. "Go on," she said, mustering another smile as she gestured to the play space. "See if they'll play with you."

I approached gingerly; the two who were awake didn't know me, and I didn't want to scare them. I sat on the floor, tucking my skirt under me, and picked up a wooden box with holes of different shapes, looked around the toys scattered on the floor and found a star-shaped piece that would fit into one of the holes. The two children were watching, one a curly-haired brunette girl with big brown eyes, the other a smaller blond, blue-eyed boy.

"This is Eva, who's two, and Edwin, eighteen months," Masako said. "Their moms are Lisa Elbert and Sarah Fredericksen."

"I see the resemblance to Lisa—that curly hair," I said. By now, the two children had edged closer to me, watching my every move. I held up the box, turning the star-shaped hole toward them. "How do you play with this box?" I asked. "Where does this star go?"

Eva took the star piece from me and pushed it into the box, clapped her hands, giggled, and reached for another piece. Soon we had a good game going, with me pointing to a piece and Eva stuffing it into the box, while Edwin observed with thumb in mouth, his other hand resting on my shoulder. Masako sat, put her feet up on a hassock, and watched us play, a big smile on her face.

By the time the three mothers arrived, I was happily ensconced in an easy chair, with the two children in my lap while I read them a storybook, and Masako sitting next to us, giving Teddy his bottle. It was a perfect end to my day and an experience I looked forward to repeating as often as possible.

Chapter Eleven

M *arch 1942*
The day-to-day restrictions of war chafed on us all. From big things like Isao's unjustified incarceration to the niggling requirements of martial law, we all had something to complain about.

For Iris, one morning early in March, it was Girls Day, when normally the family collection of elaborately kimono-clad dolls would be on display in the living room.

"But Mom," she said, pouting, as we gathered for morning chores. "No one would know, anyway. It's not like we would be flying the carps for Boys Day. The dolls would all be inside. Who would see them, except us?"

"Iris, 'nuff already," Masako said, breaking into her at-home pidgin. "How many times I gotta tell you, the answer is no. We put all that stuff away the day the war started, and we cannot take it out until the war is *pau*. You don't touch those bags." Iris quickly looked away from her mother, her lips pressed together and her eyes aimed at the rafters. "No talk about Girls Day anymore, and no mention it to anyone outside this farm."

"Yes, Mom," Iris replied meekly, and went off to collect the eggs.

"Well, at least it was a short argument," I whispered to Masako. She frowned and looked after Iris. "Almost too easy," she said. "She usually goes on a lot longer when she wants something."

"Be grateful for small favors," I said, and we both settled to our milking chores.

Soon we all had something new to complain about, as residents from our part of the island lined up at Maui High to receive the gas masks that would become our constant companions. The masks were bulky and uncomfortable, smelling strongly of rubber. People wearing them looked rather like alien insects, with big glass eyes and a metal cylinder that dangled from the front of the face. But they were a necessary evil that might keep us alive in the event of an invasion. The officials distributing them told us to keep our masks with us at all times in special shoulder bags, but everyone managed to forget theirs from time to time.

• • • •

IN MID-MARCH, WE ALL were delighted when plantation trucks loaded with khaki-clad men began to arrive in Makawao. At last, a defending force! The Army set up headquarters at the local Japanese school, long since closed. Soon we were seeing soldiers everywhere. Little encampments appeared in pastures. At first, they were all tents, but then simple wooden buildings arrived, prefabricated barracks shipped from Honolulu. Iris and her fellow students and their teachers had moved out of Makawao Elementary School to hold classes in various buildings around town, and we learned from the coconut wireless—the island grapevine—that the school would become a hospital.

An enormous and well-organized war machine was setting up on Maui at amazing speed. The very air seemed to hum with energy and purpose.

Suddenly young men in uniform filled the quiet streets of Makawao, exploring our tiny town, looking for something to do. We had never seen such crowds. Shopkeepers were thrilled with all the new business they brought, and the rest of us smiled indulgently as we dodged clusters of soldiers. Trucks rumbled through, packed with more young men in khaki, off to build something, somewhere. No one told us anything officially, but it was plain to see a lot of building was going on.

Riding on the bus to Wailuku a few days after the Army arrived, I saw new construction all over the place. I was on my way with a dozen other Maui High teachers to a meeting about our next war job, registering and fingerprinting the citizens of Maui. The military had decided it was essential to our defense to be able to locate every citizen of the Islands, and teachers had been ordered to find them. The military made the rules these days. We simply obeyed.

I made sure I sat on the left side of the bus, so I would be able to look out over the island. The road to the busy coastal town of Paia ran down the slopes of Haleakala, the mountain that makes up the larger, eastern part of the island of Maui. Below us stretched the isthmus that connects this side of the island with the west side. I always loved seeing the stunning view of the green-velvet West Maui Mountains with their shadowed valleys rising from the flat plain of the isthmus and the sea sparkling around the edges of the island.

I had heard that the airbase near Puunene was expanding. As we rounded a bend and the view opened up, I saw that the base on the plain was indeed bigger, its runways and buildings spreading into what used to be cane fields. Dust clouds rose from the edges of the base as large machines cleared more cane out of the way.

In Kahului, the military presence was everywhere, as one might expect of the island's main port. When our bus circled the bay, I looked back to see huge gray ships around the piers, and from one, a line of men disembarking, each with a large duffel bag over his shoulder. In Wailuku, soldiers and sailors crowded the sidewalks, peering into shop windows, smoking on the corner, getting their shoes shined by grubby barefoot boys. A friendly and certainly welcome invasion had engulfed the entire island. If Japanese ships approached our shores, armed soldiers would be here to meet them.

The bus dropped us off at the old settlement house, now turned to military use. We chose our seats and pulled out our notebooks. Teachers from all over Central and East Maui filled the room, most of them women. I waved to a few acquaintances scattered among the crowd. At the front of the room, women in the uniforms adopted by the Office of Civilian Defense organized stacks of papers on long tables. Finally, one of them stood before the group and clapped her hands.

"Your attention please," she said in a stern voice. The crowd quieted and turned to face her. "As you no doubt know, teachers around the territory are joining in the war effort by registering every citizen, one household at a time. We have finished with Oahu, and now it's Maui's turn. Beginning next week, all schools will close early each day so that you may be free to take on this important job."

She held up a white card, explaining that we would record the name and age of each resident in a household. "The card will include a physical description of the person. It will be used to verify identity if, for example, someone is stopped for being outside after curfew." She looked around the room, "And, of course, in the event of invasion, these cards will be even more important. Particularly for identifying a body."

People around the room stirred. Chicken skin prickled my arms.

"You are also to describe the interviewees' housing—we might need that information in case we need to place evacuees, whether from Oahu or from your own shoreline communities," the presenter continued. We were to list equipment that might be of aid either to our military or, in case of invasion, to the enemy—items such as radios, flashlights, and cameras.

Finally, we would make an appointment for each resident over the age of six to come to our schools to be fingerprinted. Student helpers would assist us in fingerprinting and issuing identification cards.

"It will be a miracle if our students learn half of what they're supposed to this year," the teacher next to me whispered. I quirked an eyebrow at her and gave her a tight smile. *Shikata ga nai*, I thought; it cannot be helped.

I was happy to hear that the Office of Civilian Defense would be giving us extra gas rations because in my rural neighborhood, this job would use up a lot of gas, much more than the monthly ten gallons we were allowed. That's also why I had ridden the bus to the training. Anything to save gas; I had even begun to ride the bus to school sometimes when I did not have to arrive early or stay late—unless it was a day when Masako was babysitting, and then I drove so I could spend a precious hour or so with her little clients.

Unfortunately, I did have to miss some of those times with the babies when we started the registration process the next week. Each day, we turned our students loose from school after lunch and headed off to our assigned routes, usually finishing just in time for blackout. My route often required me to get out of the truck to open and close gates when I arrived and again when I left. After the first day, I recruited Henry or Iris to go with me, so I could stay behind the wheel while one of them hopped out to deal with the gate.

My route covered homes in every stratum of island society. Up the hill from us, the matriarch of one of the island's leading families greeted us on her wide, covered lanai, surrounded by giant potted ferns and luxurious hanging flower baskets. She sat in a rocking chair wearing a dress with a high neckline and long skirt that looked like it belonged in the last Great War. Graciously, she answered my questions regarding her household, its inhabitants (only her), and its contents, while Iris sat wide-eyed next to me on the porch swing. After we finished her interview and set her fingerprint appointment, the lady called for the housekeeper, who lived with her husband, the groundskeeper, in one of the cottages behind the big house.

"Patsy," the matriarch said when the housekeeper had answered all my questions, "ask Polly to make a pot of tea and set out a few cookies, and tell her to come so that Miss McKenzie can register her. And please ask Shigeru to come as well. I believe he's pruning trees on the back lot." She turned to me. "Now do tell me, Miss McKenzie, how are your students faring in this dreadful time?" It was a rather lengthy visit, considering my busy schedule, but Iris and I politely drank our tea and enjoyed a few gingersnaps, then headed back out to the road to drive a mile uphill to the home of another neighbor, a large Hawaiian family.

A feisty dog ran barking to the gate. Iris and I both hesitated to leave the truck's safety until a boy came running from the house, grabbed the dog's collar, swatted the dog a couple of times, and pulled open the gate. We climbed the rickety steps to a spacious porch as wide, though not as elegant, as the one we had just left.

"Come, come," said the grandmother of the house, who sat with a plump baby on her wide lap. "Sit here," she said, patting the edge of a *punee* next to her. She turned to call into the house. "Honey Girl, try bring guava juice and bananas for Miss McKenzie and Iris." She turned back to me. "Now, what you like know?" I could see we were in for another long visit, and we might need to make a quick stop at home after all these fluids we were imbibing. If this project went on much longer, my waistline surely would expand.

Most of the people we visited were fluent in English, but at one home, Henry ended up in a conversation with a tiny, wrinkled old *issei* woman.

"She says she came to Hawaii in 1905, Auntie," Henry told me after much back and forth as my little interpreter stretched the limits of his Japanese school lessons. "And she already signed up, before the war started." This lonely old lady was not part of our target group, being an *issei*, forbidden by U.S. law to become a citizen and already registered as part of pre-war preparation, so we extricated ourselves from the conversation and headed to the next homestead. We'd have to come back another time to interview her son and daughter-in-law after work.

After a week of driving up dirt roads and hollering "*Hui*!" to draw someone to the front door, I finally turned in my notes and started on the next phase of our project. Early Monday afternoon, after most of the students had boarded the bus for home, teachers and members of the school service clubs gathered in the school's gymnasium. Outside the gym, a long line formed, with people of all ages. Mr. Crowder opened the front door and directed the first in line to the tables where we sat.

"Ready to go, Tad?" I asked my fingerprinting assistant.

"Yes, Miss McKenzie," he replied. He held up a hand with ink-stained fingertips. "I practiced on myself."

"Me too, Miss McKenzie. All set up and ready to type," Mildred Kalama said, pointing to the blank identification card already in her typewriter.

Our first customer approached, her little girl clinging to her side and a baby in her arms. She handed me her appointment card.

"Hello, Mrs. De Rego," I said, examining the card. "And, Cornelia, I see you are seven years old, so you'll be getting fingerprinted too. And you will have your own registration card, so be careful not to lose it, okay?" The little girl nodded shyly. I filled out the record book and passed it to Tad. He carefully pressed first Mrs. De Rego's fingers and then Cornelia's to an ink pad and to the record book. Mildred finished their identification cards and handed them to Mrs. De Rego.

Our first registration successfully completed, Tad, Mildred, and I exchanged smiles and greeted the next person. With such a long line, we'd be here for hours, and back again every day this week. My teacher friend had been right about how this war work would cut into our students' class time and academic learning. But seeing the care with which Tad and Mildred addressed this new job, I knew they were learning other traits—responsibility, cooperation, loyalty—that would stand them in good stead. And, like most everything else these days, there was no choice in the matter.

Chapter Twelve

A pril 1942

The arrival of the military had given us a reason to celebrate and new people to entertain. The island's hostesses took this mission seriously. That included my friend Jeanette.

"I've decided to adopt the doctors at the new hospital, introduce them to a few Upcountry folks," she told me. "Would you like to help? There might be a dish or two, there, Rose—doctors, no less!"

I laughed. "I'm sure they're all sixty, pot-bellied, and married. The young, fit ones are bound to be closer to the action, don't you think? But yes, of course, I'll help. What's the plan? What do you need?"

"Butter!" she said—the elusive item on everyone's shopping list, but one I could easily provide, thanks to my productive milk cow. "Cream for coffee, if you can spare it. And anything you'd like to contribute from the garden. But really, I want you to be my co-hostess. Help me greet the guests and generally circulate and talk story. Maybe come early to help set up the tables, you know. And by the way, how's your liquor card? Any empty spaces you could fill?"

"I stocked up for just such an occasion," I said. I didn't drink much myself, but I used my permit anyway, saving my liquor ration for social events.

So late one Saturday morning a couple of weeks later I parked under a tree in Jeanette's yard and unloaded a jar full of butter and one of cream, a bottle of gin, and another of whiskey. On my second trip back to my car, I picked up a large arrangement of anthuriums, orchids, and greenery that Masako had contributed, flower arranging being her way of relaxing after a week of farming and childcare. She was a wonder, I thought as I crossed the broad green lawn of the Thorntons' home with vase in hand. Even in these tough times, Masako kept chugging along in her quiet way, her calm grace the heart at her family's core.

"That's gorgeous," Jeanette said. "Masako, woman of many talents. Let's give it the place of honor." She moved a smaller bouquet and placed Masako's as the centerpiece of the *pupu* table amid the usual selection of crackers, nuts, and bacon-wrapped pineapple. Jeanette stood back, satisfied. "There. Let's pour ourselves a drink and sit for a moment. We'll be on our feet the rest of the party."

We'd no sooner sat, however, when an Army jeep appeared in the driveway, and three men in uniform climbed out.

"Not a pot-belly among them, you will notice," Jeanette said, turning to me with an impish look. She called down the hall to let Jim know that guests had arrived and went to the door to welcome them. I stood to one side, watching as one by one, smiling men entered to shake hands first with Jeanette and then with me.

When the third man turned from Jeanette to me and our eyes met, an electric shock of connection made my skin tingle. Those bright blue eyes locked with mine as our hands met, and for a few seconds, the social chatter and laughter around us seemed dim and distant.

"Jack Quinn," he said.

"Rose McKenzie," I replied, reluctantly releasing his hand.

I wanted to say, "Let me have that hand back. Tell me everything about you." Instead, I asked, "Would you like a drink?" and introduced him to the bartender, Alfredo. I retrieved my own drink from the coffee table and stood waiting while Jack Quinn ordered a whiskey sour. He wore two silver bars: a captain, then. As soon as he had his drink, Captain Quinn turned and came straight toward me, and I felt feelings in places that had been asleep for years.

"Miss McKenzie..." he began, raising his glass. I raised mine; said, "Rose"; and smiled as our glasses clinked. "Jack," he said, grinning back. We sipped our drinks, regarding each other. He was tall, with broad shoulders, sandy hair, and wide-set eyes that made his face look open and friendly. He appeared to be around forty, and he radiated vitality and masculinity.

"Rose, how are you?"

I turned, pulled from my daze, to find Dr. Hamilton, who had been a witness for Isao. I introduced the two doctors and then was drafted into action as deputy hostess with the arrival of new guests. I glanced back as I headed to the front door and saw that, while Dr. Hamilton was shaking hands with another of the officers, Jack had turned to watch me, a little smile on his face. He winked, and my face warmed as I smiled back and turned to my job.

I was conscious of him there, during the early minutes of the party, as I helped Jeanette get guests' purses stowed and glasses filled, felt his presence drawing me to him. It was extraordinary. The only time I had experienced anything akin to this was with Vaughn, all those long years ago, and that had been a slow fire that grew over time. This was sudden, disorienting, and thrilling.

As soon as I could, I gathered my courage and a fresh drink and went over to where Jim's mother sat in her usual place on the couch. She was telling Jack the story of the men of SS *Lahaina* arriving at Spreckelsville, when she had helped tend to the men who staggered ashore near her friend's house.

"Sit down, dear," she said, indicating the sofa beside her. "I'm telling Captain Quinn about those poor sailors who came ashore in Mittee's front yard before Christmas."

Jack, who'd been listening with a look of concern to Mrs. Thornton's tale, now broke into a smile and stood as I seated myself. I stifled a girlish giggle.

The serious mood returned as Mrs. Thornton resumed the story she had told me on Christmas Eve. I pretended to listen to her tale of the lifeboat full of torpedo survivors landing on the beach in front of her friend's house. But my attention was on Jack, on the other side of Mrs. Thornton, right where I could look at him while he kept his eyes trained on her. It was a satisfactory arrangement. I could stare, unimpeded by good manners.

At last, having described her visits to the poor sailors while they recovered in the hospital from their ordeal, Mrs. Thornton finished the story.

"Now, Captain," she said, switching topics, and Jack's eyes flicked briefly at mine, his smile widening, then turned politely back to Mrs. Thornton.

"Please do tell us whatever you are allowed to about this new hospital you're opening," Mrs. Thornton said. "I understand you've taken over the elementary school. It's quite a new school—how long since it was built, Rose? Do you recall?"

"About five years." Now Jack was looking at me, and I lowered my gaze, suddenly shy.

"Yes, we're sorry to disrupt the school," he said. "But we'll be needing it, as you can imagine. I'm sure you've noticed there are a few servicemen around."

Mrs. Thornton chuckled. "Oh yes, and we're so happy to see you all. We were so worried that the Japanese would invade Maui, you know, and we had so little to defend us. Only a few National Guardsmen, and I understand they were short of arms and ammunition. The U.S. Army is very welcome. We all feel much safer now."

"Happy to be here with you," he said, still looking straight at me. My heart gave a little lurch. "Although I do wish it were under better circumstances. At any rate, we're what's called a station hospital, set up to take routine care of a general military population. Even if, God willing, we never have to deal with battle wounds, there'll always be a case of appendicitis or a broken bone."

"Do you think we'll be able to avoid having the fighting come here?" I asked, troubled by the still looming possibility. The Japanese were hopping from island to island in the Western Pacific, and who knew when they might attack Hawaii again.

Jack lifted an eyebrow. "We'll do our darndest, and you know when Uncle Sam sets out to do something, it usually works. They hit us with a sneak attack, but we're onto them now. That won't happen again."

"There you are, my dear!" We all looked up to see another white-haired lady, Mrs. Draper, a friend of Mrs. Thornton's who I knew was an incorrigible flirt. She patted her curls and batted her eyelashes at Jack, who sprang to his feet, offering her his seat. "I'm sorry to displace you," Mrs. Draper said, but Jack laughed and bowed. Both ladies gave him doting smiles, and Mrs. Thornton pointed to a hassock near the coffee table. "Do sit, Captain, if you don't mind perching for a while. We'd love to hear more about you. Where are you from? Do you have a family waiting for you at home?" I was grateful to her for having broached this question, as I had been wondering about it myself.

Jack's smile faded for a moment, but he pulled the hassock over and sat.

"I'm from Oregon," he said. "A little town called Medford. Ever heard of it?"

We all shook our heads. Jack's smile came back. "That's not surprising. It's small, just north of the California border, but we're the metropolis of our region, so a good place for a country doctor to set up. Lots of pear farms and lumber mills, and everyone coming to Medford for their shopping and doctoring."

"Rather rainy, I suppose?" Mrs. Thornton said.

"Actually, not very. I was born near Portland, and my parents still live up there, so I know about Oregon rain. We are far south of there, with many more clear days. We're in a valley, lots of green hills. You'd love it there, almost as pretty as Maui," he said, looking at me again.

"And you have a family there in Medford?" Mrs. Thornton asked the question I had not dared.

Again, the smile faded.

"I have two sons, eight and ten. Unfortunately, my wife, Jennie, passed away in 1938." Both old ladies gasped and murmured sounds of sympathy. Mrs. Draper reached to caress Jack's hand. I, meanwhile, was caught in an uncomfortable place. This poor man, losing a beloved wife, left alone with two boys. On the other hand—no wife.

Jack went on with his story. "My youngest sister came to live with us and watch the boys. Country docs work odd hours, get called out in the middle of the night. Can't have boys left to fend for themselves, so I'm grateful to my sister." He paused, looking serious. "They all went up to my folks' place when my unit was activated. They'll be there for the duration." He made a wry face. "Of course, we had to sell the livestock. Not that I had much, a couple of steers and a few chickens. But I like to think of myself as a bit of a gentleman farmer with my little homestead, and now it's just empty pastures."

"You can rebuild when you get home," Mrs. Draper said, reaching again to pat his hand. "At least your boys are well cared for."

Jeanette appeared with the other doctors in tow. "This is Capt. Joe MacLean," she said, "and Capt. Fred Lubinski." The two leaned forward to shake hands with the ladies.

"My, you're all so handsome in your uniforms," Mrs. Draper said, looking up through her eyelashes. The three officers smiled and exchanged glances. Probably used to this reaction, I thought, though Mrs. Draper was far too old for any of them.

The new arrivals set off another round of questions about hometowns and families, and Jack stood. "I'll give up my perch so you all can get better acquainted." He turned to me. "Miss McKenzie, I was wondering if you would give me a tutorial on local plant life. Like that magnificent arrangement on the hors d'oeuvres table. I've never seen such flowers!"

"I'd be happy to, Captain," I said, while my heart danced in my chest. We wove our way through the growing crowd to reach the table where Masako's flowers sat.

"These flowers barely look real," Jack said, reaching to touch the soft petals of a white orchid.

"My friend grows them," I said. "She made this arrangement to welcome you all to the island. We are so grateful to have military protection."

Jack glanced around the room, filled with people chatting, laughing, drinking. "Is she here?" he asked.

How to explain that Masako never would be invited to a party like this, that the island's social hierarchy prescribed how we socialized? "No, not today," I said, though, of course, Masako had been here only yesterday as an employee. I changed the subject.

"Would you like a tour of the garden?" I asked. "Jeanette has a wizard of a gardener—Alfredo, the same fellow who's tending bar."

"I most certainly would," he said, giving me one of those gorgeous grins.

I glanced around, hoping not to draw attention to our exit and perhaps attract other plant lovers. I wanted this man to myself. I led him through the kitchen, where Shizue looked up from filling a plate with sliced fruit to give us a smile, and out the back door.

It was mid-afternoon now, and the sun was bright and warm on my bare arms, the kind of day that filled me with a surge of love for my island. We wandered along the edge of the property, where a hibiscus hedge sported red flowers. In their shade, ferns flourished, and in one corner a giant bird of paradise lifted its orange-and-blue blossoms next to croton bushes splashed with yellow. Jack exclaimed at the red torch ginger, inhaled the sweet fragrance of the *puakenikeni* and plumeria, stroked the velvety green of a philodendron vine crawling up a tree. While he looked at the flowers, I looked at him.

"Thanks for the tour. This place is amazing," he said and turned to face me, aiming those eyes like a spotlight into my soul. "Now, Miss Rose McKenzie, tell me about yourself." He glanced at my left hand, and I knew he'd registered the fact that there was no ring there.

I gave him the basics: I was a teacher, owned a little farm above Makawao, had lived on Maui most of my life. "I have been to the mainland," I said. "I was born there, moved to Maui so young I barely remember anything from before that, but I went to normal school for my initial teacher training and later to university in California and did my practice teaching in San Jose, where my sister and her family live."

"But you like it here better?"

"Yes, I love it here. This is home."

"No desire to go back to the States to live?"

I shook my head. "None."

"Hmmm." He regarded me thoughtfully. "So, what do you grow on your farm?"

I gave him a rundown of the crops and livestock. "Of course, we've increased our planting to meet war needs," I said. "But it's been tough." I hesitated. If explaining why Masako wasn't at the party had been impossible, how could I tell this *malihini*, a military man no less, about Isao? I had to try.

He listened, frowning, as I told him about Isao's absence, emphasizing as usual the "farm manager" aspect.

"How do you know this fellow is not helping the Japs somehow?" he asked when I finished.

I gritted my teeth and forced a smile. "Because I know Isao," I replied, "and there's not a bad bone nor a disloyal impulse in him. He's a great guy, always cheerful and energetic. A wonderful carpenter and a good father and husband and community member."

To my relief, Jack's face relaxed, and he smiled. "Well, if you're sure, then I'm sure you're right," he said. "Still, you never know. Blood is thicker than water, and we can't be too careful. If the Japs were to invade, how would we tell the difference? They look the same, right? Might make it dicey to defend ourselves if we couldn't tell friend from foe."

I smiled. "I'm pretty sure I'd know the difference between the suntanned local Japanese and a pale, fanatical invader," I said. "And I'd know for sure once they opened their mouths, because even a Japanese soldier fluent in English could never imitate the local accent."

Jack nodded thoughtfully. At least he seemed to accept my revelation.

My conscience was beginning to bother me. "I guess we'd better get back to the party," I said. "I'm supposed to be co-hostess, and I've deserted my post."

"Can't have that," he said, hand cupping my elbow as we turned to go in. The warmth of his touch remained even when he let go.

"Do you suppose," he said, "that I could come up and see your farm sometime?"

"I would love that," I said, a bit breathless. We smiled at each other again, he pulled the back door open, and we rejoined the party.

• • • •

"SO, WHAT IS GOING ON with you and Dr. Jack?" Jeanette asked as the last of the guests pulled out of the driveway. "You spent a lot of time together."

"I knew you'd notice," I said. "He is a dish, isn't he? As you predicted."

"He is indeed," Jeanette agreed. "But now that he has appeared, and you two seem to hit it off, I'm a bit worried. Can't have you getting hitched to someone who's going to drag you off to the mainland."

"Who said anything about getting hitched?" I countered, though a little thrill ran through me at the thought. "I just met the man."

Jeanette cast a skeptical glance my way. "I saw how you looked at him, and he at you. But take your time, will you?"

I laughed, but inside I already was thinking about when I might see him again, this man who had revived a part of me I'd thought I had buried when Vaughn died.

Chapter Thirteen

I had tried with half my heart, when I returned to Maui after Vaughn's death, to follow the traditional path and find a man to marry. But I knew I could never love anyone as I loved Vaughn, and I feared that marriage would mean a series of horrific miscarriages. Instead, I decided I could live without love. I immersed myself in my farm and teaching, turning away occasional overtures from would-be suitors, presenting myself to the world as a happy spinster.

Jack's blue eyes had penetrated that façade, opening a gate through which flowed a rush of emotion. If only the man didn't have a farm and family to go back to. I knew I could never leave Maui, even though, unlike Jack, I didn't have parents and children to hold me in place.

But there was a war on. No one knew where we would stand a month from now. I would live for today. And today, I couldn't wait to see Jack Quinn again.

He called the morning after the party, said he was going out for a walk, and asked if he could stop by. Of course he could!

I swiftly fluffed my hair, changed from my old *muumuu* into a pretty dress, and whipped the kitchen into shape, so he wouldn't find dishes in the sink. I went outside with pruners in hand and began to search out the nicest tropical blossoms in my flower beds. I'd send him back to his barracks—or tent?—with a bouquet.

"Rose!"

I turned, a thrill running through me, to see Jack striding down the driveway with a big smile on his face.

"Did you have trouble finding it?" I asked.

"No, your directions were swell—old church, cypress trees." He looked around. "This place is beautiful, Rose."

"Thank you," I said, bending to put the flowers into a bucket half-filled with water. "Come, I'll show you around."

I led him around the side of the house, Jack exclaiming and stopping to examine the flower beds full of ferns and impatiens that edged the walls. We reached the front, where the view opened up to show the gentle green slopes of the valley and the rise on the other side where my steers grazed. He stood, hands on hips, gazing at the coconut palms along one boundary, deep green pigeon pea bushes along the other sides, white goats reaching through the wire fencing to nibble on them.

"Gosh, Rose, this is grand!"

Pleased, I flashed him a broad smile. "Come see the stable." Down the hill a bit, we stopped to look at the sturdy new home Isao had built for our animals. Hens scratched and clucked behind chicken wire, and my old horse, Penny, stretched her neck over the fence for a pat.

"Here's a sweet old thing," Jack said, stroking her velvety nose. "Do you ride?"

"Not anymore. I used to ride her to school, back in my poverty-stricken early days as a teacher, but I had to keep a spare set of clothes there for those times when the rain soaked me. And then too, times changed. Not many people ride a horse for daily transportation anymore."

Jack laughed. "I can just see you riding up to the schoolhouse in the rain. What a gal!"

"I think most people around here consider me a bit eccentric, but they're used to me."

"You're an original, that's what you are. I know a few women in Oregon who run farms on their own, but they're mostly older widows, not lovely young ladies like you."

I blushed and batted my hand at him. "Sir, you exaggerate. Not so young anymore, anyway. Come, let me show you the gardens. We've been planting like mad."

The big garden was looking its best, some rows now in lush production, others already replanted with the seedlings Masako had started when we first expanded at the beginning of the war. Butterflies fluttered and bees from the neighbor's hives buzzed between flowers. The air was rich with the scents of soil and growing things.

Jack stood, arms folded, surveying the garden. "So you're pretty self-sufficient here," he said. "Milk, meat, eggs, vegetables, fruit. I'm impressed. And you are getting produce this time of year—where I come from, they won't harvest anything for a couple of months yet."

I turned to see Masako, hoe in one hand and a bucket of tools in the other. She had hesitated when she rounded the tall row of beans growing on poles at the windward edge of the plot and saw me there with a stranger in khaki.

"Masako, come meet Captain Quinn. He's one of the doctors in the hospital at the school. Jack, Mrs. Tanaka is our gardener-in-chief."

Masako approached, bowed her head slightly, and said, "Welcome to Maui, Captain. We're so glad you're here. We were rather vulnerable with one tiny and underequipped garrison, so you folks were a welcome sight."

Jack blinked, then smiled. "Thank you. Your garden is looking swell."

Masako dipped her head again and looked around the garden. "I'm going to plant the corn today, Rose," she said. "After I get those old pea plants out of the way."

"The goats will be happy," I said, and turned to Jack. "We feed garden trimmings to them, and they love pea vines. Now, how about a cup of tea, Captain—or coffee, if you prefer."

"Yes, indeed," he said. "Nice to meet you, Mrs. Tanaka."

That went well, I thought as we walked back to the house, smiling to myself at Masako's formality and at the novelty of calling her Mrs. Tanaka. And Jack had been a perfect gentleman.

"So how did Mrs. Tanaka learn to speak such excellent English?" he asked as we entered the kitchen. I laughed.

"She grew up here and was a top student at Maui High School, and I can assure you no one graduates without being held to the highest standards for spoken English."

"And you uphold those standards, do you?"

"Yes, in all my classes, and so do the other teachers." Jack lifted an eyebrow, apparently impressed.

I shrugged. "Of course, that's in the classroom. People who grew up here often speak pidgin in daily life—even Masako, who was a straight-A student. That's why I said I'd know in a minute whether a Japanese invader spoke like a local. I can speak pidgin myself, but I usually try to set a good example to encourage my students to speak good English. Now—would you prefer coffee or tea?" I asked.

"Coffee, if you have it. I know it's hard to get these days."

"I get some from a farmer friend and roast it myself. One of the advantages of living in Hawaii. I'm a black-tea drinker most of the time, grew up surrounded by tea drinkers, but I do enjoy a cup of coffee sometimes. And it smells so wonderful!"

I filled the coffee-pot and set it on the stove over a low flame and led Jack on a quick tour of the downstairs while the coffee perked.

"This is quite some house," he said, gazing around the living room with its stone fireplace and tall windows, now partially visible with the blackout drapes pulled aside. "Did you buy this? Inherit it?" He frowned, then looked apologetic. "And I'm sorry if I was thoughtless with my earlier comment. For all I know, you are a widow, carrying on after your husband passed. I don't know much about you, Rose McKenzie. I want to hear your life story, please."

"No, don't worry, I'm not a widow. Come have a seat, and I'll explain."

Jack settled at the kitchen table, and I poured coffee and set out plates with slices of Masako's banana bread. Jack's presence brought a new atmosphere to my cozy kitchen, an electric energy that filled me with a sparkly sensation. I took a sip of coffee, wondering where to begin.

"I was born in California in December of 1900, so I'm always as old as the century," I said.

"Really? I would've thought you were several years younger," he said.

"Thank you." I hesitated. "How old are you?"

"Thirty-eight," he said, with mock seriousness, "but very mature for my age." Both of us grinned. "Okay, then what?" he continued. "How did you get to Maui? I'd never even heard of this place until I found out we'd be stationed here."

"My father met a rancher named Vaughn Spencer in California. Vaughn was there with a couple of his cowboys who were competing in roping contests. Somehow, Vaughn and my dad connected, and my father was a bit fed up with the ranch owner he was working for at the time. Soon we were on a ship to Honolulu, then another to Maui, and my father became foreman for Spencer Ranch."

I took a bite of banana bread. At this point in our friendship, I'd be giving Jack the edited version, nothing about my father's drinking, and minimal detail about my affair with Vaughn. I told him how I'd grown up on the ranch, how Auntie Lily persuaded my mother to let me stay when she left my father, about my dad's death and Auntie Lily's, and Uncle Vaughn's helping me to get to the mainland for my teacher training.

I took another sip of coffee and a deep breath. This was where things made a turn that might shock my new friend.

"When I came back and started teaching in one of the plantation villages, Vaughn used to stop by my teacher's cottage to visit." I hesitated. "Eventually, we fell in love."

Jack's eyebrows shot up, and he seemed momentarily speechless. My shoulders tensed. Finally, he spoke.

"You mean you fell in love with a man you'd been calling 'uncle' all those years? Wasn't he much older than you?"

I nodded. "He was. More than twenty years older, actually. And his daughter was my best friend, so it wasn't simple. But we planned to marry." I set my coffee cup down and stared at it for a moment. "And then he died after a fall from his horse."

Now Jack was leaning forward, his hand reaching to cover mine. It was warm and so much larger than mine, and his touch made my hand tingle.

"So you are almost a widow, in fact," he said, and I nodded, blinking away tears. I had not wept for Vaughn in many years, but something about the warmth of Jack's hand and the knowledge that he too had lost his love set me off.

"Almost," I said. "He was a good businessman, one of the most successful ranchers on Maui, and he'd acquired a few pieces of land in addition to his ranch acreage. This place was one of them. He'd bought it for his old ranch foreman, who had a big family, but it was empty when Vaughn died, and he left it to me."

Jack lifted my hand and held it in both of his. He gently moved my fingers, a gesture both intimate and comforting.

"Vaughn sounds like quite a fellow," he said, his voice soft. "No wonder you fell for him."

"He was a wonderful man," I said, sniffing. I reached into my pocket for the clean handkerchief I always carried and dabbed at my eyes and nose. "Sorry, I didn't mean to start blubbering," I said.

"No, I understand." Jack was blinking a bit now, I noticed. "I truly do. Some people we never stop loving and missing, even after they're gone."

We didn't speak for a few moments. Finally, I looked up, trying to smile as I wiped my cheeks dry. "Perhaps we should return to the present. Are you in a barracks? I see them springing up all over the place."

"No, in a house. We docs are sharing a house near the hospital—or school, I guess it was, and with luck will be again soon. Two men to a bedroom, plus a kitchen, and a living room. All furnished and quite comfortable."

"And have you had many patients so far?"

He chuckled. "Not too many, which is good, because we're barely ready, still waiting for some supplies. But I expect the patient load will increase as training gets underway."

"Lots more troops coming in?"

"Yes, there will be." He looked apologetic. "I'm sorry, I can't talk about it much," he said.

"I know," I replied. "Loose lips sink ships."

"That's right, ma'am." He smiled again, and I smiled back, happy to be in this man's presence. I couldn't stop looking at him—those wide blue eyes, the smile lines radiating from their edges, his straight white teeth. He broke our gaze, glancing at his watch, then frowned.

"Dang it. I need to leave," he said. "I have night duty, so I have to get back and get ready." He reached for my hand again. "Rose, I'm so happy to have met you, and I'm grateful that you were willing to share your story, and your grief, with me. I'd like to see you again."

And so, when I waved goodbye and watched Jack walk up my driveway (carrying the bouquet he said was the first he'd ever been given), I already knew that there would be more meetings with the only man I'd ever met who might be worthy of the kind of love I had shared with Vaughn.

Jack called the next evening as I was grading papers. He'd be busy for the next few days he said—their supplies had come in, and a backlog of patients needed routine care. "I wanted to thank you again for the flowers," he said. "The other fellows are as amazed as I was. What do you call the heart-shaped red ones again?"

"Anthurium," I replied. "And the white ones are spathiphyllum."

"Nothing like them where we come from," Jack said. "Listen, I have to get back to work. But I wonder if we can get together again, if we can line up our schedules. You work days; I work nights. So I guess it's going to have to be on the weekends, though I do have duty then too."

"Wouldn't that cut into your sleeping time?"

"Nah. I can get some shut-eye in the early morning if you can find time in the afternoon."

"Okay, that sounds swell," I said, joy bubbling up in my chest.

"Great!" he said, sounding as pleased as I felt. "I'm not sure what we can do, though. No restaurants around here where I can take you for a meal. Any suggestions?"

I thought for a moment. There was little to do, day or night, in Makawao, as the bored soldiers who roamed the streets of our little town were learning. And gas rationing meant we couldn't drive to Wailuku or explore any of the remote beauty spots of the island.

"Do you like to walk? I could take you for a walk around the neighborhood," I said.

"I do! I'll wear my hiking boots. And maybe we can at least manage a Coke or something in Makawao."

"Sounds exciting," I said, smiling. Something to look forward to—a date with Jack!

That little hum of excitement carried me through a week of classes and clubs, of milking goats and harvesting vegetables. Often, preparing for a lesson or grading a test, I found my thoughts drifting and a smile on my face. Saturday couldn't come soon enough.

Jack arrived in the early afternoon. It was a beautiful day, sunny but not too hot, with a soft eucalyptus-scented breeze. I greeted him at the back door, both of us wearing wide grins. We'd spoken every evening in the days since he first visited, quick calls when he had a break. Now we had all afternoon, the luxury of time to share stories of our lives and our dreams.

"Got your gas mask?" he asked. I grabbed it from the hook by the door, set a wide-brimmed straw hat on my head, and stepped out to join him. Jack reached for my hand, those blue eyes focused on my face. "It's so nice to see you again," he said.

"You too," I said, blushing. This really was the most extraordinary thing—thinking about him all day, waiting for the phone to ring each evening, and now blushing like a kid when I saw him. "Are you ready to walk? We're heading uphill."

"I'm ready," he said. "Brought my canteen, in case we get thirsty."

"Then we're off."

The route I'd chosen took us up through the ranchland above mine, through emerald-green pastures filled with dairy cattle, past red-painted ranch headquarters, and back down to Makawao Avenue. Tall trees lined the narrow road, casting their shade through golden sunshine. A gorgeous walk at any time, but Jack's pleasure at the beauty of Upcountry Maui made me all the more appreciative of the lovely place where I lived. He was a good walker, matching his pace to mine. And as in our phone conversations, we found plenty to talk about: his patients back home (he spoke little of his military work, of course), funny things his boys had done, my students and their activities, our memories of growing up in the country, with similarities that spanned an ocean.

"I'm glad I grew up on a farm," he said as we strode along one of the flatter stretches through the dairy fields. "Good to take care of the animals, milk the cows, and so on. I'm glad my boys are having that experience as well. It makes you realize the importance of work and discipline and keeps you close to nature." He shrugged. "But I'm glad I spent time in the city too. Got a glimpse of the big world, plus of course an education."

I laughed. "You know I'm all in favor of education. Where did you go to college?"

"Earned my bachelor's degree in Eugene, about a hundred miles south of Portland. Then I went for my medical degree in Portland."

"Tell me about Jennie. How did you two meet?"

"We met in a chemistry class in Eugene and dated through college, got married after graduation. It was tough, making it through medical school. Jennie worked—she was a great typist, did not only her secretarial job but a lot of my school papers. Of course, I worked, though I didn't have much free time as a medical student. My parents helped all they could, but you know what farming is like. Plenty to eat, but not a lot of cash to spare." He shook his head, frowning. "Thank goodness I finished and was set up in practice before the Depression hit, or I'd never have made it."

"And how did you end up in Medford?"

"One of my buddies from med school was from there. He was headed for the bright lights, didn't want to go back to work in his father's practice. So I did instead. Neither Jennie nor I had any desire to live in some smoky, noisy city, surrounded by people and concrete. Now the old man is on his own again, a one-doc practice in a one-horse town—well, not exactly. Plenty of horses around, actually."

"You must feel right at home in Makawao," I said, and we both laughed. We were doing a lot of laughing.

But then he sobered. "Actually, as beautiful as this place is, I'd go home in an instant if I could. I miss my boys."

"I'll bet you do," I said.

He smiled again. "Roy's the big brother, ten years old. He's my little scholar. Always comes home from school and gets right down to his homework, makes top grades in every subject. He's following the war closely—he has a big map up on his side of the bedroom he shares with his little brother, Mark, and he puts pins in it to show where different battles take place," he said, chuckling.

"Now, Mark, he's full of beans, has to be coaxed—or ordered—to get that homework done, though he makes excellent grades when he's interested enough to focus on a subject. He's eight, always climbing something. Broke his arm when he tried to get to the peak of our barn. Quite the outdoorsman." He smiled fondly. "What a pair. I'm so grateful to my family for caring for them while I'm gone." He slowed his steps and reached into his back pocket. "Want to see pictures?"

"Of course I do!"

He took out his wallet and pulled two small photographs from it and held one in each hand for me to examine. Two handsome little boys faced the camera, both with shocks of blond hair and light-colored eyes that I imagined were the same blue as their father's. Each wore a plaid shirt, and each stood beside a sheep, Roy at attention beside the larger of the two animals, Mark with one arm thrown around the neck of his.

"These are the sheep they raised last year in 4-H, back in Medford. They were so proud of them! This year, my dad has given them charge of two calves, got them involved in the local 4-H as soon as they moved up there."

"They're wonderful," I said, smiling at the sight of these sweet faces. "What a treasure you've had to leave behind. Thank goodness for your family."

He turned the pictures, slightly creased from his wallet and, I was sure, much handling, and gazed at them for a moment before returning them to the wallet. "Yes," he said. "They are my treasure indeed." He sighed. "Well, shall we get on with our walk?" We turned back to the road and set off again.

By the time we completed the square that led us back to Makawao town, I knew the names of not only his sons but of his parents and five siblings, and the horse he'd loved as a youngster. We stopped at the corner outside Tam Chow Store to contemplate our next move—up the hill to my place or down to the shops and businesses of Makawao. The clusters of little buildings that met at this intersection to make an L-shaped town were crowded as they'd never been before the war.

"Are you hungry?" Jack asked. "We could get a hamburger or something and take it back up to your place or mine." The two cafes in town offered counter service only, and both were down the road. I glanced around and noticed two girls from one of my classes smirking as one whispered in the other's ear, both with eyes on us. Soldiers and residents glanced at us curiously as they passed.

"Or you could come up and have an early dinner of beef stew," I said, not wanting to face the stares we'd encounter if we headed into the town. "If you have time before your shift." I'd made a batch of stew that morning, hoping this might be a possibility.

"I'd love some stew, and I have a couple of hours, plenty of time to eat and get home for a shower before work."

"Okay, it's all uphill from here," I said. "Ready for the final push?"

"You bet," he replied, and we swung into step as if we'd been walking together forever.

Hungry, we gobbled the stew, still talking between bites; we had so much to share. When it was time for him to leave, we stood close together in the back entryway, our eyes locked on each other. Jack leaned forward, I did too, and we kissed, long and deep.

"I wish I didn't have to go, but it's probably a good thing that I do," he said at last, as he leaned back, one arm pulling me close, the other hand stroking my hair.

"Duty calls," I said, trying to catch my breath. Our lips met again in a surge of passion that I feared would be unstoppable if not for that call.

Jack released me and took his gas mask, canteen, and cap from the hook by the door and looked at me as he turned to leave. "I'll see you soon."

"Yes," I said, and watched him turn to wave as he headed up the driveway. Soon, I thought, sounded wonderful. But it also sounded scary. I knew where kisses like that could lead. And I could not afford to go there.

Chapter Fourteen

As the week went by, I found myself daydreaming as I worked, needing to force myself to focus on a student's oral presentation, smiling so much as I milked the cow one evening that Masako stopped to stare.

"What's gotten into you lately, Rose?" she asked, quirking an eyebrow as she filled a pail with grain for the goats. "It wouldn't be that good-looking doctor, would it?" She clapped a hand over her mouth. "Sorry, that sounded kind of rude." We both erupted in laughter, the kind that goes on and on, with one of us starting up again each time the other began to calm down. Lani turned her head to see what was happening as I stopped in mid-squeeze, and Iris, who had been scattering scratch feed for the hens, peered through the chicken coop fence.

"What's so funny?" she asked.

"Mommy said something silly," Masako replied, and we were both off again in gales of laughter.

The next Saturday, I picked up Jack and his colleague Fred for an afternoon bridge game at the Thorntons'.

Jack hopped into the truck first and slid over close to me, leaning in to give me a quick kiss. Fred shot us a knowing look as he settled into the passenger seat and pulled the door shut.

"Ready for a tough game?" I asked, redirecting attention from our kiss as I pulled out onto the road.

"Hell, yeah," said Fred. "I need a break from all those poor bozos and their aches and pains."

"I'm glad you have the dengue fever corralled," I said. "It would be terrible to let that get loose in the community."

Jack had been gazing at me as I drove, and now his head tilted in surprise. "How did you know about that?" he asked. "It's supposed to be top secret, so the Japs don't know we're vulnerable."

"Coconut wireless," I said, shrugging. "Word of mouth. People who live in Haliimaile know a ship came in full of sick soldiers and the Army put them up in the gym there. Don't worry," I glanced at the two doctors, both staring at me. "I won't be telling the enemy. Or about the volcano eruption on the Big Island. Did you see the glow?"

"Yeah, we did," Jack said. "Climbed up on the hospital roof to see it. I guess they're keeping it out of the papers, but it's hard to miss. Like a big lantern inviting the Japs to fly by with a few bombs."

"Let's hope they don't fly that far east," I said. "Or anywhere near our neighborhood, for that matter."

Ahead, I saw a group of soldiers beside the road turning hopefully at the sound of my engine. I slowed and stuck my head out the window. "Want a ride, fellows? We're only going a few miles."

"Yes, ma'am!" one shouted, and they all ran to jump into the back of my truck. "We're headed to the beach," one said as he passed my window.

"Poor guys, not a lot for them to do around here," I said as I started back down the road, shifting into neutral to take advantage of the slope.

"There's a USO dance every week in Wailuku, and I suppose other things to do there," Fred said. "But it's so damn far to hitchhike if they miss the bus, and they have to get back up the hill before curfew."

"War is hell," Jack said, and we were all silent for a moment. Our little problems, from rationing to boredom and even dengue fever, paled in comparison to the real hell others were experiencing.

"Things are looking bad in the Philippines," Fred said.

"Yeah. First Bataan gone, and now Corregidor. Our guys and the P.I. forces have really been up against it." Jack shook his head. "Bad situation. But at least Doolittle hit the Japs hard, bombing their capital. Gave them what they deserve, the bastards.

"Hard to imagine what they're going through in other places, looking at this peaceful scene. Much closer to heaven than hell here," Jack said, gazing out across the island as the road curved around the hill. Fluffy clouds topped the West Maui Mountains, and shades of green varied from the dark pineapple fields just below us to the bright sugarcane of the central plain, across to the mountains' blue-shadowed emerald.

I pulled over near the Thorntons' driveway to let our passengers out. They waved cheerfully and set off walking, on their way down to the wide white sandy beaches at Paia. They would have to crawl through the narrow holes left in the coils of barbed wire lining the beach, but at least they'd get a chance to wear themselves out in the waves, forgetting for a while that war loomed over our lives.

We parked under monkeypod trees on the Thorntons' lawn and gathered up our contributions to lunch—deviled eggs and a salad from me, a bottle of whiskey from the two doctors. Jack balanced the egg platter with one hand and put the other arm around my waist as we crossed the Thorntons' lawn. Fred walked ahead of us, oblivious, but I could see Jeanette peering through the window. As she and I organized lunch in the kitchen while the men poured drinks in the living room, she turned to me with a big smile.

"I see things are progressing with you and the captain," she said.

"What makes you say that?" I asked, tossing the salad.

"I have eyes. You two are obviously an item." She cocked her head, giving me a look. "I'll be blunt, Rose. How are you going to handle this? I know you must be thinking about it."

I shrugged, momentarily at a loss for words. Jeanette knew my story, the whole shocking story, the reason I'd stayed single all these years.

And now Jeanette was about to shock me.

"What you need, Rose, is a diaphragm," she said in a near whisper, glancing over at the closed swinging door that separated kitchen and living room. "You've been an absolute iron woman, staying single and celibate all these years. You need a diaphragm so you can give that man what you both so clearly want, and I'm going to see that you get one."

I stared at her, open-mouthed, not sure how to respond. I had a vague idea of what a diaphragm was, but I'd never thought I would need one.

Just then, the swinging door opened, and the twins came in. "*Tutu* says we should come help you so we can eat lunch and start the game," said Carolyn. Her sister, Madelyn, peered over my shoulder. "Is the salad ready?"

I handed it to her, Carolyn took the plate of deviled eggs, and they headed for the dining room.

"You mark my words, Rose," Jeanette whispered as the door swung shut. "Life is short and uncertain, and that man is in love with you. I don't want you to leave Maui, but I do want you to be happy. Now, come on." She picked up a platter of roast beef sandwiches. "Let's eat."

• • • •

LATE THAT AFTERNOON, after I had dropped off Jack and Fred and was starting dinner, Aiko knocked on my back door.

"Auntie, may I use your typewriter?" she asked.

"Yes, of course," I said. "What's up?"

She handed me a slightly crumpled sheet of paper on which I recognized Isao's tidy handwriting. "Dad's asking for parole," she said, grinning.

I stopped slicing onions and turned to face Aiko. "How wonderful! They finally let them apply! Oh, I hope it works, and he comes home quickly. Is that his request? May I see it?"

I skimmed the letter and handed it back to her. "Good for your father. This should convince them. My goodness, this is so exciting! Go right ahead, you know where the typewriter is, and of course, the paper's in the drawer, along with carbon paper if you want to make copies."

I went back to my dinner preparation, hearing the click-clack of typewriter keys from my little office. I decided I would write a letter too, this one to the local provost marshal offering to be Isao's sponsor, repeating my request to the hearing board that he be released to work on the farm.

Soon, Aiko returned and set the newly typed letter on the kitchen table. "Will you proofread it for me, Auntie?" she asked.

"Sure thing." I rinsed my hands, wiped them dry, and sat across the table from Aiko. The letter was formally composed, directed to the military governor of the Territory of Hawaii.

Dear General, it read. *"May I respectfully request that I be released from internment. I was interned on December 8, 1941, and in February 1942 was informed I would be interned for the duration of the war. I am a loyal American citizen. I do not support the Japanese attack on America in any way. My wife and four children on Maui are all working to win the war. My two boys helped clear brush away from the beaches with the Kiawe Corps, and my wife and daughters roll bandages with the Red Cross. They all work hard on the farm and at school and war jobs. I want to go back to the farm where we live and join in the work of raising food to support our community. A favorable reply to my appeal will be greatly appreciated.*

Yours truly,

Isao Tanaka

"Letter perfect," I said, giving Aiko a smile. "I don't even see any erasures. Miss Cawdry would be proud."

Aiko laughed. "Yes, she is a great teacher. A little too strict, but I guess that's how we learned." Then, wistfully, she said, "I only wish I could use my typing to get off that cannery line. I am so sick of the pineapple smell, my feet hurt, and my arms burn from pineapple juice." She rubbed her forearm and wrist, chronically red and irritated from the acidic juice. "Even though I always use lotion and cornstarch before I put on my gloves, it runs down my arm."

"Have you thought of looking for a job elsewhere? The war has opened up a lot of possibilities."

She shrugged. "Yes, but what I'd really like to do is go to Honolulu. And I doubt my folks would let me do that."

"Why Honolulu?"

"Exciting!" She looked sheepish. "I know, it's bad to think of a war as exciting. But it would be something new and different for me to be in the city, and I know I could make good money. Leona Ventura's sister Malia has a job at a construction company, and she is going to get Leona a job. Leona says I can come too, and we can share a room at Malia's house, so I'd have a place to live. You remember Malia, don't you, Auntie? She graduated a couple of years ahead of Leona and me."

I did remember Malia, and Leona, daughters of a big Hawaiian-Portuguese family whose father ran a gas station in Paia. Nice girls. Living with them would provide a safe base for Aiko to explore life more than she could working at the cannery and sharing a bedroom with her little sister. And Aiko was an excellent typist, with straight-A grades all the way through Miss Cawdry's famously difficult classes.

A couple of days later, when I was at the Tanakas', Aiko brought up the question to her mother. Masako's reaction was predictable.

"Why do you want to move over there? It's dangerous. There's a war on. And Honolulu got bombed a few months ago. Stay here, Aiko. I have enough to worry about with your father gone."

Aiko shrugged and quit arguing. But a few days later, she was back with more ammunition. "Leona is going to work in the construction company office, Mommy, and guess what they're going to pay her—$120 a month!"

That captured everyone's attention. It was twice the average wage on Maui.

"Leona says they're looking for good typists," Aiko continued. "And I can send plenty money home to you folks." Masako simply pressed her lips together and shook her head.

I kept my mouth shut. This was Masako and Isao's decision. But I was secretly cheering for Aiko. She was twenty-one years old, single, sociable, and ready to take on the world. If it were me, I knew I would want to go. When I was her age, I was already teaching in California and responsible for my own life. But I didn't have a tight-knit family with strict but doting parents, not to mention a family whose father was locked away. No wonder Masako didn't want Aiko to leave.

• • • •

MAY 1942

Jack came up the next two Saturdays, and we took long walks, talking and holding hands. Each time, we kissed goodbye a little longer and breathed a little faster.

"Good thing we don't start smooching until I'm ready to leave," Jack said with a rueful grin as he pulled his gas mask from the hook by the back door. "Uncle Sam's work schedule is forcing me to resist temptation."

I felt a blush rise. "It's pretty darn tempting," I agreed, then blushed more.

"One more kiss," he said, pulling me close. It was the longest kiss yet, and I had to lean against the door-frame as he walked away. Slowly, my heartbeat went back to normal, and I sighed and turned to the kitchen, frustration warring with exhilaration.

Jeanette showed up late one afternoon, knocking on my back door after she'd dropped off Masako. "I got it," she said with a conspiratorial wink. She glanced around. "No one here, right?"

"No, of course not," I replied. "You got the, uh, the thing?"

"The diaphragm, silly," she said, dropping her gas mask and her purse onto the table. "One of the girls I work with knows where to get one that will fit pretty much any woman who hasn't had a child, so I ordered one for you." She plopped onto a kitchen chair. "Whew. What a day. Any chance of a glass of iced tea? This full-time work is exhausting. At least I have the girls keeping an eye on Teddy until I get back, and Shizue is cooking dinner. How on earth do working girls do it if they don't have servants?"

"It's a struggle," I said, casting a wry glance her way as I opened the fridge to pull out an ice tray. "That's why women who want a career have to make a choice."

"Now, don't tell me that's why you made the choice," Jeanette said, cocking her head at me. "I know better. I know you love teaching, but I also know you'd have been happy to be a wife and mother. At least let yourself have some fun." She reached into her purse and pulled out a paper bag from which she took a little round case that opened to reveal an odd-looking circular ring with a thin dome of rubber attached.

"So this is a diaphragm?"

"Yep. And if it hadn't been for a bottle of champagne one night a couple of years ago, I'd have used mine, and we wouldn't have little Teddy." She sighed. "Children are such a mixed blessing. Jim and I were going to travel when the girls went off to college. Oh well, no use crying over spilt milk." She laughed. "And there's plenty of that to go around with young Theodore. Not to mention, this war would have messed up our travel plans anyway." She turned serious again. "Anyway, do you have any idea how to use this?"

I shook my head.

"It's pretty simple. You put it up your da kine before you make love, and it blocks the guy's stuff from getting to your eggs."

My eyebrows rose at the rather blunt response from my plainspoken friend. I wasn't even used to thinking about such matters, never mind talking about them. I eyed the diaphragm, wondering how to get that rather large circle into my da kine—"da kine" being the catchall island phrase for whatever was the object of discussion.

So Jeanette showed me, squeezing the flexible disc into a half circle. "You use tampons, right?"

I nodded; something else Jeanette had introduced me to, a few years earlier.

"Well, you insert this the way you'd insert a tampon. But first..." She reached into the bag and pulled out a cardboard box, from which she took a tube. Both box and tube were marked "medicated jelly for feminine hygiene."

"Now, this is important," Jeanette said, "because the jelly kills any of the little seeds that might get past the diaphragm. You put some into the diaphragm, and spread it around the edge before you put it in." She grinned. "And if you want to do the deed again, don't take out the diaphragm, just put some more jelly in."

There was more—how long to leave the diaphragm in, how to check it for holes—but by the time we finished our tea, I had a good idea of how to protect myself.

And boy, did I need that protection. Jack had been letting me set the limits, but I was finding it awfully hard to set any limits at all.

The next Saturday, while Masako and the kids were gone to visit Isao, guaranteeing our privacy, I put my diaphragm in place and waited for Jack to arrive. He came in, smiling, gave me a big kiss, and said, "So, where are we walking today?"

I leaned back in his arms, shy but certain, and said, "How about we walk back to my bedroom?"

His eyes widened. "Are you sure?"

"I'm sure."

He hesitated. "I don't have any, uh, protection," he said.

"Don't worry, I do. Let's go."

It had been so long. I was afraid I might have forgotten how to do this strange and wonderful thing. But, like riding a bike, making love is an unforgettable skill. I had forgotten how marvelous it was, however, or perhaps I'd blocked the memory, never expecting to have this experience again. I had to use a second dose of the jelly. And then we lay wrapped around each other, breathing in the scents of our bodies and our lovemaking.

"I'm sure you're wondering why I suddenly became willing to make love," I said after a while.

"Me, question a gift from the gods?" he said, nuzzling my neck. I giggled.

"Well, I managed to get my hands on a diaphragm," I said. "I'm not the sort of girl who does this sort of thing often, and I haven't met anyone I wanted to do it with for many, many years."

"Not since Vaughn," he said softly, and my eyes filled with tears. I'd told him only that Vaughn and I had been in love. Now he held me as I spilled the whole story, wiping the tears from my cheeks with gentle hands.

"My poor baby, dealing with all that loss. I'm so glad we found each other," he said at last and kissed me until I had to excuse myself to get more jelly.

• • • •

FOR SEVERAL DAYS, THE coconut wireless had buzzed with rumors: Something major was going to happen. No one knew what that might be, but our big fear, as usual, was of an invasion. All eyes were on the skies, and ears listened for the drone of enemy engines.

At night, I lay sweating in my bed, choosing the fragile security of locked doors and windows over the cooling comfort of the trade winds' breeze blowing across my body. Alone, with Jack at work and the Tanakas down the hill, I slept little. I kept an axe beside my bed and, for the first time in my life, wished I had a gun. But the military government had confiscated civilian firearms in the days after the Pearl Harbor attack, and I had no idea where I could get one. My axe would have to do.

Finally, on June 4, the Navy informed us that Midway was under attack. Two tense days later, word of a victory reached Hawaii. Our immense relief belied the relative size of that tiny atoll thirteen hundred miles to our west. Our side lost two ships, 145 planes, and more than three hundred men. But the Japanese limped away with such great losses that they might never come our way again.

We celebrated with a party at Jeanette's. Jack and I arrived early to help push the furniture out of the way and roll up the rugs that covered hardwood floors.

"Man, that's a relief," Jim said as he and Jack edged the sofa closer to the wall. "If they'd taken Midway, we'd have been on thin ice."

"No kidding," Jack replied. "We have them on the run now. Four Jap carriers out of commission! Revenge for Pearl Harbor."

"At least they can't use Midway as a base for another big attack," Jeanette said, as she and I each lifted the end of a rolled-up rug. "I feel like I can breathe easily again for the first time in months." We dropped the rug against one wall and stood up, dusting off our hands. I looked out the big window and saw the first car full of guests arrive. "Here come the people, Jeanette."

"Oh dear," she said, smoothing her hair. "And there's another one! They're early." She stripped off her apron and handed it to me. "Can you help Shizue bring the rest of the *pupus* in from the kitchen while the boys finish up in here?" She turned to call down the hall to the twins' room. "Carolyn, come put on a record! Time to start the party!"

By the time I got back from the kitchen, the first arrivals were gathered around Alfredo, who wore a huge smile as he poured drinks, Jeanette was at the door greeting another group, and Jack was waiting, leaning against the wall with his arms folded and a smile on his face. As soon as I set down my plates full of little sandwiches, he took my hand, put his other arm firmly around my waist, and swung me onto the still-empty dance floor. I hadn't danced the jitterbug for years, but Jack's strong arms soon had me twirling. Laughing, we let "In The Mood" lift our feet and our bodies as the Midway victory had lifted our spirits.

Chapter Fifteen

June 1942

Jack went home with me after the Midway victory party, and he stayed over for the first time.

"You know," I said as we lay in bed the next morning, my head on his shoulder, "this is the first time I've ever actually spent the night with a man."

"Really? Not even with Vaughn?" Jack always spoke so gently of Vaughn, as if our love had been a true marriage. He reached to smooth my hair from my forehead.

"No, Vaughn never spent the night. He visited me in the afternoons, but he headed home before dark," I said. "We were together other times, of course. I spent many weekends at his home, part of the family even after I was launched as an adult on my own. But we never were able to be together like this."

"We'll have to make up for that lack in your life," Jack said, rolling onto his side to kiss my cheek. "Unless I snored too much, and you never invite me back."

I giggled. "You didn't snore. Did I?"

"I'll never tell," he said and turned my head to kiss my lips.

We had gotten back from the party shortly before sunset yesterday, and Jack had joined us in the evening chores, helping me with the pigs and bringing the goats in from their tethers. Masako watched discreetly as she filled feed troughs, a little smile on her face, and whispered that she and the kids could handle the morning chores if I wanted. Already self-conscious about having Jack here after curfew, I gave her an embarrassed nod.

Now I was so glad I had. We spent half the morning in bed, dozing and making love, and then I showered and dressed and went to cook breakfast while Jack showered.

"I feel so domestic," I said. I set half a papaya before him, flipped the eggs in the frying pan, and pulled toast from the oven.

"It suits you," Jack said with a wink. He took a long drink of milk. "And what a treat to have fresh real milk, not that powdered junk the Army gives us. Paradise! A quiet morning, no one making demands—hey! What about the animals? I almost forgot you're a bona fide farmer with chores to do."

"Masako said she'd do them."

He looked sheepish. "Oh. She figured out I'd be staying?"

"Yes. I guess we're a bit obvious."

"Good! I want everyone to know you're my girl. And how kind of Mrs. Tanaka to relieve you of farm duty for this morning." He set his cup down and looked at his watch with a sigh. "Now, Uncle Sam, on the other hand, is not so considerate. I start my shift in an hour."

"Damn. This war. Can't get a day off from it, can we? Even when our team just won a big victory." I took a bite of toast, and Jack finished off his papaya.

"On the other hand," he said, "without the war, we'd never have met."

"That's right. Can you imagine any way a boy from Medford and a girl from Maui ever would have gotten together?" We both grinned, amazed at fate.

Jack left after breakfast. A little while later, washing dishes, I looked out the window to see the Tanakas' truck heading up the driveway. Off to see Isao. I finished cleaning up and pulled out my book bag. School was finished for the year; I had a bit of leftover paperwork to wrap up, and I would be done for the summer.

My mind drifted in the afterglow of my night with Jack. In truth, I had slept little. I wasn't used to having someone in my bed, and I had half dozed, aware of the warm solidity of his body, the rhythm of his breathing, the scent of his skin. I set my paperwork aside and lay on my bed, falling into a deep sleep.

I had just awakened from that long nap when I heard a knock on my back door.

"Rose, are you here?" Masako's voice was hoarse. I went to the door and found her with a handkerchief in one hand and a laundry bag in the other. Her eyes were red and swollen.

"Masako, what's wrong?" I held the screen open. "Come in, sit down."

"They denied his parole. And they're sending him to Honolulu on the steamer Monday night." She dropped the laundry bag, sank into a chair, and slumped, sobbing into her handkerchief.

I gasped. "But that's tomorrow! Why would they do such a thing? And I can't believe they'd send him with such short notice."

Masako nodded, dabbing her eyes. "I know. Just like that, off to another island. Who knows how long until we see him?" She broke down again, then squared her shoulders and wiped her cheeks. "We have to go say goodbye tomorrow. Will you come?"

"Of course I will!" I put my hand on hers. "Oh Masako, I'm so sorry. I really hoped they'd grant parole. Now this."

"At least they can't send him to the mainland," Masako said. "At least U.S. law holds up that much. But there's still an ocean between us and Oahu. We can't drive over to have a picnic, and he'll be all alone in Honolulu, with no family to visit. And what will I do now? The one thing keeping me going is being able to see him."

She held her handkerchief to trembling lips, took a deep breath, and sat up straight.

"I need to do some laundry, so I can send him off with everything clean. You're not using the machine right now, are you?"

"No, go ahead," I said. The Tanakas' washer had broken down, and neither Sam nor our neighbor Frank had been able to fix it, so Masako had been using mine. "And if you want, hang them overnight on the porch, so they don't get rained on."

Masako nodded as she pushed herself up from her chair, sorrow on her face. "Yes, good idea. I don't want him to leave with a suitcase full of damp clothes." She dragged the laundry to my wringer washer in the tool room and began the last task she could do for her love before he departed for an even greater separation.

The next morning, Sam stayed home from his new construction job at the air base, and Henry from his job picking kiawe beans for the plantation dairy. Aiko went to work as usual but planned to tell her boss that she needed the afternoon off. After chores, Masako put Henry and Iris to work helping to make banana bread and rice balls. Sam slaughtered a chicken for katsu. By noon, Masako had ironed and packed Isao's clothes and filled the picnic basket with a farewell feast. We all piled into the Tanakas' truck, with Sam driving, and headed for the camp.

Aiko and Isao were already in the family's regular spot when we arrived. She rose from the grass and helped me spread the blankets and unload the basket while Isao greeted the rest of the family through the barbed wire stretched tight around the camp. Along the fence line, other families were gathered, sharing food and stories with their incarcerated loved ones. I wondered if any of them also were being sent away.

I stood back as Isao spoke with each child. Sam asked the question that had been plaguing us all.

"Pop, why are they doing this? Why can't they leave you here, where we can see you? Did you do something to make them mad?"

"No, son, I didn't do anything," Isao said with a weary smile. "No one knows why they do these things. I guess the Army has some big plan we don't know." He glanced around the green grassy camp behind him, where a couple of dejected-looking men sat under the shade of tents. "Maybe they want to close this place. Maybe they want to use the dorms for something else, for the Army." He shrugged. "Some guys already went to Honolulu, only a few left now."

"Daddy, when will we see you again?" Iris asked, her voice breaking.

"I don't know, honey. When the war is over."

"And that's why they should let me and all the other guys who want to join up," Sam said. He pounded the ground in frustration. "We gotta win this war!"

"Please, Hiroki, don't think about doing that right now. It's bad enough your father will be gone," Masako pleaded.

"I will write as many letters as they'll let me," Isao said, reaching through the wire to grasp Masako's hand. "We're going to be all right. We are a strong family. This war can't last forever. And maybe you'll be able to visit me sometime. You kids have never been to Honolulu, so that would be good fun, yeah?"

"I guess," Henry muttered, plucking at a clump of grass at the edge of the blanket.

"What if I moved over there?" Aiko said. "I could come and visit you, bring you things to eat, take your clothes home to wash. And it's not so dangerous, now that we won Midway."

"Oh, please, Aiko," Masako said, turning to give her a frown. "No start that again. We talked about this last time we came, and your father agrees with me. Stay here."

"I still think it's a good idea, Mom," Aiko said stubbornly. "And now it's an even better idea, since Dad will be over there by himself. I can be his connection to home, make plenty of money to send back to you, and use my typing skills instead of standing up in the cannery all day."

"Leona went already?" Isao asked.

"Yes, and she loves it," Aiko said. "I would share Leona's room and ride the bus to the office every day with her and Malia. They're doing defense work, and isn't that how to win the war and get Dad out of jail?"

Isao stroked his beard, looking thoughtful. "That kind of work pays pretty good, huh?"

"Yeah," Aiko said. "Even after she pays her share of rent and food, Leona can save some and send some home to her folks."

"Maybe we should consider this, Masako," Isao said. "You could use the money. Not have to work so hard."

"Taking care of three babies is not that hard," Masako insisted.

"Yeah, but already we took some out of savings before you started that job, yeah? So we gotta catch up. And we gotta save up for the kids to go to college. Who knows when I'm going to be able to earn money again?"

"And what about taking care of all the animals?" Masako said. "Who's going to help with the milking if Aiko goes away?" She turned to me. "Rose, we need Aiko's help, yeah?"

I hesitated. I'd been trying to keep out of this argument, and I could certainly see both sides of it. Before I could say anything, Iris piped up. "I can learn to milk," she said. "The goats at least. And even Henry can learn. I think we should let Aiko go to Honolulu so she can take care of Daddy."

"Hah! You just want to have your own room," Henry interjected. Iris stuck out her tongue at him.

"No fighting, you folks," Isao said, though he had a smile on his face. He sobered as he turned to Masako. "You know, it might be a good idea to let her go." Masako scoffed and rolled her eyes, while Aiko sat up straight, looking hopeful.

Isao turned to me, repeating Masako's question. "What you think, Rose? Can you get by without Aiko's help?"

I took a deep breath. "Well, it's up to you and Masako. I suppose we could manage. Masako, how many goat-milk customers do we have these days? Could we let one of the goats go dry?"

"Only a couple right now," Masako said reluctantly. "But you never know. Someone could have a baby with colic any time now, and they would need our goat milk."

Isao looked down as he twisted his hands in his lap. "Well, let's think about it," he said at last, turning his gaze to Masako. "No need rush." Masako's face relaxed. Aiko shot me an exasperated glance, but she said nothing more.

The guards were kind today. They let us stay, talking, for far longer than usual. At last, one approached.

"Okay, Tanaka, time to go."

Isao's face fell, and Masako looked alarmed. "Already? The boat doesn't leave for hours yet."

"Things to do first," the soldier said. As we stood up, a truck pulled in, the kind we saw everywhere these days, with an Army-green canvas cover over a bed lined with benches. "You folks wait. We'll bring him outside and you can say goodbye before the truck goes."

Sam passed the suitcase full of clean clothes over the fence, and Isao picked it up and followed the guard to the barracks. We watched as another guard opened it and pawed through all the clothes, then closed it again. A few minutes later, Isao came out with a second bag, and guards led him and two other men to the gate where the truck was parked. We walked over and waited. Isao stowed his bags in the truck and turned toward us, and the guards stood back as the family gathered around him.

At least they had allowed that, I thought, as Masako and Isao for once shared a public embrace. The children stood by, trying to look brave. Isao spoke to each child in turn.

"Keep studying hard, Iris. I'm proud of you for getting such good grades. And write me plenty letters, okay?" He hugged her and stepped back. Iris sniffled and chewed the end of her braid, a toddler habit that recently had reappeared.

"Henry, you too—keep up the grades. You are so smart." Henry nodded, eyes gleaming with tears behind his horn-rims, and Isao hugged him. "Education, that's one thing they cannot take away from you, so take advantage, study hard," Isao said, and paused, his face wistful. Then he turned to Sam.

"Hiroki, you're the man of the family now. I wish you were off to college, but do your best no matter what. You're doing a man's work now, and you'll have time for college later. Take care your mother and your brother and sisters for me, please." They shook hands, and Isao pulled his tight-lipped son close for a final hug.

"Aiko, you do what your mother wants, okay? I appreciate that you want to help me, but she needs you more." Isao gave her a hug and a kiss on the forehead. "You're a good girl. I'm proud of you." Aiko bowed her head, eyes streaming.

Isao faced Masako again and reached for both her hands. They stood gazing at each other for a moment, until the guard said, "Time for go now, Tanaka." Isao leaned to whisper in Masako's ear, then turned toward me.

I stepped forward and offered my hand. "We'll miss you, Isao."

"Thank you, Rose. Take care my family for me, please."

"Don't worry. They're safe and well-fed, and I couldn't manage without them. We just need you to come home," I replied, trying to keep my voice steady. Isao clasped Masako's hand once more before the soldiers led him away to the truck where the two other men waited, their families huddled near us beneath the hard gaze of armed guards. Inside the barbed wire fence, the few men left watched somberly, no doubt wondering if they would be next.

No one spoke on the way home. Sam kept his eyes on the road, and Masako sat staring at her lap. As Sam pulled up to their back door, she looked up and spoke at last.

"If it's all right with you, Rose, I've decided I will give Aiko permission to go to Honolulu. I can't bear the thought of Isao being over there with no family to visit him."

"It's all up to you, Masako," I said. "If you're willing to let her go, we will get by."

"As long as the Army won't let Japanese boys sign up, we still have Hiroki here, and we can rely on him to help us."

Sam looked at his mother for a moment, pulled the keys from the ignition, and got out of the truck without a word. He didn't quite slam the door, but he shut it hard enough to let us know he was not happy. Masako and I watched him stride off.

"You know he'd sign up in an instant if they'd let him, don't you?" I said.

Masako nodded, then bent her head, her lip quivering. "I know. And I know it would be important to the way people look at us if our boys joined the fight. But Rose, I couldn't let him go. I just couldn't."

Iris and Henry had already climbed down from their orange-crate seats in the truck bed and carried the picnic basket and blankets into the house. Aiko was the last out, and now she appeared at the truck window.

"What's going on? How come you folks didn't get out yet?" she asked.

"We're coming now," I said, and Aiko pulled the door open for us. I stepped out, and Masako scooted across the seat to the open door.

"Mom, are you okay?" Aiko said.

"I'll manage," Masako said. "And Aiko, you may go to Honolulu. But promise me you'll see your father every time you can."

Aiko's eyes widened. "Mom! Are you serious?"

Masako reached back for her purse and turned wearily toward her daughter. "Yes. You know I don't want you to go, but it will help your father, and I know you want to get out into the world. But you must be very careful over there. Even though we're probably past the threat of an invasion, there are all those military people on Oahu. Some of them are bad people. You stay close to Leona and Malia. And you visit your father every time you get a chance, understand?"

"Yes, Mom, of course. I'll be careful, and I'll go see Pop every weekend if they'll let me." She hugged her mother. "Thank you, Mommy, thank you so much! I have to go write to Leona and make sure she can get me a job." She turned and ran up the steps and into the house, looking back to flash us a brilliant smile.

Aiko's joy was infectious, and yet I wanted to weep. This girl I'd known all her life was going to step out into an adult world far different than the one where she had grown up.

Masako and I didn't speak for a moment. Then I said, "You are very brave," and squeezed her shoulder.

Masako smiled sadly and looked up at the sky. "It's getting late. I'm going to take a little rest before it's time for chores."

I watched her go, then turned to walk up the driveway to my own home.

• • • •

LEONA RESPONDED ENTHUSIASTICALLY to Aiko's letter. "Mr. Dawson says Malia is the best secretary he's ever had, and I am the best typist in the typing pool, so he is happy to hire another of Miss Cawdry's students. You should receive a letter from him in the next day or so," she wrote.

The Honolulu company's offer to hire Aiko was only the first step. Wartime labor regulations and paperwork delayed her departure for almost a month. She needed a release from her employer, allowing her to change jobs. And she had to get a travel permit from the military government. When at last the day came, I kissed Aiko goodbye and waved as Sam steered the truck up the driveway, Masako sitting stoically in the front seat, off to put her daughter on the boat to Honolulu.

• • • •

JULY 1942

Now, in place of her visits to Isao, Masako lived for his letters. Often, they were censored, words or lines cut out, dates and locations apparently forbidden information. The mailbox was Masako's first stop when she came home from work, and Iris told me that after everyone had read each letter, Masako placed it carefully in a polished wooden box Isao had made for her few bits of jewelry.

"She keeps it by her bed and reads them again before she goes to sleep every night," Iris told me one day when she brought one of her own letters to show me. It was Iris's description of her activities that week, the highlight of which had been a visit by a school chum. Iris had illustrated the letter with drawings of her favorite chicken (a Rhode Island Red, appropriately colored with an orange crayon) and of a sunflower she had planted, now in glorious bloom.

Dear Daddy,

> *We are all working hard to win the war. I help Mom with the garden and the babysitting, Henry still picks kiawe beans for the dairy, and Sam is using your tools to help build barracks at the Puunene airport. He says he promises not to lose them!*

> *My classmate Alice came over the other day and I showed her how to milk Lily. Alice never drank goat milk before, but she liked it. I showed her how to skim the cream from the cow's milk and make butter. Alice never made butter before*

either. I am used to it, so I could shake the jar much longer than Alice. Mom gave her some butter to take home, because Alice's mother can't find any in the store. I showed her how to feed the chickens, and we cut some pigeon peas to feed the goats. They have a garden at Alice's house, but they don't have any animals, and she really liked ours. Next week I will visit Alice and she will show me how to play the piano. When you come home, could we get a piano so I can take lessons? I promise I'll practice every day.

I smiled at the idea of a piano in the Tanakas' little front room. "You would have to practice a lot to play the piano," I told Iris. "Ukulele is easier. Maybe you can learn to play ukulele as well as your dad."

"I wish they'd let my daddy come home," she said. "When do you think they will, Auntie?"

"I don't know, sweetheart. We'll have to wait and see."

Masako sometimes showed me Isao's letters. He was allowed to write a one-page letter twice a week. His first letter from Honolulu, short but reassuring, described the barracks that had replaced tents originally set up on the coral shore of Sand Island. "The barracks are new, and so much nicer than the ones I was repairing in Haiku," he wrote. "Hot water in the showers and good food. I'm glad it is summer and dry, and we can be outside. I am working in the garden and the carpenter shop. I will send you *geta* soon." I smiled; Isao often made the traditional wooden slippers for his family and friends.

I folded the letter and handed it back to Masako. "It sounds okay," I said. "Much better than some of the stories we heard in the beginning—living in tents, soldiers making them stand out in the rain, punishing everyone if they thought someone broke a rule."

"I guess. Isao, you know how he is—always looking on the bright side, always *shikata ga nai*, cannot be helped, so get on with things. And maybe he's just trying to sound cheerful, so I won't worry. I wish I could go see him," she said. "Have you ever seen this Sand Island place where he is? I would like to be able to visualize it when I read his letters."

"No, I've never seen it. I think it's right there in the harbor area. But that's a great idea. Why don't you go? You could see where Aiko lives too."

"Oh, Rose, how would you cope without me? All those chores every morning and evening, and the boys gone so much. What about the kids? And what about my job?"

"We could figure it all out. If you went on a Friday night and came home Monday morning, it might work." I thought for a minute. "The kids can sleep at home, with Sam to watch over them, and come up to eat here, of course. Iris can spend Saturday with me while the boys are at work. We can handle the chores between us. Iris is getting pretty good at milking goats, and I can milk Lani."

"Well, it might work," Masako said, looking brighter than I'd seen her for weeks.

The next day, she caught the bus to Wailuku to fill out the paperwork required to go to Oahu. Late that afternoon, after I came home from my USO volunteer job at Maui High, Masako appeared at my back door. I had expected her to be smiling, but she looked sadder than ever.

"They won't let me go, Rose," she said, pulling out a chair.

"What? Who's 'they'? Why not?"

"The provost marshal. I told him I'm *nisei*, an American citizen, but he said because Isao is imprisoned, and I'm registered as a citizen of Japan, I'm in 'a suspect class.' That's how he put it: 'a suspect class.'"

I sank into the chair next to my friend, once again in need of more comfort than I could possibly provide.

Chapter Sixteen

I pitched the last shovelful of bagasse from the wheelbarrow into the chicken coop and stepped back into the shade of the shed, took off my hat to fan myself, and looked up at the sky. Almost noon. Time to stop this outdoor work as the day heated up. I scraped the chicken manure off the shovel, sat on a bucket, and pulled a file off the shelf to sharpen the shovel. As silver gleamed along the edge dulled by use, I considered the rest of my day. First a shower—I could smell my sweat even amid the barnyard smells around me. Then I'd have time to make a batch of cookies before I caught the bus to the USO for my afternoon shift.

I enjoyed those peaceful afternoons in the cool of the Maui High School library, where soldiers gathered to write letters, read, and get away from the mud and monotony of the little camps scattered around the area.

And the soldiers loved cookies. A couple of them looked up, curious, as I walked in and set my plate on the counter where another volunteer, Madge Henderson, sat knitting.

"Those look good. You boys are going to be happy about this," Madge said to the dozen or so men scattered at various tables. One table held a chessboard, and at another, four guys played bridge, while a couple of others read *The Maui News*. Heads lifted around the room, and young men rose to inspect the plate I was unwrapping.

"Thank you, ma'am," one said as he munched a cookie. "You make the best ginger cookies."

I smiled, offering the plate to another eager young man. "I bet you say that to all the girls," I said. That got a few laughs from the soldiers clustered around the desk. "Just be sure you clean your fingers before you touch any library books, or we'll be in big trouble."

"Yes, ma'am," the first fellow said, wiping his fingers on one of the makeshift napkins I'd cut from an old sheet. A scrawny fellow with big brown eyes and a prominent Adam's apple, he had what I guessed was a New York accent, something I'd heard only in movies. "How do you make them so good, with sugar rationing?"

"I use honey from my neighbor's hives and molasses from the plantation," I replied.

The soldier seemed inclined to conversation, leaning against the desk as the others helped themselves to cookies and went back to their books, games, and letters. "What's your name, Private?" I asked him. "And where are you from?"

"Jerry Giordano, ma'am," he replied. "I'm from Brooklyn."

"My, you're a long way from home. Do you have family to write to?"

"Oh, yes, ma'am," Jerry said, and he was off and running, telling me about his little brothers and sister, his father who worked so hard, his mother who was a great cook and who had made all the boys' shirts as they were growing up. He paused, looking forlorn. "I miss them all so much." He took a deep breath and continued. "Of course, we live in the city, so we don't have any neighbors with bees. Everything is so country around here, plantations and everything. Do you live on a plantation, like Mrs. Henderson?" Madge lived in Hamakuapoko, the plantation camp across the gulch from the school.

"No, I have a little farm up above Makawao."

Jerry's eyes widened. "A real farm? With cows and everything?"

I laughed. "I have one cow and some steers in the pasture, two goats, a couple of pigs, an old horse who mostly eats grass all day, and a bunch of chickens."

"I've never been on a farm," Jerry said.

"Well, maybe I should start giving farm tours," I said, and Jerry's eyes grew even wider. "That would be swell," he said. "I hope you invite me if you do."

. . . .

"WHAT DO YOU THINK ABOUT putting on a party here?" I said to Jack the next time I saw him. "Jeanette has done so many, and I've been helping, but I could be doing more for the troops. These poor kids are so bored."

"Who would you invite?"

"One of the soldiers the other day gave me an idea," I said. "His name is Jerry, and he's from Brooklyn. So many of these fellows are city boys, and they would love to see what a farm on Maui looks like. Even some of the farm kids would be interested, I bet, because it probably would be different from what they have at home. Jerry's a nice kid, so I'll ask him to bring a few friends. I'll invite some teachers from school; there are a few single girls who'll be glad to come. And of course, the hospital folks who go to Jeanette's parties, if she's ready for a break."

"Sounds like a good idea," Jack said, reaching to give me a hug. "A lot of work, though, so let me know how I can help. How about if I ask a couple of the nurses to pitch in too? I know Connie and Joanie would love to help."

Jeanette was enthusiastic about my idea. "Oh, that would be swell," she said. "I might not even come! I'd love a weekend with no social obligations, lazing around with Jim and the kids."

So I began to host parties, with me doing most of the preparation, though Masako offered to make flower arrangements and banana bread. "I don't want to come, Rose," she said. "I'm not ready to socialize with a bunch of mainland-*haole* soldiers, considering that they're the ones who keep Isao locked up. But I do appreciate that they're protecting us, so I'll stay in the background and help you give them a good party."

I spent a few days cleaning house and preparing food. We always had eggs to devil, and our peanut crop had come in, so I made salty boiled peanuts, great with cold drinks. I minced cloves of Masako's homegrown garlic and mixed it with butter to put on thin-cut bread, toasted in the oven just before guests arrived. With plates of sliced fruit and avocados, and whatever potluck odds and ends people brought, we had an acceptable *pupu* table. I made and stored ice cubes for days ahead, people brought bottles, and the harvest from my prolific lemon tree made lemonade for the few teetotalers.

"This is great, honey," Jack said as he surveyed the crowd in the living room at the first party. There were people everywhere, wandering in and out the door to the front porch.

I was sitting, watching the party go on. My feet hurt from all the cleaning and cooking over the past couple of days. But I was content. People were laughing and chatting, admiring the flowerbeds, having a good time.

"Not bad for a gal who hasn't put on a party in an untold number of years, huh?"

He leaned down to give me a quick kiss. "I knew you could do it. And you just enjoy yourself, let me and the nurses do the running around and cleaning up, okay?"

I stood up when I heard Jerry's Brooklyn accent and went to greet him and his friends, then settled back onto the couch, sipped my drink, and watched the party. The Tanaka kids were all here, enthusiastically hospitable. Sam was bartender, having been coached by Jack in drink making. Iris circulated with a plate laden with garlic toast, and I watched as a nurse in conversation with a sergeant smiled and stroked Iris's head before taking a piece. The smile stayed on her face and her eyes followed Iris for a moment before the conversation resumed. Another one missing a baby sister? Henry was giving tours of the farm, and now he returned with a little group, the women with fresh plumerias tucked behind their ears.

"Hello there!" It was Jeanette, covered plate in hand, and Jim right behind her. "I know I said I'd stay home and be lazy, but I couldn't help myself—had to come to your party." She turned to Jim. "Honey, will you get me a drink, please? And set this stuffed celery on the *pupu* table?" She sat next to me, looking around the room full of military people in conversation with locals.

"I see the gang's all here. They might decide they like your place better than mine."

"Oh, I doubt that. And I have no plans to usurp your place as queen of Makawao parties. Too damn much work! But I'm willing to do one a month, if you're ready for a change."

Jim returned with Jeanette's gin and tonic, and she took a sip. "Ahh, that's good. I see you've put the kids to work."

"They volunteered. Too exciting to be left out of the first social event in years. Plus, Sam is dying to sign up and loves to be around military men, and Henry wants to be a doctor and loves to be around doctors, so they're in heaven."

"I don't see Masako."

"No. I gave her the latest Agatha Christie novel, and Iris took her a plate of *pupus*, and I'm sure she's happy to be reading with her feet up and no kids around."

"She's a hard worker, that girl. Good for her to have an afternoon to herself."

I stood up to greet another group of guests, led them to the dining room to get drinks and food, and had just rejoined Jeanette when one of those odd moments occurred when everyone in a crowd seems to stop talking at once. In the sudden silence, I heard clearly a man's voice.

"How do we know that little Jap bartender isn't dropping something nasty into the drinks?"

Eyes around the room turned to the open front door, where a newly arrived corporal stood, flinching as he realized everyone there had heard him. A surge of anger had me on my feet, but Jack strode past, touching my arm briefly and shaking his head, a frown on his face, heading straight for the offending corporal. Conversation resumed and people averted their eyes as he grasped the man's elbow and, without pausing, ushered him out and down the porch steps.

I sat, heart still pounding, and Jeanette patted my hand. "Thank goodness for Jack," she said. "That's the last we'll see of that fellow. How rude! He won't dare show up here again."

Jack returned, his face carefully neutral, and sat next to me.

"Did Sam hear that?" I asked in a low voice.

"I heard it from the doorway to the dining room, but I think he was busy taking an order. I certainly hope he didn't."

"I need to find out," I said, and stood up to look through the door into the dining room.

Sam's face was flushed, his jaw was clenched, and his hands seemed to shake a bit as he poured a drink. But half a dozen people were clustered around, and I heard one of the teachers say, "My goodness, Sam, your drinks are as good as your math grades."

Several people in the cluster laughed, and one of the soldiers clapped Sam on the back, and said, "So if you decide not to be a math professor, you can always fall back on bartending." More laughter, and I saw Sam's face relax into a little smile. Relieved and grateful for supportive friends, I looked around for Iris. She was standing in the doorway to the kitchen with her plate of garlic toast, her face stricken. As I watched, one of the nurses distracted her with a comment I couldn't hear, and in a moment they were both laughing.

I went back to sit between Jeanette and Jack and held his hand for a moment. "Thank you for chasing that fellow away, Jack. Sam and Iris seem to be okay. And Henry is busy with another farm tour, so he wouldn't have heard it." I tried to keep my voice low, not wanting to spoil my party further. "I'm so tired of all these rumors of sabotage. You know, there have been official reports saying there has been no sabotage, damn it. When are people going to quit this nonsense?"

"Honey, you have to accept that it's going to be that way in wartime," Jack said, shaking his head. "But that doesn't excuse that guy's rudeness. If you don't like what you find at a party, leave quietly. That guy's kind of a jerk anyway, and he just got here from the mainland. Better he's gone, probably get tight and start making passes at the nurses."

"I thought that was against the rules," Jeanette said, looking puzzled. "Isn't that why they make them lieutenants, so the enlisted men don't harass them?"

"Yeah, and it works most of the time, but you know how drunks are."

"Maybe it's a good thing liquor is so scarce," I said, lifting an eyebrow.

"Unless you want to drink that awful Five Ulcers stuff," Jeanette said, and we all chuckled at the nickname given to the locally made rotgut, "Five Island."

Iris appeared, holding an empty plate. "Auntie, we're out of garlic toast."

I pushed myself up from the couch. "Come on, let's toast a new batch," I said, heading for the kitchen. As usual, it was a gathering place, and I had to shoo a few people out of the way to get to the refrigerator and stove.

Madge Henderson stood to one side, drink in hand, watching Iris and me lay the buttered slices out onto baking trays. "So this is the kitchen that produces those famous ginger-honey cookies," she said.

"This is the place. Those boys love their cookies."

"They do," Madge agreed. "But I wish we could offer them more activity. There's only so much you can do in a library. Plus, we're out of the way for a lot of the troops."

I set the baking trays in the oven and leaned against the counter to wait while the toast browned.

"It would be great if we could set up something in Makawao town," I said, "but the hospital created a domino situation. They took over the school, and the school took over every available space in town, so where would we put a USO?"

Iris, standing by with her empty plate, piped up. "How about Tam Chow Store, where we have our classes?" she said.

"Where would you folks go? Madge asked.

"The Army might build us a new school," Iris replied.

"Really? Why do you say that?" I asked, opening the oven door to peek in and check the toast.

Iris shrugged. "I heard some teachers talk about it," she said. "Is the toast ready yet, Auntie? I think the people are getting hungry."

Chapter Seventeen

August 1942

At Jeanette's regular shindig the following week, Madge joined me as I sat on the couch listening to a group sing-along. Her husband, a plantation executive who worked with Jim, was playing the piano while a group gathered around him to sing lustily to old favorites. I smiled, watching Jack, an enthusiastic member of the impromptu chorus.

"I had no idea Jack had such a great voice," I commented. "And Howard is doing a swell job on the piano."

"Yes, Howard's quite musical," Madge agreed. "The product of many years of piano lessons. He tells me he'd rather have been out on the softball field, but now he's grateful to be able to play." She sipped her drink and turned to me with a sly smile. "So, Miss McKenzie, what's going on with you and the handsome tenor? Any wedding bells in the future?"

I laughed. "Who knows? There's a war on; I'm sure you've heard. It's a bit difficult to make plans for the future."

The song ended, and Jack shot me a glance, a big grin on his face, then turned back as Howard began to play "I'm Looking Over a Four Leaf Clover."

"You two do seem well suited, though," Madge continued. "And he certainly seems to like you."

"Yes, he's a dear," I replied, but I had enough questions of my own about the future of this relationship; I didn't want to try to answer Madge's. I changed the subject "And I hear your girl is getting married soon. She's so bright. I enjoyed having her in my classes."

My tactic worked. Madge was off on elaborate descriptions of the wedding plans for young Loretta and her beau. I let her talk while I sipped my drink and watched the singers enjoy themselves. Better to live for today and let tomorrow take care of itself.

. . . .

IT WAS EASY ENOUGH to see how Jack could fit in around my place, if only he didn't have a life and a family back in Oregon. He and Masako were on a first-name basis now. Iris liked his silly jokes. Henry wanted to hear stories of dramatic medical situations, and Sam quizzed him about military life. It became a bit of a ritual, when Jack was over on a Saturday afternoon, to sit on my porch after chores and talk story with Captain Jack.

"I don't understand why they won't let us sign up," Sam complained one evening as Jack and I sat with Iris on the porch swing, and Sam and Henry perched on the porch steps. "How are we gonna prove we're real Americans if they won't let us join?"

"You can help on the home front too," Jack said. "And you already are, doing carpentry work at the air base and helping with farm work here. We need food to win the war, you know."

Sam was not convinced. "Yeah, but I'd be doing that anyway. And I gotta do something extra to prove this family is loyal, and maybe they'll let my dad out."

"The best thing you can do now is help your mom and take care of Henry and Iris," I said.

"He doesn't need to take care of me!" Henry said, indignant.

"We all have to take care of each other," I said, as Sam rolled his eyes. "And anyway, Sam, whatever happened to the idea of you going to college? They're still having classes over in Honolulu, you know. Have you looked into that?"

Sam shrugged, frowning as he scratched dirt off the porch step with a twig. "I don't know. Gotta think about the war now. Maybe after we win. Plus, no more 'nuff money. Gotta stay home, work to help Mom."

"I'd like to see you all go to college," I said, "and I know your parents would too."

"I could be a doctor, couldn't I, Captain Jack?" Henry piped up.

"Sure thing, kid," Jack replied. "How about you, Iris?" He smiled at her fondly. "Want to be a nurse like Connie and Joanie?"

"I want to be a lawyer," Iris said. We all looked at her, surprised. That wasn't a profession most girls would even consider.

"Why do you want to do that?" I asked.

"Because lawyers help people get out of jail when they're innocent and they didn't do anything wrong," she replied.

Jack and I glanced at each other. I cleared my throat.

"Well, both of you are very ambitious, and I'm proud of you," I said. "Just make sure you study hard and make good grades, the way Sam did, and you'll be ready to do whatever you want," though I had to admit to myself that I wasn't so sure about Iris being a lawyer. Lady lawyers were few and far between. But the war was changing things. Women were working at all kinds of jobs they'd never have done before the war.

"Kids, time for dinner. Come home now, please." Masako appeared in the twilight glow. "Hello, Jack, how are you?"

"Fine, thank you, Masako. You have some great kids here."

She laughed. "Most of the time, yeah, kids?"

"Mom! We're great all the time," Iris said, bouncing off the porch swing and down the steps to stand by her mother.

"Ha! Maybe me, but not you!" Henry said, and as he pulled himself up from the steps, the wooden banister made a cracking sound.

"What was that?" Iris said. "See, you're not so perfect, Henry Tanaka. You wen' break Auntie's stairs."

Sam reached over and gave the banister a nudge, and sure enough, it moved when he pushed it. Jack stood up and went to look, giving the banister another push and bending to check its connection with the steps

"Hard to see what's going on when it's so dark, but I'll look at it tomorrow morning," he said.

"You're going to be here tomorrow morning?" Iris asked, and we grown-ups exchanged looks.

"Captain Jack will come back when it's light enough," Masako said. "Now, come on, you folks, let's go eat before it gets cold."

We were careful, the next morning, as always, to be discreet about Jack's presence. I even shut my back door on those days, rather than have only the screen door between the kids' eyes and Jack at breakfast.

When we did go out to the porch with my toolbox, it took him only half an hour to fix the loose banister.

"Anything else need fixing?" he asked as he set the hammer into the toolbox.

"Could you look at the hinge on the stable gate? It's loose, and the gate is sagging and dragging in the dirt. I tried to fix it, but it came loose again."

We walked to the stable, and I sharpened a couple of tools while he removed the hinge and placed it where the wood was still solid. "We might want to replace that whole post," he said, standing back to survey the gate and the fence to which it was attached. He walked along the fence, pushing each post to test its strength. "Yep, it wouldn't hurt to replace all these posts. I think they're beginning to rot."

"Jack, I don't want to ask you to do all that work on your days off," I protested.

He smiled. "Well, you didn't ask. I offered. I want my sweetheart to be happy, and I know this farm makes you happy."

I looked around quickly—no kids in sight—pulled him into the shelter of the alcove where we kept feed and tools and gave him a kiss. "You make me happy," I said. "Let's go back to bed."

"Now, that you can ask me any time," he said, gathering the tools, and I led the way back up to the house.

Chapter Eighteen

F *all 1942*
The first summer of the war had passed in a constant round of activity—farm work, USO work, bandage making with the Red Cross, entertaining. I had fallen into a regular rhythm of a party each month, plus having a few hospital folks for lunch every week or so. In between were Jeanette's parties and an occasional invitation to someone else's do, all planned to keep our military guests in good spirits. I, of course, did my bit, keeping both Jack and myself happy through trying times. Jeanette gave me a big smile when I asked her to get more "hygiene" jelly.

When school began, we were busier than ever. The various service groups sold war bonds and stamps, baked cookies for soldiers, and collected salvage materials. The shop classes made model airplanes, using plans supplied by the naval air base, for use in training spotters to identify real planes aloft. Homemaking classes sewed gowns for patients at the Makawao hospital.

One Friday afternoon I set out after school to deliver a batch of slippers the Junior Red Cross had made. With limited resources, the kids had figured out how to put together a cardboard sole with straps made of folded newspaper, all covered in bright fabric, and the patients could use as many as the kids could make. I loaded the boxes of slippers into my truck, next to the burlap bags full of half-ripe papayas and bananas I'd packed up that morning, and I headed to the hospital.

A clerk greeted me at the front desk, set the box of slippers on his desk, and went to pull the heavy bags of fruit from my front seat. He returned and began to fill out paperwork accepting the donations, and I peered over his shoulder, hoping, as always, to catch a glimpse of Jack. A dozen or so young men in maroon bathrobes sunned themselves in the open courtyard where schoolchildren used to play.

171

Some sat on benches, some in wheelchairs. I smiled when I saw Jack, striding along the covered walkway across the courtyard. But his face was grim. He must be having a tough day.

Just then, I heard a heavy truck barreling around the corner behind me. I looked over my shoulder to see an ambulance with mud splattered over its army-green body and the red cross on its side. It turned into the driveway behind the hospital, brakes screeching. A voice barked something unintelligible over the PA system. Hospital staff poured out of various doors and raced to the back of the building. Jack was the first one there, and he shouted instructions as others arrived.

Another vehicle roared around the corner, a jeep crowded with men, all covered in mud and blood. One's arm was in a sling, another had a bloody bandage around his forehead, another slumped with his head resting on his forearms.

The front desk clerk had jumped up to join the crowd rushing to the ambulance. My heart was pounding, and I clasped my hands, fighting the urge to run and try to help. But civilians were not allowed in the hospital, and I knew the professionals there didn't need me. I moved nearer to the entrance, where I could see the open back of the U-shaped building that made up the hospital. In the courtyard between the wings, the recovering patients sat up as best they could, eyes riveted on the drama across the way.

One by one, workers carried four stretchers from the ambulance, each holding a bleeding, mud-covered man with what looked like serious injuries. Jack stood just inside the courtyard, briefly examining each man before the litter bearers carried the patient into the building. Other medical workers were helping soldiers from the jeep. The soldiers moaned and cried out as they climbed from their seats.

As the last of the men limped or were carried into the shade of the walkway, I saw Jack, walking fast as he stripped off his now-bloodstained white coat, following the litters that carried the worst of the injured into what must be the operating room.

I stepped back, shaken by the scene, by the sight of all that suffering. I couldn't imagine the work that lay ahead of Jack and the others as they stanched bleeding, cleaned mud from horrific wounds, and tried to put these soldiers back together. It would be a long evening for them.

I had trouble sleeping that night, remembering what I'd witnessed, wondering how those poor men were doing.

Jack called the next morning and said he would be coming over, but late. When he arrived at sunset, he looked exhausted, with dark shadows under his eyes.

"A jeep loaded with soldiers went over the edge into a gulch," he told me. "The gulch was so deep that medics had to rappel down to get them, patch them up as best they could, and haul them back up by tying ropes to the stretchers. A lot of jungle in the way, trees and bushes, uneven ground, so it was a pretty rough ride back up. Then one of the medics slipped in the mud and broke an arm, and another one got hit by a falling rock."

"I hope they all survived," I said.

He shook his head. "No, we lost one on the operating table. And it took a hell of an effort to save a couple of the others. Good thing the local docs collected the blood types of everybody on the island when the war first started. We had to call in a lot of blood donors. You know, I've seen plenty of farm accidents, mill accidents, even a tree falling on a logger once or twice. But nothing like this." He closed his eyes briefly. "I'm not going to be much good to you tonight, honey. I need sleep."

"And a hot bath?"

"That would be wonderful," he said and leaned over to give me a quick kiss. "And I have to leave early tomorrow. I probably should have gone back to quarters for the night, but I needed this dose of normality with you." He smiled briefly. "Can you wake me up after chores tomorrow? I have to get back to the hospital and relieve Fred."

Jack went straight from the bath to bed and slept deeply until sometime in the early hours, when he woke me by tossing and turning, moaning and mumbling. I hugged him and spoke gently until he woke up, his eyes dazed and darting. At last, he settled, turned to embrace me, and we slept. In the morning, I cooked him breakfast, and he set off wearily to work.

The next day, the teachers' lounge was humming with rumors about the big accident out past Haiku, but I kept my mouth shut. As a doctor, and because we were all aware of the "loose lips" warning, Jack rarely spoke of his work. When he did, it was because he needed to talk, and anything he said was for my ears only.

· · · ·

IN NOVEMBER, THE TERRITORIAL Department of Public Instruction decreed that our school week would be cut by one day. On Fridays, our students would work—in the fields, preferably, or if not, in some other job that needed filling, in a restaurant, an office, or wherever war work had left vacancies. To make up for the lost day, school hours were lengthened for the rest of the week.

On Monday mornings, I gave Henry a ride to school to save him the walk to Makawao and the bus ride with many stops.

"Good morning, Auntie," he said blinking sleepily as he climbed into the truck.

"Good morning. Were you able to finish all your homework yesterday?"

"Uh-uh. I still have a little bit of math to do."

"Okay," I said, pulling out onto the road. "You'll still have about half an hour when we get to school. How many bags of kiawe beans did you pick this week?"

"Three on Friday, but only a little over two on Saturday. I brought some home for the goats."

I smiled. "Goat candy. I'm sure they were happy to see you."

At school, Henry settled into one of the desks in my classroom and opened his math book while I organized myself for the week. When it was time for flag raising, he gathered his papers and books, and we both went outside for the daily ceremony.

Back in homeroom class, the students looked as tired as Henry did. They listened, with drooping eyelids and shoulders slumping, as each described their weekend jobs.

"I harvested potatoes for the plantation," one boy said. Like the others who were doing fieldwork, he was brown and lean.

"I waited on tables in my auntie's restaurant in Paia," a girl said.

"And I wen' wash all the dishes," said her cousin, seated across the room. "I rather wait on tables and get tips, but my mom says the soldiers like girls better for waiting on tables." That got a few laughs.

"I worked in the cannery," another girl said. "I'm never drinking pineapple juice again." More laughs.

"Better than hoeing weeds in the cane fields," a third girl insisted. She raised her arm and flexed her biceps. "But at least I'm getting muscles."

"Miss McKenzie, what do teachers do for workdays?" one boy asked. "You folks gotta get extra job too?"

"We're getting a bit careless with our good English," I said. "I know everyone is tired, but let's keep up our standards, please.

"As for workdays, I don't know about all the other teachers," I continued. "I work on my farm. Friday, I weeded and pulled up dead plants and harvested vegetables. Saturday, I canned tomatoes and made pineapple-papaya jam. Sunday afternoon I came to school and volunteered at the USO." It had been, as usual, an exhausting weekend of work. I looked around the room at the students' weary faces. Poor kids. What a way to spend the last years of childhood. "Now, we have ten minutes before the end of homeroom. You can use this time to finish up any homework you couldn't get done yesterday or just sit quietly. If you fall asleep though, I'll have to wake you up, so try to keep your eyes open." I smiled, and most of them returned the smile.

• • • •

WE WORKED HARD, AND we grabbed whatever pleasure we could find. Jack was my pleasure, and I knew I was his. We had so little time together that we cherished every moment. But we couldn't spend all our time in bed, and Jack often helped me with my farm work.

"Where do you want these? They must weigh close to a hundred pounds," Jack asked me one afternoon. He groaned as he shouldered a four-foot-long stalk of bananas he'd cut from the tree. "This way," I said, leading him to the hook in the front-porch ceiling where a thick rope dangled. He held the stalk in place while I pulled the loop of rope tight. "Before you head home, let's cut off a few hands for you to take," I said.

Jack rubbed his shoulder, surveying the stalk of plump green bananas. "That's a lot of fruit."

"Yes, and they will all ripen in quick order, so one stalk gets spread around the neighborhood, and Masako will bake lots of banana bread."

"Now what, boss?"

"How about we go walk the fences? Poor Sam is home so late, and so exhausted, I don't think he's done that for a while."

We gathered a few tools and set off to inspect posts, hammer in loose connections, and tighten slack wires. By the time we circled the big pasture where the steers grazed, we were both ready to call it a day. We stopped to look over the green acres, and I broke off a few pigeon-pea branches from the row just out of reach of the fence. I offered them to the steers, who had been observing us calmly as we made our way around the fence line.

"This is quite a setup you have here," Jack said. "Took you years to put this together, huh?"

"Yes, it's been a lot of work. I'm glad to have it all now, with the war."

He was staring at the cattle as they munched on the pigeon-pea leaves. "Yes, quite an investment of your time and money and labor. I guess you'd never consider selling up and moving somewhere else." He looked at me with a question in his eyes. I cleared my throat, not wanting to face up to that unspoken question. I put my arm through Jack's. "Come on, cowboy, let's go rustle up some grub. We should get an early night. My neighbor Frank is coming tomorrow morning to pick up a steer."

It was to be our second steer sent to slaughter this year. Normally, we'd slaughter one a year to provide for me and the Tanakas, plus some to sell or share with friends and neighbors. This year, we had started early, sending one of our five steers to slaughter because of the feed rationing and drought. Now we were sending another, in time for the holidays.

I knew my fridge would fill, and then be emptied over the next week or so as I shared the bounty of beef with friends. I'd bought a big new refrigerator a year ago, one with plenty of space for bottles of milk and garden surplus and a freezer much larger than the tiny one in my old fridge that held only a couple of ice trays. I was glad I'd bought it when I did. Refrigerators were one of many items impossible to find these days, and no telling when they might be available to buy again.

Early the next morning, I heard the rumble of Frank's big truck. I left Jack in the kitchen, sipping a second cup of coffee, and went out to greet him.

"Eh, howzit, Rose," Frank said, sticking his head out the window of his truck. "You want to ride or walk over?"

"I'll walk, Frank. Meet you there."

Frank backed up and set off toward the gravel-covered road past the Tanakas' back door and to the fence that edged the big pasture. I grabbed a bucket I had filled with kiawe beans and followed on foot. Henry and Iris peered out the back door as I passed and ran to join us. I was glad we'd decided Jack should stay in the kitchen. Of course the kids knew by now that we were a couple, but we still maintained some discretion. I couldn't afford to have my schoolteacher reputation ruined by an innocent comment from one of the kids, and there was no way to explain why Captain Jack might be spending nights at my house, so he kept his head down until a decent hour.

"Can I hold the can, Auntie?" Iris asked.

"And I can help herd, right?" Henry said.

"Sure, but you folks be careful. You don't want to get trampled."

Frank turned his truck and backed up to the fence, opened the doors of the wooden stock rack, and lowered a ramp next to the pasture gate. Iris climbed up the side of the truck close to the cab so she could lure the steer in with *kiawe* beans. Frank took a handful to draw the steer we had chosen toward the truck, while Henry and I distracted the others with pigeon-pea branches. It took a little maneuvering, but soon the steer was following Frank up the ramp. Iris rattled the bucket of beans, the steer went to the front, and Frank jumped out and slammed shut the doors of the stock rack.

"Good job, you folks," I said as we all gathered at the back of the truck.

"My mom has something for you, Uncle Frank," Henry said, and the two kids took off running to get the box of treats Masako and I had assembled for Frank. He didn't need a share of the beef—he had plenty of his own—but I insisted on donating a gallon of gas siphoned from my truck (though I wasn't sure that would pass muster under the rationing rules). Frank had been true to his word, always willing to help us cope in the absence of Isao.

Jack was waiting at the kitchen table when I came back, staring at his empty coffee cup. He looked up with a little smile that quickly faded.

"Why so gloomy?" I asked, settling into my chair.

He sat looking at me for a moment. "You have quite a life here, don't you, Rose?"

I blinked. Of course I did.

"Well, yes. After all, I've been here since I was a kid."

Jack fiddled with the handle of his coffee cup, then met my eyes.

"It's just ... well, I guess it would be really hard for you to uproot yourself from this place."

Neither of us said anything for a moment. I looked away, picked up the teapot, filled my cup. Jack was coming close to speaking aloud what I, for one, had been thinking for months. It was hard to imagine how this relationship, so wonderful, so rich, could endure past the end of the war. I'd realized, from the beginning, that we'd face a choice at some point, assuming Jack wasn't transferred off to some dangerous and maybe deadly battlefield.

Would I be willing to move, giving up everything I'd worked to build in a place I loved, perhaps never to return? Would he? Or was this a wartime romance, destined to end when this dreadful war concluded?

We let the conversation drop, but I couldn't get it out of my mind, and I knew, from Jack's distracted silence, that it was on his mind too as we walked downhill to the Saturday matinee.

Jack headed back to quarters after the movie, and I walked home alone, still thinking of this choice we might face. When I got home, I wandered around, looking at my house and trying to imagine what it would be like to leave it and all its memories. I had transformed the old house Vaughn gave me into a restful, peaceful home. I took delight in the rose-patterned wallpaper in my bedroom, the window seat where I sometimes piled pillows for a reading nook, and the stone fireplace, where the crackle and flames of a wood fire warmed rainy Makawao days.

On the wide front porch, I stopped to enjoy the scent of the *lauae* fern growing next to the steps, then turned to look out toward my pastures. The cow grazed peacefully. My old horse Penny saw me and neighed as if to say hello. A goat bleated. Birds chirped. A black mynah bird strutted on yellow legs, bending to snatch a bug from thick grass. I walked barefoot onto that soft lawn, taking it all in, the wide blue skies over green slopes, the brisk scent of eucalyptus. Branches danced in the soft trade winds as if to some unheard melody, and a rainbow shone against a distant gray cloud.

I had been born in California, but in my heart, I was a child of the land, a *kamaaina*. I felt this island in my bones. The *aina* had fed me from childhood, and I had dedicated so much of my life to nurturing it in return. I was rooted here. How could I ever pull those roots loose?

Did Jack feel the same way about his land? I wasn't sure if mainland people had this attachment to the earth at their feet that people of the Islands did. But I knew he had an unshakeable love for the little boys who waited for him, the sister who so faithfully took responsibility for their care, the aging parents who someday would need his help.

It was a conundrum, a problem that ran in circles. I could see no way out but to go forward and hope a solution would appear. I took a deep breath of crisp Upcountry air and climbed back up the stairs to home.

Chapter Nineteen

Winter 1943

As 1943 began, Makawao was abuzz with the local society ladies' new project—a USO in the Tam Chow Store. Iris had been right. She and her classmates had moved to a temporary building across from the Catholic church, on the edge of town, and the old store was being transformed.

Tam Chow Store was perfect for this purpose—a large one-story building with a long porch where soldiers could congregate out of the Makawao rain to smoke and watch town life without clogging up the sidewalks. It was right at the crossroads of Makawao—hence its name, the Crossroads USO. No longer would young men in uniform perch on the town's curbs, whiling away off-duty time. I bid goodbye to the soldiers and volunteers at the Hamakuapoko USO and switched my volunteer time to this new USO, closer to home than the school library. Now I walked with Jack every Sunday after lunch to spend my afternoons in the lovely ranch-themed recreation center the community had created for the soldiers who'd made us all so much more secure.

• • • •

ONE DAY IN FEBRUARY, Sam came home early. Masako and I were in the garden, and we stopped our hoeing and raking when he appeared.

"Son, why are you home? Is something wrong? You sick?" Masako asked.

Sam stood at the edge of the garden and looked down at the gas-mask bag he was tossing from one hand to the other. After a moment, he looked up, with that familiar stubborn expression on his face. "Mom, I enlisted," he said. Masako dropped her hoe.

182

"Oh, Hiroki," she said, her face anguished.

I stood silent, tense, not sure how to react to this news. The president had just approved the enlistment of Japanese American volunteers, and young men had flooded enlistment offices in Hawaii. Though the volunteers far exceeded the available slots, the army had accepted additional men. Now we knew that Sam was among them.

Masako seemed to be struggling with her own reaction, wringing her hands and biting her lips as if to stop their trembling. First her husband, then her daughter, and now her son caught up in this all-encompassing war.

"Can you get out of it? Can you change your mind? Tell them your father is gone and your mother—and your auntie—need you on the farm."

Sam shook his head. "No, Mom, it's done. Cannot change now."

"Why didn't you ask me? We could have written to your father to see what he would say."

"Mom, I'm eighteen. I need to do this. Pop will understand."

The sorrow that shadowed Masako's face all the time lately grew deeper. She shook her head and dropped her gaze to the ground.

Sam's eyes filled with tears, and he crossed the garden to his mother and put his arm around her shoulders, his head bent toward hers. Masako's shoulders shook. Sam shot me a pained glance and turned back to his mother.

"Mom, I'm sorry. It's something I have to do. We gotta win the war. We gotta get Pop out."

"Why does it have to be you?" she replied, her voice raw. "Plenty of other boys volunteered whose fathers are home. I can't lose you, Hiroki."

"Please, Mom. I need to do this. And I cannot back out now. I already signed up. Too late."

Finally, Masako lifted her head and looked up into her son's face. "All right," she said. "I guess you have to go. I know you want to. Maybe it will do some good, make people think better of us. But you must do your best, Hiroki. Don't shame your country, and don't shame your family."

Eyes fixed on his mother, Sam nodded. "I won't, Mom. I promise."

"Let's go write to your father. It's early. We can get it in the mail today." Sam nodded again. "Yes, Mom." Masako gave me a pained smile, and they turned toward home. I watched them go. At last, I picked up Masako's hoe and set it to one side, wiped away my tears, and went back to raking rocks from the garden soil.

This damn war. It was so hard.

· · · ·

"OKAY, AUNTIE, YOUR oil should be good for a few months," Sam said, pulling himself out from under my truck on the wheeled platform Isao had made for such chores. "It's up to Henry next time. He did most of the work on this one."

Henry scooted out from under my truck. "And next time I can use the trolley, and not some junk piece of cardboard," he said as he stood.

"Thank you, gentlemen," I said. "What are you up to next, Sam?"

Sam wiped his hands with a rag and dropped it into the box of tools he and Henry had used to change the oil in his mother's truck and then mine. "Going to a goodbye party. A bunch of classmates are getting together in Kihei, build a fire, cook some hotdogs, have a few laughs."

"Well, don't stay out so late that you can't get up in time for your swearing-in tomorrow morning."

He flashed me a brilliant smile. He seemed a lot happier since he had enlisted. "No worry, Auntie," he said. "I wouldn't do that. I'm ready to go."

Sam might've been ready, but his mother wasn't. This morning we had worked in the garden, Sam doing heavy jobs like digging in compost and harvesting bananas. Masako followed him around, mournful eyes rarely leaving her son, getting her fill of him while she still could.

The next day we all went down to Wailuku. Young men, their faces bright with excitement, lined up on the steps of the courthouse to raise their hands and swear to defend their country. Families watched with a combination of pride and trepidation. More than one mother dabbed tears from her cheeks, fathers stood rigid, and one enlistee's girlfriend sobbed on a friend's shoulder.

Once the swearing-in was done, we all stepped forward to drape flower lei around the new soldiers' necks. I added a fat red carnation lei to the pile on Sam's shoulders and gave him a quick peck on the cheek. "You be careful, Sam. Come home to us in one piece," I said.

He gave me a little hug, and said, "Of course, Auntie. I'll see you soon." But I could see the youthful certainty in his eyes that he was bulletproof and would live forever.

The next day, I drove the family to the dock. The boys who'd been sworn in yesterday joined another group, from Lahaina, to board *Waialeale*, the steamer that would take them to Oahu.

I stood behind Masako, my hand on her shoulder, while Iris clung to her side. Henry stood apart, erect, now the man of the family, and while we all waved, Henry saluted. We watched the ship pull out, young men hanging over its sides, laughing, waving until we could no longer distinguish Sam's face. We turned and plodded to the truck, to begin the latest chapter in this tragedy we hoped would somehow, someday, have a happy ending.

The day after Sam left, I was at Masako's house when Aiko called. Masako listened intently. "Let me call you back," she said, and hung up. She turned to me, downcast.

"Aiko says they're having a big farewell rally at Iolani Palace Sunday, and she wants me and the kids to come over. She says we could stay with her at Leona's house and go see Isao. I didn't have the heart to tell her the authorities wouldn't let me go. I guess I'll have to call her back and explain. Poor Hiroki, no mother or father to see him honored before he leaves. At least Aiko will be there." She looked up. "And I could have seen Isao too, in his new camp, and taken him some treats, banana bread and musubi. And butter for Aiko folks. She says they hardly ever get any."

Somehow Masako's list of simple gifts drove home the injustice of the authorities' cavalier decision. "Hell's bells, what is wrong with these people? To deprive you of the chance to see your family—how dare they! Oh, no, we're not letting them get away with that," I said. "You need to be at that rally. Come on—let's go to Wailuku right now."

"Rose, they won't listen."

"Masako, you can just stand there quietly and let me talk. I'll make them do it."

"Well, they might listen to you, I guess. More than they listen to me." She sat chewing her lip for a moment, then straightened her shoulders and lifted her chin. "Okay. Might as well try. All they can do is say no, and who knows, maybe they'll say yes."

We arrived at the provost marshal's office shortly before closing time and found the receptionist frowning over her typewriter. A plump dark-haired woman who wore a cluster of plumeria flowers tucked behind one ear, she radiated anything but the friendly island aloha the flowers implied. Her grumpy expression didn't change when she looked up at us. I'd been fuming all the way to town, but I did my best to contain my anger and speak in a pleasant voice.

"We're here because Mrs. Tanaka, my farm manager's wife, needs to get to Honolulu to attend the farewell rally they're putting on for her son and all the AJA boys who've been sworn into the Army," I said. "Unfortunately, the provost marshal denied her the necessary travel papers when she asked to visit her husband at the Honouliuli camp, but I believe her son's enlistment should earn her and her other two children the right to travel."

Still frowning, the receptionist jotted down Masako's name and those of Isao and Sam. She knocked on a closed door and entered. She returned a few moments later. "I'm sorry, the decision stands. We will not be giving you travel papers, Mrs. Tanaka." She sat at her desk, poised to return to her typing. "Is there anything else?"

I was ready to explode by this time and started to argue, but Masako put her hand on my arm. "Please, Rose, no," she said. She leaned closer to me and whispered, "Why don't you go?"

Surprised, I stood with my mouth open. Masako gestured for me to follow her out the office door to the waiting room.

"Are you serious, Masako? I'm ready to take this thing to the top—uh, wherever that might be. I've had enough of this martial law nonsense. They should let you go!"

"Yes, Rose, I'm serious. Challenging the authorities won't do any good, and it might make things worse. I don't want to call attention to myself. Please, Rose. I would be so grateful if you would go." She looked at me with pleading in her eyes. "You could take the gifts, see Isao, go to the ceremony, and bring me back a report." She attempted a smile. "You know how curious I am about how Aiko has been living over there."

I thought for a moment, then said, "All right, I'll go." I looked at my watch. "I'd better get back in there to get the paperwork done before they close."

"Thank you, Rose, so much. I'll wait here." Masako sat in one of the chairs along the wall, her purse in her lap, and stared straight ahead.

I was glad Masako had stopped me from making a scene. The receptionist was still grumpy, but she filled out the paperwork, took it back to the powerful man behind the closed door, and returned with a signed copy. Masako and I rushed to the steamship office to buy a ticket before closing time. No one there questioned my right to travel, which was nice for me but did nothing to soothe my anger with these bureaucrats who were able to forbid Masako to travel.

Friday afternoon, I hurried home and took my suitcase to her house. I could tell it required all of Masako's strength to maintain a cheerful face as she stuffed the suitcase with banana bread and jars of butter and honey. The kids added letters with the usual decorative drawings. I padded everything with my nightgown, blouses, and a dress for school on Monday. With the teacher shortage we were facing, I had to get back to work. For the rest of the weekend, I would wear practical trousers topped with a clean blouse each day.

I drove myself down to Kahului and lugged my suitcase to the steamer. People who'd paid only for deck passage were settling in with mats, blankets, and bento boxes. One family had a little cage of chickens, and another held a baby goat by a leash. We steamed into the sunset and a darkening night. Our ship was blacked out, so only the stars and a half-full moon lit our zigzag course, designed to evade possible attack. I stayed on the dark deck listening to a group of passengers play ukulele and sing Hawaiian songs until fatigue overtook me. Early the next morning, after a decent night's sleep in my little cabin, I went back up to watch the sunrise as we neared Honolulu Harbor.

This was not the Honolulu Harbor I knew, languid in the morning sun, fragrant with hundreds of lei, serenaded by Hawaiian singers. The Aloha Tower was camouflaged with shades of olive drab and beige, and the only people around were dock hands and military men, the only smell a mixture of seaweed and fuel oil. In pre-war times, people filled the docks to greet arriving passengers. Now we had to walk to the crowd awaiting our arrival on the other side of a fence at the far end of the pier. I hauled my heavy suitcase toward the fence. Finally, I spotted Aiko and Leona, waving enthusiastically. I handed my bag to Leona, a husky Hawaiian-Portuguese girl, and turned to greet Aiko, who threw her arms around me.

"Come, Auntie, we'll get you settled and have breakfast, and then we'll go see my dad," Aiko said, leading the way through the crowd to a bus stop.

"Sorry, Auntie, we don't have a car to come get you, but not too far a ride," Leona said, as Aiko helped her lift the suitcase up the steps. The bus driver frowned but said nothing, and we squeezed through the crowd of soldiers, sailors, and civilians, keeping the precious luggage between us as we clung to poles while the bus made its way through more traffic than I'd ever seen.

Honolulu's streets were full of men in uniform, even more than I was used to on Maui. They lined up outside restaurants and shops and posed with girls in hula outfits against painted backdrops. Little boys waved newspapers with big headlines, and, as in Wailuku, other little boys knelt to shine soldiers' shoes. I craned my neck to look at one particularly long line outside a nondescript building, wondering if it might be leading men to one of the legal brothels I had heard about.

Civilians made their way through these throngs, children clutching their mothers' hands, and stood in long lines outside grocery stores.

"I feel like a country bumpkin, with all these people around," I told Aiko, who laughed.

"I know what you mean, Auntie. I'm kind of used to it now."

After many stops, where a few riders exited and others squeezed into the bus, we finally reached our destination, a neighborhood of pleasant one-story houses just *mauka* of the Ala Wai Canal. Leona and Aiko parted the crowd, Leona still carrying my suitcase. I was glad to step back into the fresh air.

Leona turned into an open gate, and Aiko and I followed her up the steps. The house was big, with three bedrooms and a spacious living room, where Leona set my suitcase next to a *punee* in one corner.

"And this is where we sleep," Aiko said, opening one door to reveal a small room with two single beds and a chest of drawers. "We're lucky we have our own beds. Lots of civilian war workers gotta share with someone who works a different shift—so hard to find housing. This door is Malia and her husband, Joseph. And this door is Joseph's brother Antone and his wife, Pua. They're all at work now."

"Your mother would have loved to see this," I said. "And she sent treats for you." I opened my suitcase to show her Masako's gifts.

"Dad will be so happy to see this," Aiko said. "And to see you, Auntie!" She frowned. "If only they would let my mom come."

"Yes. I was ready to fight them, but she made me cool down."

"That's my mom," Aiko said. "Tough, but never wants to make trouble. And she knew Dad and Sam would be happy to see you, even if she couldn't come."

"The eggs are ready now," Leona called from the kitchen. "And let's have some of that banana bread!"

After breakfast, Aiko and I headed out. Anticipation rose in my chest as we walked several blocks to the pickup point for the military bus that would take us to see Isao. Both of us carried full bags. Besides what Masako had sent, Aiko had made *musubi,* rice balls wrapped in dried seaweed, for both Isao and Sam.

I was the only *haole* in the group gathered at the bus stop, standing a head or more above the middle-aged women and younger ones with worried-looking children at their side.

"How far to the camp?" I asked Aiko as we settled onto seats on the bus.

"This is the first time I visited this camp, but I think it's long—all the way past Pearl Harbor, near Waipahu. They just moved there a few weeks ago from Sand Island."

"Aiko, have you talked to him about applying for parole again?"

She shrugged. "I mentioned it, but he doesn't believe it will work. I know Sam thinks he should. He talked about it in the letter he sent me after he enlisted. How can they keep our dad in prison when Sam's going off to fight?"

"Let's see if we can persuade him to try again," I said.

"He's so discouraged now," Aiko said, her face sad. "Maybe if we all encourage him, he'll be willing to try."

When at last we turned off the main road, the murmur of conversation in the bus died. We drove on a narrow road between walls of sugarcane, then bus turned onto a road that led down the side of a gulch. At the bottom were guard towers, the pointed tops of dozens of tents, and the roofs of small wooden buildings in orderly rows. Barbed wire fences surrounded it all.

We filed off the bus and stood in line, the sun beating down on us. I was glad I had worn a wide-brimmed hat. At the gate to the camp, tall soldiers inspected the passes the women presented. When it was my turn, I got the usual suspicious frown as the soldier rifled through my bag of treats.

"How do you know this Tanaka, ma'am?"

"He's my farm manager, and his family lives on my farm," I said and added, just to make a point, "I'm here to see his son welcomed into the U.S. Army tomorrow, so I thought I'd visit Mr. Tanaka as well."

"Hmph," was the response, but at least he handed back my pass and bag of gifts and let me follow Aiko into the camp.

Armed soldiers with bayonets ready escorted our group over a dirt path between the little barracks-like buildings where bored-looking men in sleeveless undershirts watched us pass. It was a far cry from the green Haiku camp, where I'd last seen Isao. This place was hot and dusty, shaded by only a few trees. A mosquito whined near my ear.

The soldiers led us to the mess hall, a large building where wooden tables with attached benches lined up in rows. As we entered, Isao looked over, his face lighting up as he saw us. He stood from the bench where he sat, reaching to take our hands, and across the table, Sam turned, breaking into a smile. He wore a khaki uniform, and his hair was trimmed short. Isao's hair and beard had grown grayer since I last saw him, and he was even thinner.

"Ho, Rose, I'm so glad to see you," Isao said. He craned his neck to search the cluster of women entering the room. "Masako—is she here?"

"No, I'm so sorry, Isao," I said, resting a hand on Sam's shoulder as I settled onto the bench next to him. "The government wouldn't let her come, so she asked me to come instead." Isao sank back onto his seat, crestfallen. "We wanted someone to go with Aiko tomorrow when they have the sendoff rally for these new soldiers, and of course I wanted to see you." I patted Sam's hand, trying to change the subject and give Isao a little time to swallow his disappointment. "You look great in a uniform, Sam!"

Sam sat up straight, smoothed the front of his khaki shirt, and placed his cap on his head at a jaunty angle.

"Ho, da handsome, you," Aiko said, and we all chuckled. I glanced over at Isao, who was making a brave effort to look cheerful. It hurt to imagine how he must feel. Guilt surged through me about being the one to take Masako's place. But it wasn't something we could speak of; the kids kept up their banter.

"I guess you decided it's okay for me to sign up after all," Sam said, raising an eyebrow at his sister.

Aiko shrugged. "Cannot help. You're such a stubborn donkey, you were gonna do it no matter what I thought. At least you look good in uniform."

"They've been teaching us basic stuff like how to march," Sam said. "You'll see it tomorrow."

Isao's eyes, fixed on his son, were bright with unshed tears. "I am proud of you, son," he said. "I only wish I could go to see you off."

"Me too, Pop. I'm just glad they let us come visit our families today."

I reached into my bag to pull out loaves of banana bread. "Your mother sent this—two for you and two for your dad."

"And we made *musubi*, and here's a little jar of honey, Dad, from Maui," Aiko said.

Isao blinked as he accepted the gifts. "Masako's banana bread. I'm so grateful to you for bringing it, Rose. If only she and the kids could have come too."

We were all silent for a moment. Then Isao smiled and tucked his treats into the bag Aiko had carried. "I will share one with my barracks friends tonight," he said. "They will appreciate that Maui banana bread made by Masako Tanaka is number one."

We all laughed, the mood lightened a bit, and we began to talk story, following Isao's example of finding whatever joy he could in the situation.

Sam told us a little about life as a soldier. "Lots of marching, following orders, learning who to salute, like that. After all that work, we get together and play uke, some guys throw dice, good fun. You folks know plenty of these guys," he said, listing boys he had known as a child, others who'd been my students or played football at Maui High School. "You know Franklin Odo from Paia, right? He's the shortest guy, has to roll up his uniform pants practically to his knees." It did me good to see the family dimples deepen in all three Tanaka faces as they laughed at Sam's stories.

Sam turned serious. "Pop, have you applied for parole again?"

Isao's smile dimmed. He looked at his hands. "No use," he said. "They already said no. Why try again?"

"No, Dad, do it again." Sam leaned forward, intense, his eyes on his father. "You raised us to be patriotic Americans, right? This proves it, that I'm willing to go off to war. How can you be loyal to Japan when you got a son in the U.S. Army?"

Isao leaned forward, his face troubled. "Hiroki, I hope you didn't sign up hoping to get me out. I no like take advantage of you risking your life. Mo' bettah I stay here, and you stay safe."

"No, Dad, I was going to do this anyway, as soon as they'd let me, so you're not taking advantage. But use it! Please, Dad, keep trying. Mom needs you at home. Henry and Iris are growing up without their father. Even Auntie Rose needs you, so she doesn't have to haul the goats out to graze every day. Right, Auntie?"

"I agree you should try again, Isao," I said. "Sam is right. Use whatever benefit Sam's enlistment offers and get out of this damn place."

Isao cocked an eyebrow and half smiled. "You mean, my new home, Hell Valley?"

"Is that what you folks call it? Well, let's get you out of hell," I said.

"I can type it up nicely, Dad, if you'll write a letter," Aiko said. She reached across the table and placed her hand on her father's. "Please, Dad, don't give up. Keep trying. You know you don't belong here. Tell them I'm doing defense work, and even Henry is picking *kiawe* beans, and the family on Maui produces food to help our neighbors. We're doing our bit, and the government should let you go."

Isao thought for a moment, then nodded. "Okay, I'll give it another try. You still willing to be my sponsor, Rose?"

"Of course! You write that letter and let's get this process going."

"Okay, okay. I will. I'll mail it to you, Aiko, and you can type it up before next visiting day, yeah?"

"I will," Aiko said, and looked around the dining hall and out the windows at the sere slopes of the valley. "So, how is it here, Dad? Better than Sand Island?"

"Not especially. We're starting over with our gardens," Isao said. "We had Sand Island all fixed up, but here, no more nothing. But plenty of rocks here, so we're building a Japanese garden, nicely arranged with some plants." He swatted at a mosquito. "Too many mosquitoes, but."

"And so hot," I said. "No trade winds down here."

Isao shrugged, and in my head, I heard as if he'd said it aloud, "*Shikata ga nai.*" Cannot be helped.

The visit ended too soon, first for Sam, when a soldier called out that the Schofield bus was leaving. Sam stood and stepped around the table to embrace his father.

Isao leaned back, hands on his son's shoulders, and his advice echoed that Masako had given. "Do your best, Hiroki. Do your duty. America is your country. Try to come back alive, but whatever you do, make us proud."

Sam nodded, his face serious, shook his father's hand, gave brief hugs to Aiko and me, and was gone.

Then the soldier came back to shout that the downtown bus was ready for boarding. Aiko and I stood.

"Thank you for coming, Rose," Isao said as he took my hand. "Please tell Masako I will try for parole again."

"And I will write another letter offering to be your sponsor," I said. "I hope you'll be home with us soon."

Aiko gave him a kiss on the cheek, and we followed the other visitors, turning once to wave. Isao stood where we had left him, looking so forlorn that I had to wipe away tears as we trudged back along the dusty path to our bus. I had wept more in the past couple of years than I had in my whole life.

On the bus, I stared out at the dusty landscape. There must be something I could do to help free Isao, something beyond the simple letter I'd promised to send. If only I could figure out what it might be.

Chapter Twenty

March 28, 1943

M The next day, Aiko, Leona, and I left after lunch for Iolani Palace. People were already gathering when we arrived. Military police guarded the perimeter of a large space where the soldiers would stand, so we found a shady spot near the entrance gate and spread our blanket. The girls lay down and promptly fell asleep. I leaned against the trunk of a monkeypod tree and looked around.

People were scattered across the broad lawn surrounding the old palace, home of Hawaiian royalty before the kingdom was overthrown and the capital of the short-lived Hawaiian republic that was annexed to become the Territory of Hawaii. The palace was ornate and elegant, with its pillars, towers, long verandas, a wide staircase, and the U.S. and Hawaii flags flying from the central tower.

But the grounds looked very different from the last time I'd seen them. A long, low building blocked most of our view of the open square in front of the palace where the soldiers would stand. Other buildings were scattered across the tree-dotted green grounds, which once had been like a park in the middle of downtown Honolulu. Now there were slit trenches and piles of dirt indicating underground air-raid shelters, and all those ugly temporary buildings.

People were arriving to fill the remaining open spaces, mostly Japanese, of all ages from infants to elders. Many had brought picnics, and mamas were feeding little ones while grownups nibbled on *musubi*.

It was a relatively cheerful crowd, with much chatter and here and there a youngster playing ukulele. The enlistment of more than twenty-six hundred young men was an occasion to celebrate, a validation of the patriotism of the entire local Japanese community.

Only a few seemed to be brooding over the battles these boys would march off to or worrying about how many of them might never come home.

After a while, I lay next to Aiko and dozed. We were awakened by a buzz of excitement, the military sound of a band playing a marching tune, and voices calling, "Here they come!" I pushed myself up and looked around, as Aiko and Leona scrambled to their feet. "Wow, this place filled up while we were napping. There must be thousands of people here."

"Look, here come the soldiers! Lucky we're by the fence," Leona said. "Can you folks see?"

Aiko and I, both shorter than Leona by several inches, stretched our necks to peer over the crowd gathered at the palace fence and jamming the sidewalks outside.

"Good thing we wen' sit on the King Street side," Leona said. "Look how many guys marching!"

Aiko and I squeezed closer to the fence with its iron rails atop a low concrete wall. From where I stood, I could see only one khaki cap after another, like the one Sam had worn yesterday. Aiko slipped through the crowd to peek between the rails. After a few minutes, she gestured to me and stepped back to let me take her place.

Now I could look across the four columns of young men marching side by side. All so young, but already looking like soldiers. Yes, as Sam said, they had indeed learned to march. Soon they would leave for the mainland, to Camp Shelby in Mississippi, the papers said, and I didn't like to imagine what they would have to learn there.

I stepped back and let another eager viewer take my place and turned to see what was going on in front of the palace. Crowds of civilians had wedged themselves between the buildings along the side of the palace entry and the area reserved for the soldiers. The men lined up in orderly rows as they arrived, and young women moved along the lines, draping each man's shoulders with what looked like a crepe paper lei. The lei were a golden yellow, like the *ilima* lei made from hundreds of tiny, fragile blossoms, once reserved for royalty. It seemed a fitting tribute to these young men who had so nobly volunteered to face death far away from home.

By now, the courtyard in front of the palace was almost filled as more soldiers arrived, and we could see some of their faces from our vantage point near the front gate.

"Ho, da handsome," Leona said. "So many of them! I wish they didn't have to leave. But they look so nice in their uniforms."

Searching as they passed by, I'd seen a couple of familiar Maui faces in the mass of men, but none of us had yet glimpsed Sam. Then Aiko shouted, "There he is!" She pointed to one of the columns, so alike in their khaki uniforms, and at last, I saw him. Sam's face was even more serious than usual, stern, determined. He was off to war, into unknown dangers.

Somewhere up near the palace, the Royal Hawaiian Glee Club began to sing the Hawaiian anthem, *Hawaii Ponoi*. The last of the marchers arrived, forming a sea of khaki, their dark hair trimmed to military length, their faces forward. We all listened as one bigwig after another came to the second-floor balcony of the palace, each extolling the young men, telling how proud the community was. The event had been put on by government and business leaders, a farewell rally for these boys on whom so many hopes rested.

We were listening to one of the older volunteers (whom I recognized as a Maui politician) thank the crowd and pledge "to pick up arms and fight for our homes, our country, and our freedom" when it struck me: I was within a few hundred feet of the leading men of Hawaii. I would ask one of them to help free Isao.

I tapped Aiko's shoulder, and she turned to me with a big smile.

"Aiko, I am going to go up and talk to one of those men up there. Wait for me by the gate," I said.

Her smile turned into a look of confusion. "Auntie, why?" she asked.

"I'll tell you when I get back. I need to hurry. I think it's almost over. How's my hair? My lipstick?"

"Fine," she said, staring at me as if I was crazy.

"I'll be back. See you at the gate," I said and turned to squeeze my way through the crowd to the rear of the temporary building edging the square. Everyone had crowded as close as they could to the soldiers, and I made quick progress through the empty space behind the building. My mind raced, considering which of the powerful men standing on the third-floor balcony could help me. I wished one of them was part of the military government, but this was a civilian ceremony. My best bet, I decided, was the retired major general who'd opened the ceremony. Surely he would have some connections to General Emmons, the military governor who was the true power in Hawaii these days.

When I reached the military policeman at the end of the line guarding the front steps of the palace, I stopped, took a breath, then stepped forward and gave the MP a sweet smile. I remembered Masako's warning the other day when we had tried to get permission for her to attend this gathering. Challenging authority could make things worse. I knew that being a *haole* gave me some advantage in dealing with these men. I would build on that privileged status by being as diplomatic as I could.

"Corporal, can you help me? I need to speak to Major General Welch," I said. The guard frowned at me.

"I'm sorry, ma'am, you can't go up there."

"I really do need to speak to the major general. Is there someone in charge that I can ask for permission?"

The MP looked almost as confused as Aiko. Clearly, this was not a situation his orders had prepared him to handle. A middle-aged white woman attending this rally was enough of a novelty, never mind one who wanted to approach one of the bigwigs. He looked relieved when a sergeant who'd been standing behind the banister on the first-floor porch came rapidly down the steps.

"What's going on? Why are you here, ma'am?"

"I need to speak to Major General Welch," I said. "My name is Rose McKenzie, I am a schoolteacher from Maui, and I must leave on the steamer tonight. The only way I can speak to the major general is if you'll let me see him right now." The crowd was applauding, and an officer facing the rows of young men shouted orders at them. They turned, and at the next call from the officer, began to march toward the gate.

"It looks like the ceremony is over," I said. "So this would be a perfect time, Sergeant, for you to escort me up the steps before those gentlemen go on their way." I put on my most appealing face. "Please, Sergeant. It's important for the future of a family who live on my farm."

The sergeant thought for a moment, looking nervous. I opened my purse to show it contained nothing dangerous. "I'm harmless, I promise. You can search me if you want," I said raising my arms and turning slowly, suddenly very aware of how my slacks showed off my slim waist and the curve of my hips. When I faced him again, the sergeant was blushing. Abruptly, he waved me forward.

"Okay, let's go, ma'am. I don't want any trouble. I'll take you to my captain, and we'll see what he says."

Within a few minutes, I managed to persuade the captain that my cause was innocent and just, and he led me up the steps to the third-floor balcony, the sergeant following close behind. If I had been a saboteur, the two of them could easily have tackled me, and I'm sure that was exactly their plan.

When we reached the third floor, the captain looked at me, said "Stay put," and strode toward the group of men clustered at the center of the balcony. Someone was passing around cigars, and the rich, sweet scent of their smoke filled the air. I recognized the major general, a portly fellow who was lighting his cigar. The captain spoke to him, and he looked over at me, surprised. I gave him my most beguiling smile. He smiled back and came toward me.

"Well, madam, what's on your mind?"

I widened my smile and introduced myself, then continued. "Major General, thank you for your stirring remarks today. This is such a glorious occasion, isn't it? To see these young men march off to defend our country—so inspiring." He chuckled, took a drag on his cigar, and turned his head to blow the smoke away from me.

"Thank you, ma'am. Now, how can I help you?"

"I have come regarding an American family who live on my farm. Their son is one of the boys down there today. He could not wait to sign up to prove his patriotism and that of his family. But you see, Major General, the problem is that his father has been locked up and is now at Honouliuli camp." I gave him my usual speech about needing my farm manager but hammed it up a bit.

"Now, my manager's son has signed up, and we are left with no man on the farm, just two women and two young children. How will we cope, sir? I need my farm manager back at work. We are doing all we can to support our community, and all of us are doing defense work, even the children. We frequently entertain staff members from the Army hospital at the farm, and we take boxes of produce to their mess hall.

"We raise goats whose milk is so helpful to new babies with colic and their poor mothers, who can do nothing to calm them. Our goat milk works wonders for them, but with young Sam gone off to war, we've had to dry up half of our little herd, and what will happen when another young mother comes begging for this wonderful milk?" I tried to draw up some tears, but the best I could do was look mournful and hope that would touch his heart.

"I was thinking, sir," I continued, "with the great influence you wield and your many connections with the military, if I gave you this man's name, perhaps you could pass it on to someone in authority. My manager has agreed to my begging and will apply for parole, and of course, I will be his sponsor. But I'm sure it would help if someone of your stature were to speak for him. If you're willing, I'll give you his name, and mine as well, so you can check that I am all that I say I am."

Welch pursed his lips and tapped the ash off his cigar, looking at me. Finally, he said, "All right. There is no guarantee that this will result in the release of your farm manager. But I appreciate your spunkiness, coming all the way up here, talking your way past the guards. Have you a piece of paper and a pencil?"

"Oh, yes sir, I certainly do." I quickly pulled out the little notebook I always carried and wrote Isao's name and mine, adding our address and my phone number for good measure. Welch accepted the paper, said "Good day, madame, and good luck to you," then turned and walked away.

Weak and shaky, my strength drained by this encounter, I took a couple of deep breaths and looked at the captain, who had a little smile on his face. "Well, congratulations, ma'am. Spunky indeed," he said, and turned briskly to the sergeant. "Escort Miss McKenzie back out. No detours, no stops, all the way down." The sergeant clicked his heels together, saluted, and turned to lead me downstairs.

My heart pounded as I squeezed my way through the excited crowd. I craned my neck, watching the marching soldiers for a final glimpse of Sam, scanning the crowd to find Aiko and Leona. Now that I'd succeeded in my spontaneous invasion of Iolani Palace, second thoughts took hold. Elation warred with embarrassment. I didn't know how it had occurred to me to twirl so suggestively before the sergeant. It made him blush, and now it made me blush. I was not usually the kind of woman who used my body to get what I wanted. But today I had, and I prayed that it had worked.

• • • •

MASAKO WAS THRILLED, when I arrived at Jeanette's after school the next day, to hear that Isao was going to apply for parole a second time, and wide-eyed as she listened to my story of talking my way up the ranks of soldiers to get to the major general. "Oh, my goodness, Rose, I'm amazed you had the nerve, but I'm so grateful you did," she said.

I told the story again when Jeanette came home. She threw her head back and laughed. "I can't believe you did that, Rose," she said. "It's the sort of thing I would have tried." She paused, her face becoming serious. "You know," she said, "I can't imagine you doing something like that a year ago. You would've put on your stern schoolteacher voice, not flirted your way past all those soldiers. Being with Jack has changed you. You've learned to use your womanly charm, girl. Good for you! It's about time!"

I hadn't thought of that, but she was right. Jack brought out the woman in me. And my newfound confidence in my femininity had given me power to use it as I never would have thought to do before.

I had skipped a weekend with Jack to make this journey, and I was eager to tell him my Honolulu stories when he came up for a quick visit that evening. He listened intently, nodding and smiling. His eyebrows rose when I gave him a slightly edited version of my success with getting to the bigwigs at Iolani Palace, skipping the part about making the sergeant blush.

"Those guys shouldn't have let you through," he said, frowning. "I wonder if their superiors are going to hear about that. They might be in trouble."

"I hope not," I said. "It never occurred to me that they could get in trouble, to tell the truth. But I did achieve my objective. I gave Isao's name to the retired major general who's the Chamber of Commerce liaison with the military and asked him to pass it along to someone in authority. Sam and Aiko and I talked Isao into applying for parole again, and I'm going to be his sponsor. I hope my connecting with that major general will nudge things in the right direction."

Jack's lips thinned, and his frown deepened.

"Rose, I have to ask," he said. "Are you sure this is a good idea? Putting yourself out like that to someone in authority? How do you know your name's not on some list now? And you're going to act as sponsor?"

"Well, of course I am," I said, astonished to hear him question the plan. "We've been working on this for more than a year. Why would I not be his sponsor?"

Jack looked away, shaking his head, then looked back up at me. "Are you sure it's safe? Are you sure he is not involved with Japan in some way? If anything went wrong, it would be bad not only for the country but for you personally, as his sponsor."

I sat up straight, set my coffee cup down, and looked at Jack. "How can you even consider that?" I tried to keep my voice calm. "You have known this family for months. You see what kind of people they are. Do you think their husband and father could be a spy for our enemies?"

Jack looked apologetic, sitting back, hands up. "Okay, okay. If you say so, I'll trust your judgment. I know you've worked on this for a long time. But I don't want you to do anything that is going to cause you trouble in the future."

"It won't." I picked up my cup and took a sip to cover my anger. I turned to look at him. "I hope you will find it in your heart to be kind to Isao. Imagine if you had gone through what he just did."

"Of course I will, honey," Jack said, sipping his own coffee and staring out at the darkening pasture from our seat on the porch. "I'll be my usual gentlemanly self."

I watched him for a moment, doubtful. I hoped that would be enough. As much as I loved Jack, our different attitudes about other races kept cropping up. Probably Army indoctrination to hate anything Japanese reinforced his lack of experience; from what he said, Oregon was almost entirely white. He was kind to Masako and the kids, if a bit patronizing. But I wondered if he could get past his mainland prejudice to be friends with Isao.

· · · ·

THE NEXT DAY, THE PHONE was ringing when I came home from school, and I rushed to answer it. The caller identified herself as Major General Welch's secretary.

"The major general asked me to let you know that he has passed on your request to the military governor. He said to wish you luck."

"Thank you! Did he say anything about how the governor responded?"

"No, I'm sorry. That's the entire message. Goodbye now." And she hung up.

I dumped my books on the table and ran to give Masako the good news.

Then we waited, watching every day for the mailman's arrival. On the days when Masako was home, she'd station herself near the road around the time he usually arrived. He didn't even leave his truck to put our mail in the box because Masako would step forward to take it with eager hands. She'd stop by my house to drop off anything addressed to me and sometimes share a letter she'd received, and already read, from one of her scattered flock.

Isao's letters were the usual recounting of camp life. He had made a chess set out of cardboard and pebbles, tried his hand at Japanese calligraphy, and read books by Jack London and Zane Grey. Aiko wrote to let us know she'd typed up her father's new request for parole and sent it off. But he'd heard no word on a decision, pro or con.

If the waiting was hard for me, it was agonizing for Masako.

"The days seem so long now," she said. "All I care about is what's in the mail. And when I check, and there's nothing about Isao coming home, it's so disappointing. The only way I can get myself moving is to look forward to the next mail. And then I'm disappointed all over again."

But Masako was considerably happier when she appeared at my doorstep the next day. She'd received a letter from Sam, the first since he had been inducted.

The new soldiers, now known as the 442nd Regimental Combat Team, had shipped out of Honolulu a few days after the gathering at the palace.

Some guys were seasick, Sam wrote, leaving us to guess details like the ship's name, the number of days spent at sea, and the destination port. *I wasn't, but I still had blisters from marching to the ship in Honolulu. These boots don't fit so well! Better than being seasick, but.*

After we landed, we got on a train, but we didn't see much on the trip because the windows were covered with blinds. Now we're in Mississippi near a little town called Hattiesburg. We haven't had a chance to look it over because they're keeping us in camp. But when we were at the railroad station after we arrived, we saw signs on the men's room and drinking fountains saying "white" and "colored." Our officer told us to use the "white" ones. Some crazy, this place.

Us Hawaii guys stick together. The mainland guys are kind of stuck up. We have a good time when we pau training, we play ukulele and sing, throw dice, joke around. But they don't join in so much. I speak good English (thank you, Mom and Auntie Rose), but plenty of the Hawaii guys only talk pidgin, and the mainland guys don't like that.

I miss the fresh food from our farm. And rice—never enough here. No more shoyu, so we use bouillon cubes to season our food.

They keep us working hard. But we are learning a lot, getting strong, and our officers are good to us. It's cold here! Nighttime, we freeze, with only screens, no glass in the windows. Lucky thing we have a pot-belly stove, but still cold.

I will write again soon, and I will write to Pop. Have you heard anything about his parole? Tell Henry I hope he's looking after all you ladies.

Predictably, Henry puffed up with importance at Sam's comment, and Masako carefully folded her son's letter and put it in her wooden box.

I tried to think of anything else I could do to move Isao's case forward. But I'd already done everything I could. As soon as I'd heard that General Welch had passed Isao's information to the military governor, I'd written three letters. The first was a thank-you to General Welch. A second one went to the military governor, repeating my defense of Isao and offering to act as sponsor. And finally, I wrote a similar letter to the local provost marshal, who would be in charge of Isao if and when he was paroled. None of the men replied.

Isao's letters continued to be cheerful, but Aiko's gave us a glimpse of the reality he was living.

"Dad seems distracted when I see him," she wrote. "He stares off into space, and sometimes I have to say something twice before he notices. He is thinner, too. I hope they decide on the parole soon. And of course I hope they decide in our favor!"

Days became weeks, and weeks months. We had no way to know how this decision was being made or who was making it. We had no way to track the progress of Isao's request. We could only wait.

At last, two months after he had applied, Isao sent good news. Masako appeared as I stepped out of my truck late one afternoon, waving a letter.

"One of the camp officers interviewed Isao about his parole application!" Masako said, her face bright with excitement. "Listen to this. 'He asked me many questions, and he seemed to like my answers. He also seemed happy to hear that Hiroki joined up. So I'm hopeful.'"

She looked up from the letter, grinning. "It sounds good, doesn't it?"

I grinned back. "It does indeed."

A couple of weeks later, Masako came straight to my door after her ride home from Jeanette's.

"Rose, are you here?" she called from the back door, and I went to push open the screen. Masako had stopped at the mailbox, and with an enormous smile on her face, she waved a letter. "He's getting paroled!" she exclaimed.

"Oh, Masako, that's such good news!" I opened the door wider. "Come inside, tell me all about it." We sat at the breakfast nook, both of us beaming.

"When will he get to come home?" I asked.

Her smile faded slightly as she reread Isao's letter. "Well, that part's not clear. It might be a while. He says his friend was granted parole but didn't go home for a couple of months."

"Oh. Well, that's too bad. But at least things are on the right track!"

The next day's mail brought a letter for me. "Dear Miss McKenzie: Enclosed please find the forms you must fill out in order to be named parole sponsor for Isao Tanaka. Complete the forms and bring them in person ..." The letter gave me a number to call for an appointment at an office in Wailuku, which I dialed immediately. I arrived promptly on the day of my appointment and turned in the paperwork, promising to keep an eye on Isao, make sure he remained employed and out of trouble. We waited a full six weeks for the letter that told us we could pick him up at the dock.

• • • •

SEPTEMBER 1943

I drove Masako and the kids to the harbor that day. It was a perfect Maui morning, the air fresh, the sky clear and blue, the ocean still and shining. The air at the dock had that familiar scent of ocean, seaweed, and molasses from bags of raw sugar ready for shipment.

Iris jumped up and down with excitement as we watched *Waialeale* dock. "There he is!" Henry called, and Isao waved from his place on deck. He was one of the first ones off the gangplank, and he hesitated for a moment, looking around at the deep-green West Maui Mountains, the purple slope of Haleakala, breathing deeply. Then he came straight to us, the kids meeting him halfway down the dock and clinging to him as he walked into Masako's open arms.

I hung back, letting them have their moment. At last, my old friend was home, where he belonged.

Henry had taken charge of his father's bags. Iris held one of Isao's hands, smiling up at her father, whose other arm was around Masako. When they reached me, he let go of Iris to take my hand. "Rose, thank you so much for your help. Without you, I'd still be in Hell Valley."

"Isao," I replied, gripping his hand with both of mine, "I'm so happy you're back. Let's go home and get you some good breakfast."

Our conversation on the ride home, I admit, was not memorable, mostly the usual travel small talk about how rough the voyage had been. Unlike me, Isao had spent the night on deck, rather than in a cabin, pulling extra clothes from his suitcase for warmth and rolling up a sweater for a pillow.

"So you'll be even more thankful to sleep in your own bed tonight," I said.

"Yes, I will," Isao said, and out of the corner of my eye, I saw him share a tender glance with Masako.

I had set up the ingredients for a celebratory breakfast in the predawn hours, and after I dropped the Tanakas at their house, I backed up to my own place and went inside to cook. The rice in its cast-iron pot was still warm. I heated the broth Masako had made yesterday and added miso paste and cubed tofu. Meanwhile, bacon sizzled in a frying pan, and eggs were ready to scramble when the family arrived. I set out sliced papaya and Masako's pickled vegetables and sat with a cup of tea until I heard their footsteps at my back door.

Isao was home at last. His body was, at least.

Chapter Twenty-one

After breakfast, the Tanaka family went home, and I washed the dishes and sat down to do my bookkeeping. Late in the afternoon, I headed to the stable for chores. I thought Isao might want to take the day off, but he was there ahead of me. Masako was putting Luna into her stanchion for milking, Iris scooped chicken feed from the barrel, and Henry stood close to his father, gazing up at him. Isao was in front of the stable gate, frowning as he pushed back and forth on the gate post—the one Jack had replaced. If it moved at all, it was only a tiny bit, but that didn't seem to meet Isao's standards.

"Who did this?" he asked. Masako and I looked at each other. I had no idea what she had or hadn't told him.

"My friend, Jack Quinn," I said. "He's an Army doc at the school—you know it's a hospital now, right?"

"Mmm." Isao nodded, gave the gate post a final slap and turned to look around, hands in his back pockets.

"Things have grown," he said. "Everything a little bigger. Looks good, Rose. You folks got along fine without me."

"I wouldn't say that. It was tough," I said. "But think of what we can do now that you're home! We need you, Isao—you're the backbone of this operation."

He ducked his head. "I'm glad to be back. I better go get the cow in." He turned and walked away, head still down, one hand on Henry's shoulder as the boy strode to keep up with his father. I watched them go, a weight descending on my heart. I had expected us all to be so happy today. But Isao was subdued, his re-entry awkward. Where was the bubbly, happy Isao I'd hoped to see, today of all days?

The next morning, Isao was up early, leading the goats out to their lines, feeding the pigs, checking the water tanks in the pasture.

"My, it's good to have you home," I said when he came back to the barn, where I'd just finished milking Lani. "I wasn't making it up when I kept telling all those officials how much we needed our farm manager."

Isao smiled tightly but said nothing as he rummaged in a toolbox and pulled out a pair of pliers.

"And of course, Masako and the kids are thrilled," I said, desperate to lift the mood. "Masako has been so happy since we heard you were coming home."

He smiled a bit more at that but didn't look at me. "Yeah. I'm going to check the fences." With that, he turned and walked away. I watched him go, biting my lip, feeling as if I'd said something wrong. But I didn't know what I should say.

A couple of days later, I picked up Masako from her babysitting job.

"I'm worried about Isao," she said as we drove home. "He's not doing much. He doesn't talk. He doesn't want to go visit his friends. He's afraid of how people will react when they see him. And you know how some of them have been. No matter what you tell them, they still believe there must be a good reason for someone to get arrested and locked up."

"I hope this is temporary," I said. "Maybe time will heal him." But I couldn't help but think that Isao had come home with some vital element of his personality missing. It was as if he'd used up all his cheer in those reassuring letters he'd written from camp.

That evening, our neighbor Frank De Silva dropped by to welcome Isao home. Isao was working in the garden, and he dropped his hoe to grasp Frank's outstretched hand.

"Ho, Isao, you buggah, we missed you, you know!" Frank said, slapping Isao on the shoulder. "You folks gotta come over, play a little music, drink a few beers. So good to see you again."

I was happy to see that big-dimpled smile on Isao's face in response to Frank's enthusiasm. But none of Isao's other buddies showed up to welcome him home. And the longer he stayed home, the more reluctant he seemed to get back out to see people and to look for work anywhere but here.

I was nervous about how Jack and Isao would interact when they met. In my dreams, I imagined them laughing and singing together, as each did with other friends. Jack came up on Saturday as usual, the weekend after Isao returned, and I took him over to the garden, where Isao was replanting sweet potatoes. He looked up as we approached, then slowly straightened, hoe in one hand, potato vine dangling from the other, and stood frozen in place, eyes on Jack in his uniform. I wished I'd waited to introduce these two until Jack had changed into the jeans and shirt he kept in my closet.

"Isao, I want you to meet my friend, Jack Quinn," I said, trying to ignore the tension coming from both men.

"How do you do," Jack said formally, and Isao bowed his head briefly and said, "Nice to meet you." He made no move to shake hands, which I guess made sense since both hands were full and rather dirty from gardening. But it didn't strike me that either of these men was likely to reach out in friendship in any case. They stood stiffly, barely meeting each other's gaze. I tried to make conversation.

"Good sweet potato harvest from the last crop. Masako has worked so hard on this garden."

"Yes." That was all Isao said. I tried another tack.

"Jack is one of the doctors at the hospital, you know, and that's where Sam and the other boys went for their physicals. Jack was so impressed with how fit they are, weren't you Jack?"

"Oh, yes. Great kids," he said, his voice tense.

Isao nodded but said nothing, still standing there with his hoe and his vine, directing his gaze at the ground. I was not having any luck stirring up a conversation here, and this little gathering was making me increasingly uncomfortable.

"I guess we'll let you get back to work," I said. Jack followed me from the garden as Isao returned to his planting.

"Well, that was a lively conversation," I said when we were back in the house. "I certainly hope you two can get to know each other and maybe become friends."

Jack snorted. "You were worried about me not trusting him, but I'd say it's pretty clear he wants nothing to do with me."

"Can you blame him? He's been imprisoned by *haoles* in Army uniforms for nearly two years. Then he comes home to find another man has been doing the jobs he would have done around here, and that man wears the same uniform."

Jack stiffened, sitting up straight. "I seem to recall that those jobs needed doing, and also that pretty much everyone on Maui was extremely happy to see this uniform arrive by the truckload not so long ago."

Remorseful, I leaned over to kiss his forehead as I set his cup of coffee on the table, then stroked his shoulders. "I know, honey. I've appreciated every bit of help you've given me. And Lord knows we're all glad of the protection you've brought. But please try to see it from Isao's point of view."

Jack took a sip of coffee and rolled his eyes. "Okay, okay, I'll keep it in mind. I don't want to get into a pissing contest here."

I laughed. "A what? Never heard of it—no, don't explain, I can figure it out for myself—but yes, please avoid that, literally or figuratively." I changed the subject. "Meanwhile, since we're relieved of chore duty, do you want to go to the movies this afternoon?"

• • • •

JACK DID TRY. "CAN I give you a hand with that?" he asked one day when we came home from a walk and found Isao harvesting a stalk of bananas. He had propped the stalk up with a board while he whacked at the base of the tree and was maneuvering the falling stem so the bananas would have a soft landing. He glanced Jack's way briefly. "No, thanks," he said, and went on with his task. Jack shot me a look and raised one eyebrow, as if to say, "You see, he doesn't want to make friends."

Later that afternoon, Henry came to sit on the porch steps while Jack and I were watching the sky turn pink. Jack had just made a joke, and we were all laughing when Isao appeared. "Henry," he said. "Come. I need your help." With that, he turned and strode back to the stable without even looking in our direction. Henry hesitated, then said, "Bye, Captain Jack and Auntie." He followed his father, head hanging. Jack shot me a disgusted look but must have seen the hurt on my face. He took my hand and squeezed it, and we sat silently watching the sunset.

When he ran out of farm chores, Isao sat on his porch, staring off into space or reading a book. He went nowhere. He made no attempt to find jobs, this man who'd been in constant motion only a couple of years ago.

"He really needs to work," Masako told me when I picked her up one afternoon. "I know he's doing stuff around the farm, but he needs to get out in the world! Or something. At least he needs to work. I know he's hesitant to approach his old clients. Remember how awful that Mr. Breeze was when you asked him for help in the beginning?"

"Yes, that was terrible," I said. "I don't blame Isao for being sensitive. There have been so many bad feelings."

"Rose, I've been thinking." Masako turned to look at me. "Remember before the war when you were talking about building another cottage to rent out to teachers? Do you still want to do that? Could Isao get to work on it?"

"Yes! Masako, you're a genius. That's a great idea," I said, energized by the prospect of a solution, or at least a beginning of one. Giving Isao a big job like this might spark him back into action. "Let's talk to him when we get home."

We found Isao reading at the kitchen table. He looked up as both of us sat, Masako next to him and me across the table.

"Isao, do we have enough material put away to start on that rental cottage we were going to build?" I asked.

He cocked his head, considering. "The stuff we've been stockpiling should be enough to frame it and put in a floor and a roof."

"Well, I've been thinking we should get started before your regular clients realize you're back and start signing you up for their projects. And if you do get outside jobs, there's no rush, so you can work on it when you have time." I was pleased, as I presented the idea, to see Isao perk up, purpose returning to the face that had seemed so detached since he returned. "Maybe you could draw up a plan and do an inventory of the materials we've collected," I said. "Start a timesheet, and I'll pay you every couple of weeks."

Isao stood up, pulled paper and pencil from a drawer, and came back to the kitchen table. "Okay, let's get started," he said. "How many bedrooms you want?"

That evening, Isao was actually whistling as he hauled the pig-food buckets to the pen. A couple of days later, he brought me his building plan, plus the list of materials the little house would require.

"We might not be able to finish until the war's over," he said. "When we can get building supplies again." He looked thoughtful. "You know, they've built a lot of things no one's going to need when the military leaves. I bet we can get whatever they leave behind for cheap."

I nodded. "Good idea. And if we're already working on this, we'll have a head start."

He straightened the papers spread on the table of my breakfast nook. "We'll see. Meanwhile, it will be good to build something. I'll get started tomorrow." He looked up, smiling. "I might need you to hold a board or two, with Hiroki gone."

"I think I can remember how to do that," I said, smiling back. I had been Isao's helper on other building projects, beginning with the goat pen we'd added to the old stable and including the house his family lived in now. "It will be like old times," I said.

. . . .

BUT WHAT WAS GOOD FOR Isao did not particularly please Jack.

"What's going on out there?" he asked as he hung up his hat and gas-mask bag the next time he came to visit. "Cleared land, strings lined up—construction project?"

"Isao is building me a rental cottage," I said, setting my teacup on its saucer. "We've talked about it for years, and he's still at loose ends, so I decided it was a good time to go ahead."

"A rental cottage? Why?"

I shrugged. "Good way to bring in extra income. I don't need it now, but with no kids to look after me, I figure I need to build up savings for my old age."

Jack sat in his usual chair, frowning. "So ... it sounds like you're expecting to grow old here, alone."

I couldn't meet his eyes, fiddled with the salt-and-pepper shaker, brushed crumbs off the tabletop.

"I guess I am," I said at last. My heart beat fast, and my breath was short, as if I'd issued an ultimatum in an argument. We gazed at each other. Jack held his mouth in a grim line. A trickle of sweat ran down my back.

"Rose, if I asked, would you reconsider that?" He reached across the table to take both my hands. "Come home with me after the war. I have a beautiful little farm, and you'd love my boys. They'd love you too, and they'd take care of us both when we're old. What do you say? Will you think about it, at least?"

I hesitated and broke our gaze to look at his hands clasping mine. "I have thought about it. A lot. Somehow, I can't imagine leaving here."

He nodded, chewing on his lower lip.

"I was afraid of that," he said, his voice almost a whisper.

"How about you?" I had to ask, though I feared the answer was preordained. "Is there a chance you could move here? There's plenty of room upstairs for Mark and Roy."

He shook his head. "I can't imagine that either. So many ties to Oregon. I can't see my boys here, going to school barefoot, learning to speak pidgin. Would the local kids even accept them? They'd be fish out of water. And I can't take them from their grandparents. You know how hard it would be to ever get back to Oregon for a visit."

I nodded. "And as hard for me to ever get back here, to the place where I've spent my life." I stood up and went around the table to sit on his lap. "What a situation," I said, my eyes filling with tears. "Loving you has been the only bright spot this damn war has brought me."

Jack pulled me close, and I leaned my cheek against his, inhaling his scent, feeling his skin warm against mine.

"I love you, Rose, and I want to marry you," he murmured. "I don't want us to be just a wartime romance."

"It doesn't feel like a wartime romance. I love you too. I'm so happy you came into my life. But it's as if I have you on one side and Maui on the other, and each has equal strength, each tugging on me just as hard." I pulled back to look at his face and saw that his eyes also held tears. "Leaving here would rip my heart out. I can't do it, honey. I'm so sorry."

Now I was really crying. I put my head on Jack's shoulder and clung to him, as if this conversation might end with him disappearing, wafting away on the trade winds, leaving me alone and bereft.

"We'll take it day by day, okay?" Jack said, stroking my back. "Who knows what might happen? Two years ago, neither of us would have thought we'd meet and fall in love. Let's just accept the complete uncertainty of living in wartime. We have no control anyway. Uncle Sam could scoop me up and send me somewhere else. Let's love each other while we can and let the future take care of itself."

We made love then, locked into the little world of my bedroom, clinging to each other as if we could meld our bodies together, sharing tears along with our passion.

Chapter Twenty-two

November 1943

The next morning, we ate silently, poking at our scrambled eggs, taking an occasional bite of toast. What could we say, after all that had happened yesterday? My eyes were dry and burning from a night of lying sleepless, and I knew Jack had been awake much of the night as well. Here we were, unwilling to be apart, but with no future together that we could see. I tried to come up with some way to lighten the mood.

Finally, I said, "Let's do something to cheer ourselves up. Carpe diem, right? Why don't we put on a party? I wanted to let Isao settle in, and I think he's had enough time now. He and Masako won't come anyway, but the kids might." I leaned over to give him a kiss on the cheek. "Our parties are one of the best things we do together, aren't they?"

He looked up from his half-empty plate, a wan smile on his face "Yes, they are. And you're right, we might as well make the best of the time we have together. Let's live it up!"

Jack started spreading the word among our regular military guests that there'd be a party at my place the following Saturday, and I did the same among the teachers who usually attended.

"I'm glad you decided to have another party," one of the single teachers said when I invited her. She gave me a shy smile. "I like that redheaded doctor—and he's single. I only got to talk to him a couple of times, but I'd love to have another chance. Do you think he'll be there?"

I managed to return her smile. "I wouldn't be surprised. Good luck!" And I turned, perhaps a little too rapidly for politeness, and headed for my classroom. For her, a wartime romance might turn into something more. I didn't need reminding that mine would not.

Other guests were equally happy to have our parties revived, and I found myself busy every other week, preparing for the next one. As I had hoped, the parties gave us something to talk about and plan for, relieving some of the strain we both felt, knowing that our time together would be limited.

One Saturday morning, we were getting ready for the day's party. Jack had just come in from sweeping off the front porch when I went into the tool room to get potatoes for salad.

"Oh no!" I said when I opened the bag sitting on the countertop next to canned goods and dried beans. "These potatoes have gone off—look." I held up one with green leaves sprouting from its surface. "It even smells bad!" I untied my apron and hung it on its hook. "I'm going to walk to the store and get some more."

"Okay. Anything you want me to do while you're gone?"

I checked my hair in the little mirror by the back door. "Well, you could have a look at that new leak under the kitchen sink. Don't do anything if it's going to be a big job to fix—I have a bucket catching the drips. But if it only needs tightening or something you can do in a couple of minutes, that would be great."

"Yes, ma'am," Jack said, giving me a mock salute followed by a quick kiss.

Twenty minutes later, I was back. "Thank goodness they had potatoes," I said as I entered the kitchen. Then I stopped in my tracks. Jack was sitting at the breakfast nook and spread on the table before him was a Japanese flag. It was a small flag, about the size of a sheet of paper. But its crimson circle on a background of white silk was unmistakable.

"Where did that come from?" I asked, setting my bag of potatoes on the table, my eyes on that flag.

"That's what I'm wondering," Jack said, unsmiling. He reached over to the chair next to him and lifted a handful of papers covered in *kanji*. "And what the hell is this? I needed a bigger wrench than the one in your toolbox, so I went looking around the tool room, trying to find one. When I opened this one cabinet, I found feed bags carefully packed away. They clearly were not holding grain, too many lumps. I saw a piece of fabric sticking out of the top of one, and I was shocked when I pulled it out and found a Japanese flag. So I opened that bag and found these papers. What the hell, Rose? What are they, directions to Pearl Harbor? And what is all this stuff?"

He stood and walked to the door of the tool room where he gestured toward the cabinets that lined the walls. Reluctantly, I followed him to the doorway. The cabinet doors were open, empty burlap bags on the floor, and the countertops piled with the Tanakas' belongings, all the things we had packed so carefully on the first day of the war.

I turned back to the kitchen, suddenly breathless. Jack took his seat and stared at me, his mouth set in a hard line. I sat across the table and frowned back at him. "I offered to store some of their family treasures as soon as we heard of the Pearl Harbor attack. Since you went so far as to tear apart everything in my cupboards, you can see that it's all very innocent. Family pictures, a hand-carved altar, some books, the big paper carp flags people fly on Boys Day, and the dolls they display on Girls Day. Masako's wedding kimono. Things like that. Japanese, but nothing to do with the war. The papers are nothing more than writing practice that the kids did in Japanese school. I don't know how that flag got there. I've never seen it before."

"It was right at the top of one of the bags. And I tore everything open because, damn it, I'm an officer in the United States Army, and I needed to know what else was in those bags. Rose, I know you know that it's against the law to own a Japanese flag." He frowned, shaking his head. "You could go to jail for having this in your house. And if the authorities find out, Isao is on the next boat back to Honouliuli, if not worse."

"Oh, Jack, you wouldn't report it, would you?" I pleaded, reaching across the table to put my hands over his. Usually, he would have turned his hands to hold mine, but he didn't move. I took my hands away and clenched them in my lap. "I'm sure Isao doesn't know about this flag. I swear it wasn't there when we put everything away, and that was the last time I looked." Those feed bags full of the Tanakas' things had been out of sight, out of mind, for all this time, but now they might be about to reverse the work we had done to bring Isao home, not to mention what damage they might do to me.

Jack sat looking at me, his face grim. "Okay. If you say the flag wasn't there, I'll believe you," he said at last. The tension in my chest eased a bit. "Although I'd like to know where the hell a Japanese flag came from. What else is in there?" He shuffled through the stack of papers. "You say these are schoolwork?"

"Yes, Masako is sentimental about the kids' achievements."

"So whose idea was it to put this stuff away here?"

I glanced away, hating to put a spotlight on Isao. "It was my idea to put it here. Isao was going to bury everything, and I couldn't let him bury his family's few heirlooms."

"So Isao was afraid of being searched?"

"He was planning ahead," I said, defensive. "He'd been following the news and knew things were looking bad, and I guess he realized that local Japanese would be under suspicion if war came."

"You don't think it was a coincidence that he was already doing this clearing out on December 7, right after the attack?" His voice was sharp, and his eyes never left my face, as if he was interrogating me. "Sounds to me like he might have been expecting it."

"No, Jack, he was as surprised and shocked as any of us," I insisted, my mouth dry. "I'm just saying he's the kind of guy who pays attention and plans for contingencies."

"Funny this flag didn't show up until after he came home."

"Well, who knows how long it's been there? All I can tell you is that it wasn't there when we packed those bags, and I can't see any way Isao could have found a Japanese flag after he was released. Please, honey, I'll try to find out where the flag came from, but please believe me that it couldn't have been Isao and that none of us knew it was there. I'm mystified. Please ..." I stopped myself. Enough begging.

Jack sat nibbling on a thumbnail, staring at the flag and the pile of papers. I kept reminding myself to breathe, waiting to see what he would say. Finally, he tossed the flag on top of the papers. "You know, I spend a fair amount of my time up to my elbows in the blood of young Americans training to fight, maybe even to give their lives, in a war with the nation that flag stands for," he said. "I can't take it lightly when I find a Japanese flag in the home of someone I care for. I'm tired, Rose, tired of seeing young bodies mangled and destroyed because of what some imperial idiot on the other side of the ocean wants to do."

"I know, Jack. And I promise you no one on this farm is loyal to that flag." I stroked his hand again. He still didn't respond to my touch. "I will find out where it came from. As you saw, everything else in those bags is memorabilia, family treasures, nothing imperial or disloyal."

He stood up. "Okay, put these things away where no one, and I mean no one, is going to look. I'm still not sure what to do about this, Rose." He held up a hand as I started to say something. "I know you think you did nothing wrong, but I'm not convinced Isao isn't just using you and your good heart to cover for him. Right now, we have a party to put on, and you need to get that potato salad made before people start showing up, so let's let this go for the moment, shall we?"

He turned and went out to the front porch. Through the living room windows, I could see him setting up folding chairs. I wanted to go to him, hug the doubt from his heart, kiss the anger from his face. But I knew it wouldn't work. Panic fluttering in my chest, I stuffed the things Jack had unpacked back into the cabinets, rolled the washing machine to block the cabinet doors, and shut the tool room door behind me. My hands trembled as I put the potatoes on to boil.

Jack didn't have much to say to me the rest of the day. When I joined in a conversation, standing near enough to him that our shoulders touched, he refused to look at me, and soon found an excuse to move on to another group. He was kind as ever to Henry and Iris as they circulated through the crowd scattered from kitchen to porch, offering *pupu* platters and basking in the attention of homesick soldiers. I watched Henry approach with a tray of garlic toast, the usual adoring expression on his face. Jack patted Henry's shoulder and took a piece of toast, smiling down at him. How could Jack even imagine these were the children of a traitor, I wondered.

By the time everyone left, I was exhausted, drained by the effort to be a smiling hostess while inside I quaked about what Jack might do with his discovery. Would he turn us in? Stop loving me?

I was putting away leftovers when Jack tapped me on the shoulder. I turned to find him with his cap and gas mask in hand. He gave me a peck on the cheek and said, "I'm hitching a ride back to quarters with Jeanette and Jim. I need to sleep in my own bed tonight. I'll be in touch."

I'll be in touch—that sounded so impersonal. What did it mean? Stunned and afraid, I rushed to the doorway and watched him climb into the Thorntons' car, watched it head up the driveway, the tiny red slit of its taillights disappearing into the night.

I turned away from the door, all distractions gone now, knowing I had to do something about that flag. It couldn't be here, in case the unthinkable happened and the man I loved turned me in to the authorities. First, I had to talk to the Tanakas.

Chapter Twenty-three

I t was early yet, barely past sunset. Flag in hand, I walked down the hill. Blackout restrictions had been relaxed recently, so I could see dim light coming through the gaps in the Tanakas' living room curtains. As I drew near, I heard the gentle notes of Isao's ukulele, and I saw him sitting on the porch steps in the faint light from the open doorway. I stepped into that light and held up the flag. Isao stopped in mid-strum and stared with his mouth open.

"What's going on, Rose?" he asked, standing slowly, staring at the flag. "Where did that come from?"

The door opened, and Iris came out, followed by Henry. Iris stopped short, one hand over her mouth, and stared at the scrap of fabric in my hand, and Henry bumped into her.

"Hey, watchu doing, Iris?" he protested, then looked past his sister and frowned. "Is that one Japanese flag, Auntie?"

Iris still had not moved and still said nothing. As I climbed the few steps to the porch, her eyes lifted to meet mine, and she blinked and looked at the flag again.

"Is this yours, Iris?" I asked.

She ducked her head and squeezed her shoulders forward as if she was trying to make herself smaller. "Yes, Auntie," she said in a pinched voice. Henry looked from the flag to his sister and back again, shock on his face. Isao was speechless at first, but after a moment, he turned to me and said, "Come inside, please."

In the house, filled with the savory scents of dinner cooking, Masako must have heard our voices; she was already pouring me a cup of green tea. "Hi, Rose, want to stay? We're having chicken *hekka*," she said, and then she looked up and saw the flag. Her eyes widened, and she set the teapot down and wiped her hands on her apron.

227

We sat at the table, already set for dinner, and I told them the bare outline of the story, trying for the kids' sake to soft-pedal the potential damage. I didn't have to spell it out for Isao and Masako, already tense at the presence of the forbidden flag. They exchanged fearful looks. Iris sat with her head lowered, her hands clasped in her lap, her shoulders still slumped.

"I should go get rid of it all right now," Isao said as soon as I finished speaking. He pushed his chair back as if to stand, but I lifted my hand and said, "No, Isao, let's talk. Please." He hesitated, but settled back into his chair, his face rigid.

"It's too late. Jack's already seen it, and we talked about it. His word would be enough." For the kids' sake, I did not add "to convict us." I swallowed, the great chasm that had opened between me and Jack piercing my heart. My lover, the Army officer, now suspected me and my friends of treachery. I wanted to weep at that chasm, but I needed to be calm. "Besides, what would you do? Bury everything in the garden? Start a fire? That would only draw attention. We need to stay calm and wait this out. I can explain the rest of the stuff, so no need to do anything but repack it and put it away. But the flag is different. I need to get rid of this flag tonight."

I glanced at Iris and Henry to see how much they were grasping the ramifications of my story. Henry's gaze jumped from one adult to the other, his brow furrowed. Iris's head was still bowed. "I think it will be okay," I said. "I explained, and Captain Jack understands. I'll call him tomorrow to see what he's thinking, and I'll let you know," I said. I cleared my throat and spread the flag on the table. "But I'd like to know how this came to be in one of the bags. Iris?"

Masako and Isao turned to stare at their daughter.

Iris looked at her hands, a tear rolling down one cheek. "I forgot I had it, so I put it up there, way back after we first hid the bags," she said. "It was in a little purse I had last time we went to visit *Shintoku Maru*. One of the sailors gave it to me for a souvenir, and I kinda forgot about it, since I never use that purse. And when I found it, I was afraid I'd get scoldings for forgetting it. So I thought I should put it with the other stuff."

Her admission roused a vague memory in my mind, something that had never seemed quite right. "Wait a minute, Iris. Was that the day I saw you coming out of the kitchen? When you said you were looking for scraps for the chickens?" I asked.

She nodded and looked up, on the verge of a sob. "I'm so sorry, I didn't mean to get anyone in trouble. Will they arrest us all now?"

Masako and I each reached to pat one of Iris's shoulders. But as we did our best to comfort her, our eyes met across the table, and I saw fear in Masako's face to match the dread in my heart. Isao propped his elbows on the table and buried his face in his hands. That's when I noticed that his hair was damp.

"Isao, did you just take a *furo*?" I asked. "Would the fire still be hot?"

He looked up, his eyes dull. "Yes."

"Good," I said. "I'm burning this damn thing right now."

I picked up the flag, and without a word, everyone stood, and we all went out the back door. The *furo* was sheltered by a simple shed behind the house, set on a low stone wall foundation so that Isao could build a fire directly under the tub's copper bottom. He pulled open the little metal door of the firebox to show glowing coals. Plenty hot enough to burn this small square of silk, I thought, and without hesitation I tossed it in and saw its edges curl and turn brown as little flames rose. Iris took my hand and leaned against me. We all stood watching, Isao and Masako and the two children and I, waiting to see that every scrap of silk was gone and that nothing remained of that hateful flag but ashes.

• • • •

AT CHORE TIME THE NEXT morning, everyone was silent; Isao's face was set, and Iris's eyes were swollen from crying. Masako came up to wash out the milking buckets, and we sat at the breakfast nook and tried to come up with a way to make things better, but there seemed to be no solution. I couldn't get anything done all day; for the first time in my teaching career, I wouldn't finish the weekend's grading. Our lives were in Jack's hands, but though I called several times, he wasn't answering the phone.

I tried again as soon as I got home on Monday. One of the other docs answered and said Jack wasn't there; did I want to leave a message? Yes, I said, thinking carefully how to word it. "Please tell him our culprit is Iris." I did my best to laugh, as if I were sharing the punchline to a joke. "He'll know what I mean."

Then I waited, my chest hurting with anxiety as I went about my daily life of chores and teaching. At last, midway through the week, Jack called and said he was coming up to see me. I put on a pot of coffee and sat waiting until he walked in the back door, all beautiful, strong six feet of him, eyes bluer than ever in a face bronzed by Hawaii's sun.

"Rose, I've thought about this," he began. "I feel a bit better knowing that flag came from Iris, an innocent kid making an innocent mistake. And I guess, in reality, even if Isao was a spy, there's not much he could do, now that we're closing in on the Japs. They won't be coming back here, and what does Isao know anyway that might help them, right?"

"Right," I said, nodding fervently, hoping this meant he was willing to let the whole thing go. "That's what I've said all along. He's just a farmer and carpenter living near a little town on Maui. He wouldn't be any use to the Japanese even if he wanted to be, which he doesn't."

Jack cleared his throat and looked somewhere over my head.

"Okay, so let's set that aside. I won't report the flag. I trust you, and I know your heart was in the right place when you hid that stuff." He paused for a long moment. "But, Rose, honey, we both know it's not going to work out for us."

I stared at him, a chill settling over me. A moment ago, he'd seemed ready to forgive me. And now this blunt statement.

He put his hand on mine and aimed those blue eyes at me, and I was startled to see tears there. He swallowed hard. "We both already know there's no future for us once the war ends. I'm sure it'll slog on for another year or so—those Japs are stubborn bastards—but when it ends, neither of us is willing to give up our lives to make a new one together. So that tells me that maybe we are in a wartime romance, after all. Maybe the things we have in common—farm life, plants and animals, and putting on great parties—making love." He squeezed my hand. "Maybe they only mask all the things we don't have in common." He looked out the window, where clouds were reflecting the pink light of the setting sun.

I leaned toward him, pleading. "Jack, the war's still on, and we can still help each other make it through. Can't we? Even if we aren't meant to be together forever."

He looked back at me, pain on his face. "I can't do this anymore. I'm sorry. It's too different here. I know you all are part of America. But you're not really American, you know? All the races, all mixed up. It's not what I'm used to. I don't belong here." He grimaced and wiped his eyes.

"This flag thing made it clear," he continued. "Not so much the flag, but that you stored their Jap trinkets and spent all that time trying to rescue Isao, and now sponsoring him. It seems like Isao and keeping him free are more important to you than anything, even me."

"Jack! No, that's not true! You are important to me, very important," I insisted, my voice shaking.

"Nevertheless, it feels that way." He sat back, pulling his hand away from mine, and it was as if he was withdrawing his whole being, his eyes growing distant, his voice impersonal. "I've decided to make a clean break. No use sitting here, waiting for the end, maybe watching things deteriorate between us. There's an opening at the hospital in Waikapu, and they've been trying to figure out how to juggle staffing between here and there, which of the docs to send down there. I decided to make it easy on my boss, and I volunteered."

I gasped. Waikapu, all the way down country, past Wailuku, almost another world.

"They need a real surgeon up here," Jack continued, "which I'm not. I've just been making do. If I leave, maybe this hospital can move up the list to get one."

I reached for him, but he dropped both hands into his lap. I tried to look into his eyes, but he looked away.

"So I'll be heading to Waikapu soon," he said. "I came over today to tell you that I've loved our time together, and I'll never forget you. But I need to move on and let you get back to your life." Now his voice was choked with emotion. "I'm sorry, but I think it's better that way."

I sat there in shock as he stood up and leaned across the table, kissed me gently on the forehead.

"Are you saying this is it? You're leaving just like that? I won't see you again?"

"I think it's the best way to do it."

"Well, I don't. I love you, Jack," I said, panic rising in my chest as I stood to face him. This couldn't be happening. He couldn't be making such a cold, hard decision, leaving me so abruptly after all we'd shared.

"I love you too, Rose. But it will never work in the long run. You made it clear you won't leave here, even to marry me. We might as well admit it and get it over with. I wish you all the best." He turned and walked away. He closed the back door gently behind him, but it was as if he had slammed it in my face.

What could I do? Running after him would not help; I'd look like a fool. And deep inside, I knew he was right. So I didn't move. I stood stunned, trying to fathom my loss. I could find no end to it. It seemed to spread across my entire landscape, to roll through time, through all the days of my life to come.

T hat was a bad day. And so was the next, and the next, for what seemed forever, each hour weighing like lead as the days dragged by. I survived by working, burying my pain in routine, the well-worn path at school and at home. After a while, I was even able to go back to the USO and to attend Jeanette's parties, though I couldn't bear to host one myself without Jack at my side.

But gradually my heart began to heal. The drama and constant change of the war years could not fail to distract me from the loss of Jack. So many had lost so much more than me. And so many were healing from deeper wounds.

I remember the day I first heard Isao laugh again. Startled, I looked over from the laundry I was hanging and saw our neighbor Frank standing with his hands on his hips outside the half-built house where Isao squatted, hammer in hand. I don't know what Frank had said to make him laugh, but I'll never forget the joy that surged through my heart at the sound of that laughter and the sight of Isao's smiling face as the two men talked story.

And then there was Sam. Along with the rest of the Hawaii boys who'd joined the 442nd Regimental Combat Team, he'd been a part of changing history. After a year of hard training in Mississippi, they shipped out to Italy. In the first days of fierce fighting there, Sam was hit by a shell that shattered his tibia. He spent months in an English hospital and finally came limping home, unable to rejoin his buddies in the war in Europe. Those Island warriors were playing a much bigger part than anyone had expected in fighting back the Nazis. German soldiers, in awe of the tenacity and bravery of the boys from Hawaii, called them "the little iron men."

Masako's eyes streamed with tears of happiness as she embraced her son the day we all went to meet him at the dock, and even Isao wept as he embraced his son. Sam took it all stoically, though he broke into a grin as Henry and Iris rushed to hug him. He leaned on his crutches so he could use both hands to ruffle their hair.

"Sam, I'm so happy you're home and safe," I said as he hobbled to the family truck. I'd splurged with gas to meet the ship; I couldn't miss this long-awaited homecoming.

"Auntie Rose, good to see you," he said, but his smile was tight. "I'm glad to be home, but I should be fighting with my unit. They need every man, lost so many already."

"You did your bit, Sam, and we are proud of you." I patted his back and kissed his cheek, sad that he might be feeling guilty after having given so much. "Now you need to heal so you can help us get life back to normal when this war is over."

He nodded, but his eyes were distant as he turned toward the door his father held open for him. Isao had brought a sturdy wooden box for a step to help his son climb up onto the seat, but it still was obviously a struggle for Sam to lift his body into the truck. We all stood watching, not knowing how to help, and when Isao offered a hand, Sam shook his head. "No, Pop, I can. Just let me. I'm slow these days."

Iris, her face dismayed, moved closer to me, reaching for my hand, and Henry's eyes were wide as he watched his big brother hoist himself into the truck. Masako covered her mouth with both hands. This somber young man was not the boy who'd waved from the decks of *Waialeale*, laughing with his friends, only a couple of years ago.

When I came home from school a few days later, Sam was sitting on the edge of the floor of the new house, in the shade of the roof Isao had made with used beams and boards he'd salvaged from a renovation job several years earlier. Beside him was a stack of lumber, old pieces the ever-thrifty Isao had saved from other projects. Sam was pulling nails from boards, examining each critically before dropping it into one of two old cans. When I went out later, he was pounding out the straightest nails from the favored can, making them ready, one by one, for his father to use as he put up boards to make walls.

I never noticed father and son saying much to each other as they went about turning old wood into a new house. But with every sawn board and every hammered nail, their wounds, interior and exterior, began to heal. Sam grew stronger from lifting and moving building supplies, and his limp became less noticeable as he walked around the farm doing chores. Isao now sometimes whistled while he worked, glancing at his son from time to time as if to simply enjoy the sight of him. In the evenings, I could hear the two playing ukulele on their front porch, harmonizing on the old songs Isao had learned from his cowboy friends. And sometimes Sam dazzled us all with his quick finger work on popular dance tunes.

There was still plenty of war going on while the men of my homestead pulled their lives back together. A few months after Jack left, thousands of Marines set up camp in our neighborhood, just miles from our farm, my school, and the camp where Isao had been held.

The day they arrived, fresh from battle, I stood on the porch of the USO with other volunteers waving a welcome to truck after truck on the way to the new camp. Men peered through the slats of the truck's sides to return our waves, smiles on faces too young to look so exhausted. They'd returned from horrendous but successful battle in the Marshall Islands; now they would train for more battles to come. We heard them more than saw them as they learned to fight their way through bamboo forests and tangled jungles. The booms and blasts of target practice sounded from the camp itself to the barbed wire-lined seacoast of South Maui.

Camp Maui sat at the foot of a tall cinder-cone hill, with hundreds of tents lined up in orderly fashion on muddy ground. Like the Puunene air base where pilots trained twenty-four hours a day, Camp Maui was a small town with roads, offices, ball fields, movie theaters, and a post exchange. Makawao's streets, the USO, and the little hospital where Jack had worked were busier than ever.

For all the love Maui had shown the earlier arrivals, the love for this 4th Marine Division was even greater, as they marched off to battle on faraway Pacific islands and came home minus thousands of their buddies. When they returned from capturing Saipan and Tinian, Makawao hung a "Welcome Home" banner over the street, and we USO hostesses split into two groups—some to greet them at the dock and others to wave as the trucks once more rolled through Makawao. I went to meet the ships and hand out paper lei and bags of homemade candy, while the welcoming crowd cheered so loudly people could hear it for miles.

Island by island, our troops took back the territory the Japanese had devoured. They raised the flag on Iwo Jima and secured U.S. airstrips that gave our planes access to Tokyo, while in Europe, the Allies at last ended the fascist reign of terror that had held a continent in its grip.

And after the war? Nothing was ever the same. Listening to Aiko's husband, Dennis, and Sam talk one evening in 1946 brought home to me how much the Islands would change because of this war. Already there was upheaval—sugar workers around the territory had been on strike for months.

"I'm not working for no plantation," Dennis said as we all sat around the barbecue grill he and Sam had set up, with a picnic bench and a few tree stumps for seating. "I saw how my dad had to work hard and live in the plantation house, where they can throw you out anytime you act up too much against the bigwigs. I pity the buggahs striking now, marching, living on cabbage soup. The plantation going win, and they'll be outta luck." He took a sip of beer and shook his head. "Mo' bettah take my chances, start my own business. I'm as good as any of those mainland carpenters they brought in, better than a lot of 'em." He put his arm around Aiko's shoulders. "With Aiko to run the office and me to do the construction, we can make it." Aiko smiled and nodded in agreement.

"I don't know, I think the strikers going win," Sam said as he flipped steaks on the grill. "This whole plantation thing gotta change. The plantations and the *haoles* been running this place too long. We used to talk, us guys in the hospital, about what we can do to change things when we get home." He turned to look at his parents. "In fact, I got news for you folks. I'm gonna go to law school. I finally decided."

Isao and Masako broke into big smiles, and everyone joined in clapping and congratulations. "Finally going to use those brains, huh?" Aiko said, laughing.

"I wish I can go with you," Iris said.

Sam smiled. "Give it a few years, kid, and I'll share some tips with you for how to be one smart lawyer."

Sam's departure was the first big change that would transform life on my little farm in the years after the war. He went off to the university on Oahu and to law school in California, then set up his law practice in Honolulu. He worked behind the scenes on the 1954 territorial legislative campaign, once again making history as part of the Democratic revolution that overturned the longtime white Republican ruling class at the ballot box. A few years later, Sam himself was elected to the legislature.

Meanwhile, Henry and Iris finished high school and moved to the mainland to study medicine and law, just as they had planned when they were children. Both chose to live the rest of their lives in California, Henry as a pediatrician and Iris as a Legal Aid attorney.

Only Aiko remained, with the husband she'd met while working at the construction company. When military surplus building supplies became available, Dennis helped Isao and Sam build a big new house on the corner of land I'd given to Isao and Masako for a dollar and love. They'd be right next door. But it wasn't the same, with schoolteachers and hired farmworkers living in the two cottages Isao had built. No, not the same at all.

· · · ·

I NEVER HEARD FROM Jack again. A few years after the war ended, one of the regulars from Jeanette's party gang came back for a visit and told her Jack had married a girl from his hometown. By that time, the news was only a prod to an old wound, to scar tissue that, most of the time, no longer hurt. I even found I could be happy for his finding someone to share his life.

I also knew by then what I had gained from my time with Jack. I had learned that I could love a man who wasn't Vaughn, that there were men in the world worthy of my love. And I knew now that I was a woman who wanted the love of a man. The next time one came into view, I would be ready for him.

After the war, when I ran into people who hadn't seen me for a long time, and they asked the familiar question—"How was your war?"—I had to say that it was a mixed bag. Terrible things happened. There was so much loss, so much suffering, and the dislocation of great change. And yet along with that pain came the compassion and spirit that carried us through. So, when I ask myself that same question—how was my war?—my first thought is: It was full of love.

Some of the people in this book speak the Hawaii vernacular we call pidgin. A pidgin is a mixed language incorporating the vocabulary of one or more languages. Hawaii's modern version of pidgin is actually a "creole," a language descended from the pidgin that originated with early settlers. Everyday speech also includes Hawaiian words and those of the other ethnic groups who came to Hawaii over the past couple of centuries. Modern usage of the Hawaiian language includes two diacritical marks that assist with pronunciation and meaning. They would not have been in common use in the 1940s. This book does not include them due to the technical limitations of the publishing platform.

People in Hawaii still refer to themselves by their families' ethnic origins, i.e. "Japanese" or "Portuguese," even though they have been Americans for generations. The use of the slur "Jap" was common during the war years, even in newspaper headlines. It is included for historical accuracy, to demonstrate the intense fear and anger that followed the attack on Pearl Harbor.

I hope this glossary, with both Hawaiian and Japanese words, will help you understand the ways that Hawaii residents speak to each other, even if you've never had the opportunity to experience our unique culture.

Furo—A Japanese hot bath.

Ganbatte—Do your best.

Geta—Japanese wooden-soled shoes.

Hanai—Foster, adopted; to raise, feed, nourish, sustain.

Haole—Foreigner, of foreign origin. Commonly, a white person or Caucasian. This usage has come into disrepute in recent years because it is sometimes used prejudicially, in addition to being inaccurate in the case of lifetime Caucasian residents, who are not "foreign" to Hawaii.

Ilima—Native shrub bearing yellow flowers so delicate that about 500 are needed for a lei.

Kanji—A Japanese system of writing.

Kiawe—The algaroba tree.

Lauae—A scented fern.

Lei—The famous Hawaiian garland, usually made of flowers. Because there is no "s" in Hawaiian, "lei" is both singular and plural.

Malihini—Newcomer, stranger.

Manuahi—Gratis, free of charge.

Mauka—Inland, toward the mountain.

Musubi—Rice ball wrapped in seaweed.

Muumuu—Traditional loose Hawaiian dress.

Pau—Finished, ended, complete.

Poi—The Hawaiian staple food, made by mashing the cooked corms of the taro plant into a smooth paste.

Puakenikeni—Small tree with fragrant white flowers often used for lei.

Punee—Moveable couch, sometimes used for sleeping.

Shikata ga nai—It cannot be helped.

Talk story—The custom of hanging out and sharing stories.

Zabuton—A large, flat pillow used for sitting or kneeling on the floor.

AUTHOR'S NOTE AND ACKNOWLEDGMENTS

W riting *Rose's War*, a novel, required almost as much research as my nonfiction books. I wanted to present the best picture I could of World War II as experienced by ordinary citizens of Maui. But the facts of both the general wartime situation and the incarceration of U.S. citizens and others on Maui under martial law are hard to come by. Newspapers were heavily censored. Much of what has been written about the war years in Hawaii is focused on Honolulu. Shame, and the desire to get on with life, seem to have been key motives in the cover-up of Hawaii's internment camps.

So this book is pieced together from multiple sources, some of which provided as little as a sentence or so that confirmed another source. Five of the most important sources were a chapter from an unpublished book by my late friend and colleague Laurel Murphy; *Hawaii's War Years* by Gwenfread Allen; *Remembering Our Grandfathers' Exile* by Gail Y. Okawa; *Facing the Mountain* by Daniel James Brown; and *The Maui News*, particularly the "war extras" that were digitized and made available online by Kamehameha Schools. I also consulted articles I collected some years ago from microfilm copies of the newspaper, which gave an idea of how Maui residents coped.

Laurel's chapter, taken from her as-yet-unpublished history of the Baldwin family and of Hawaii during the years of their preeminence on Maui, provided an excellent overview of the war through Laurel's research and survivors' memories.

Hawaii's War Years is based on the Hawaii War Records Depository, a collection of material amassed by the University of Hawaii. Ms. Allen was a remarkable person, a journalist and active member of the Honolulu community who managed to condense six years' worth of documents into a meticulously referenced single volume about civilian life during the war.

Remembering Our Grandfathers' Exile is about the *issei*, first-generation Hawaii Japanese, who were arrested, imprisoned, and spent years in various camps on the mainland. Though Okawa's research focused on the experiences of this noncitizen first generation, I borrowed details such as the questions interrogators asked arrested individuals and applied them to the hearing before a civilian board that decided the sentence of Isao Tanaka, a Hawaii-born U.S. citizen. I also learned something of the huge impact incarceration had on the internees and their families.

Facing the Mountain is a highly readable book about the wartime experiences of Americans of Japanese ancestry in Hawaii and on the mainland, including incarceration and the establishment and battles of the much-decorated *nisei* military units, the 100th Infantry Battalion and the 442nd Regimental Combat Team. Brown's research and storytelling skills educated me about the overall situation and about several Maui individuals caught up in the war.

Excellent online resources include the Densho Encyclopedia (https://encyclopedia.densho.org) which contains thousands of articles about the forced removal and incarceration of Japanese Americans.

The Japanese Cultural Center of Hawaii (JCCH) website (https://www.hawaiiinternment.org) includes excellent and informative curricula about World War II's impact on the Islands' Japanese Americans. Volunteers at the center, trying to answer questions about internment in Hawaii, spearheaded recent study of incarceration sites around the Islands, particularly the finding of the almost-forgotten Honouliuli camp. This website includes reports on the various camps as well as primary documents, such as letters, interviews, and photographs. A DVD of the center's documentary film "The Untold Story: Internment of Japanese Americans in Hawaii" was gifted to me by the helpful staff and volunteers at Maui's Nisei Veterans Memorial Center (NVMC).

A museum display created by JCCH traveled to Maui at a time when I was unable to be there, so my friend Lorraine Tamaribuchi photographed the display at the NVMC for me, then introduced me to her cousin, Dr. Mel Inamasu, who shared a report by archaeologists Jeffery F. Burton and Mary M. Farrell on confinement sites in Hawaii. Dr. Inamasu and another volunteer, David Fukuda, did in-depth local research at the Haiku site where Isao Tanaka was interned. I have imagined the camp's layout based on their findings and on comments by Maui architect Frank Skowronski, who at one time owned and lived in the former pineapple-cannery dormitory that now houses the Roots School. It likely was the administration and living quarters for the guards at the camp, where another dorm probably used to house internees once stood behind the site of the present U.S. post office.

Editor Judith Tarr made significant critical comments on the first finished draft, and Beth Butler provided careful and insightful copyediting of the final draft. My writing group colleagues Nalani Clark, Christy Vail, and Benni D'Enbeau gave great feedback along the way. Benni helped me come up with the basic plot, and Nalani spent months teaching me how to ramp up the drama. Colleen Sotomura's review of the manuscript from a Japanese American perspective reassured me that I had accomplished what I set out to do. Lorraine Tamaribuchi, in addition to the help mentioned above, proofread the final version. Others who read earlier versions include Roy Tanaka, who had previously permitted me to borrow his father's name for *A Dollar and Love,* the book that introduced Rose McKenzie and the Tanaka family. Roy also made important comments on this author's note. Neal Engledow, Madge Walls, Connie Kent, Kathleen Jensen, and Jerry Richmond read, commented, and encouraged me. Cynthia Conrad designed a cover that subtly evokes the dramatic times in which Rose and all of Hawaii fought to survive the war.

Iolani Palace Historian Zita Cup Choy provided information about the palace, its grounds, and the farewell rally held for the first Hawaii recruits to the 442nd RCT. Michael Case, senior digital archivist for the USO, shared information and pictures about the USO in Hawaii during WWII, including the Hamakuapoko and Makawao Crossroads USOs.

Yaemi Yogi helped me begin my research when her daughter, Kathy Collins, brought her mom to Kepaniwai Park to talk story about Makawao during World War II. Aiko's experience at the beginning of the book is based on Mrs. Yogi's story of hearing about Pearl Harbor while meeting with friends before services at Pookela Church.

Maui rancher Alex Franco answered questions about cattle, and Maui farmer Stuart Nicholls advised on tree removal.

Much of the information about schoolteacher Rose McKenzie's workplace, now known as Old Maui High School, is based on research I did for the book *The Spirit Lives On*, co-authored by Barbara Long. Many of the comments attributed to Rose's fictional students came from the school's yearbooks and newspaper. Among the teachers at this school that gave so many of its students an excellent education, the only one whose real name is used in this book is the legendary typing teacher Emma Cawdry.

Essays written by Rose's students are excerpts from the 1939 *Maui Hi-Notes* supplement, *I Live in a Democracy,* for which the real Earl Isao Tanaka, then a Maui High student, did page makeup. Earl later joined the 442nd RCT and worked for *The Maui News* for forty-five years, during which time he hired me as a reporter. The real Isao Tanaka was not incarcerated and was not a farmer, but his lively personality inspired the fictional Isao.

Like most historical novelists, I had to guess, extrapolate, and make things up to meet the needs of the story, especially considering gaps in available information—the visiting schedules and setup of both the Haiku and Honouliuli camps, for example. Likewise, I pieced together what I read in various places to describe Isao's hearings. Stories differ about the New Year's Day shelling. One person said that the shells landed in the cane fields above Wailuku, causing a fire, but Dr. William Patterson's book said there was no damage. The scene in which teachers gather in Wailuku for training on how to register citizens is made up, as is the scene in the gym with student helpers. The jeep accident is not real but is a stand-in for many accidents that happened during the years when some 200,000 troops trained all over Maui.

Other helpful books:

Hawaii Under Army Rule by J. Garner Anthony. "The real story of three years of martial law in a loyal American territory."

Hawaii Goes to War by DeSoto Brown. Wonderful pictures and text about life in Hawaii from Pearl Harbor to peace.

Dust Before the Wind by Helen Troy Elmore (unpublished, available at the University of Hawaii Hamilton Library). A memoir of Mrs. Elmore's experience of the war on Maui.

Old Fashioned Recipe Book: An Encyclopedia of Country Living by Carla Emery. Detailed advice about old-fashioned farming.

Every Grain of Rice: Portraits of Maui's Japanese Community by Rita Goldman.

Judgment Without Trial: Japanese American Imprisonment During World War II by Tetsuden Kashima.

Ambassadors in Arms: The Story of Hawaii's 100th Battalion by Thomas D. Murphy (Laurel Murphy's father).

Cane Fires: The Anti-Japanese Movement in Hawaii, 1865-1945 by Gary Y. Okihiro.

From the Isle of Skye to the Isle of Maui by William Benton Patterson. Based on the diaries of a Maui physician.

Under the Blood-Red Sun, by Graham Salisbury, a young readers' novel about a Japanese family on Oahu.

Plantation Life and Beyond by Spencer Saichi Shiraishi. A memoir of growing up in Paia, Maui.

Life Behind Barbed Wire by Yasutaro Soga. A memoir of incarceration.

Lucky Come Hawaii by Jon Shirota, a novel about a Japanese family on Maui in WWII.

Bridge of Love by John Tsukano. The story of the Japanese immigrants and their soldier sons.

Other helpful websites:

Newspapers.com[1] includes full copies of the *Honolulu Star-Bulletin* and the *Honolulu Advertiser*, searchable by date or topic.

An Era of Change is a University of Hawaii oral history project. https://oralhistory.hawaii.edu/an-era-of-change-oral-histories-of-civilians-in-world-war-ii-hawaii/

https://campmauimuseum.com tells the story of the 4th Marine Division stationed on Maui from 1944 to 1945.

United States Army in World War II. The Medical Department: Hospitalization And Evacuation, Zone of Interior by Clarence McKittrick Smith. https://history.army.mil/html/books/010/10-7/CMH_Pub_10-7.pdf

The Makawao History Museum's website includes information and a great collection of photos of the Crossroads USO. https://www.makawaomuseum.org/digexhibits/the-crossroads-uso

· · · ·

---

1.   https://d.docs.live.net/5e5649b416d7b4bf/newspapers.com

ROSE'S WAR is the third book in "The Maui Trilogy," novels about independent women making their way on Maui. The others in the trilogy are *The Island Decides*[2] and *A Dollar and Love*[3]. Together, they span the first seventy-five years of the 20th century on Maui. They can be read in any order. Learn more about them, as well as my nonfiction historical works, at https://jillengledow.com

If you enjoyed this book, help others find it by leaving a review at the retailer where you purchased it or on a social networking site like Goodreads or Facebook. And tell your friends! Reviews and personal recommendations help a lot. Mahalo!

2. *https://books2read.com/The-Island-Decides*

3. *https://books2read.com/a-dollar-and-love*

Don't miss out!

Visit the website below and you can sign up to receive emails whenever Jill Engledow publishes a new book. There's no charge and no obligation.

https://books2read.com/r/B-A-NYQQ-ZWIHD

BOOKS 2 READ

Connecting independent readers to independent writers.

About the Author

Jill Engledow is an award-winning Maui journalist and nonfiction author who moved to Hawaii at the age of 13. Her books include *Island Life 101: A Newcomer's Guide to Hawaii, Haleakala: A History of the Maui Mountain, The Story of Lahaina,* and *Sugarcane Days.* Now retired in Oregon, Jill still writes about Maui. Her latest books are a trilogy of novels about women making their way on Maui between 1900 and 1975: *The Island Decides, A Dollar and Love,* and *Rose's War.*

Read more at https://www.jillengledow.com.